Praise for the novels of

# BELLA ANDRE

"Sensual, empowered stories enveloped in heady romance."
—*Publishers Weekly*

"The perfect combination of sexy heat and tender heart."
—#1 *New York Times* bestselling author Barbara Freethy

"Bella Andre writes warm, sexy contemporary romance
that always gives me a much needed pick me up.
Reading one of her books is truly a pleasure."
—*New York Times* bestselling author Maya Banks

"I can't wait for more Sullivans!"
—*New York Times* bestselling author Carly Phillips

"Loveable characters, sizzling chemistry,
and poignant emotion."
—*USA TODAY* bestselling author Christie Ridgway

"I'm hooked on the Sullivans!"
—Marie Force, bestselling author of *Falling For Love*

"No one does sexy like Bella Andre."
—*New York Times* bestselling author Sarah MacLean

"I never want this series to end."
—TalkeSupe Book Reviews Blog

# BELLA ANDRE

## *If You Were Mine*

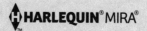

Recycling programs
for this product may
not exist in your area.

ISBN-13: 978-0-7783-1560-5

IF YOU WERE MINE

Harlequin MIRA/November 2013

First published by Bella Andre

Printed in U.S.A.

www.Harlequin.com

Dear Reader,

Can two people who have both sworn off love find forever in each other's arms? That was the driving question that fueled me as I wrote *If You Were Mine*.

Throughout the first four books in my Sullivan series, Zach Sullivan always stood out to me with his wicked sense of humor and his passion for living life to the fullest. But I never imagined it would be a puppy that would help Zach find the love of his life.

The last thing he wants is to watch his brother's new puppy for two weeks. Until he meets the dog trainer, that is. Heather is bright, beautiful, and he can't stop thinking about her. Unfortunately, she just might be the only woman on earth who wants nothing to do with him.

I laughed—and cried—my way through writing Zach and Heather's story, and I hope their very unexpected love story has you both grinning and reaching for the tissues, too.

Happy reading,

Bella Andre

# *One*

Zach Sullivan stared with disgust at the bundle of fur chewing on his shoelace.

"No way." He shifted his foot to try to get the little bugger off but, for such a tiny thing, it was tenacious. It growled a little and shook its tail as it renewed focus on his shoe. His new shoe.

"Sophie loves dogs. Ask her."

He looked up to see Gabe smirking at him. Clearly, it had been way too long since he'd wiped a grin off his little brother's face.

"Sophie's got enough to deal with lately, between her pregnancy and marrying Jake," Gabe told him. "Chloe and Chase are going to have their kid any second now. Marcus and Nicola are always on the road. Ryan is practically living at the stadium for baseball season. And I wouldn't trust Lori with a dog if she was the last person on earth. Trust me, you were at the end of my list for someone to watch the puppy while we're away on vacation, but Summer insisted you *needed* to have Cuddles."

Zach almost hurled. "Cuddles?"

"Summer named her." They both looked down at the puppy. "I think the name fits pretty well."

Gabe was incredibly protective of Summer, his fiancée Megan's daughter. Zach knew better than to insult the dog's name, even if it was, hands down, the worst one ever.

"Look," Gabe said, "Summer is convinced you're the perfect person to keep the puppy. For some reason none of us can figure out, she thinks you can do no wrong. Don't disappoint her, Zach."

Zach had thought Summer was pretty great for a seven-year-old. Until now, when she was trying to stick him with a dog he didn't want for two weeks. Especially since there was no way a puppy was going to fit into his life for even two days.

His daily—and nightly—schedule was all about fast cars and pretty women. What the hell was he going to do with a puppy?

Shaking his head, Zach said, "You've really lost your touch, Gabe, letting two girls lead you around."

Zach was still surprised by how smitten his brother was—not only with Megan, but with her daughter, too. And it wasn't just Gabe who had fallen way down deep in the bottomless pit of "true love." Chase, Marcus and Sophie had tripped into it, too.

Their mother was beyond thrilled knowing there were babies and more Sullivan weddings on the way. Zach was happy she was happy. Just as long as she had no false expectations about him falling in love.

Because it was *never* going to happen.

But Gabe clearly didn't care if he'd lost his touch, or that he'd never be able to pick up a stranger at a bar for hot sex again. If anything, his brother looked disgustingly happy about it.

"I'm not asking you to dress the puppy up in frilly doggy clothes or to spend all day rolling around in the grass with her. I just need you to keep her fed and watered and walked while we're on our trip. So, will you do it or do I have to break Summer's heart by telling her she's wrong about you being a good guy?"

As if to punctuate his brother's request, Cuddles finally let go of her grip on Zach's shoelace and looked up at him with oversize brown eyes, her little pink tongue licking at her whiskers as if she'd just finished a truly tasty meal.

Damn it, he'd always been a sucker for puppy-dog eyes.

He wasn't happy about it, but he supposed he could suck it up for a couple of weeks while Gabe, Megan and Summer took a European vacation to see castles and princesses and whatever else it was Summer had been going on and on to him about at the last Sunday lunch.

His reputation as a player with women was well deserved, and it was exactly how he liked things: no deep connections to have to deal with down the road, no woman to disappoint or leave behind one day. But his family was different. His brothers and sisters meant everything to him.

"Fine." He scowled down at the dog. "I'll do it. What breed is she, anyway?"

His brother grinned, not bothering to hide his evil pleasure at Zach's capitulation. "A Yorkshire terrier. Evidently, she's a big one."

"Big?" He bent and picked her up by the ruff with two fingers before putting her back down by his shoe. "She can't weigh more than a couple of pounds."

"Closer to three," Gabe said as he headed for Zach's front door and came back a few seconds later with a huge cardboard box. "Here are her things."

Zach knew what the food and bowls were for, but everything else looked as if it belonged in the toy box at a preschool. "Why does a three-pound puppy need all of this for just two weeks?"

He had a bad feeling about this whole thing, sensing how easily fourteen days could turn into way longer than that if he wasn't careful.

Gabe shrugged. "We've only had her a couple of days and Summer has mostly been taking care of her so far. Timing kind of sucks on having to leave her so soon, but I know Megan really appreciates you stepping up to the plate like this."

It grated that they all thought he would be such a pushover about the puppy before even talking to him about it. But that didn't bother him nearly as much as when Cuddles chose that exact moment to squat down over the toe of his shoe and empty her bladder.

Her surprisingly large bladder.

"You'd better be back for her in two weeks," Zach warned in a low voice, "or she's going straight to the pound."

Gabe's laughter rang out as he wisely hightailed it to his car.

* * *

Heather Linsey was just finishing up with the students in her preliminary-level dog trainer certification class when her cell phone buzzed. She pulled it out, but when she saw the name on her screen, she quickly shoved it back into her pocket.

"I can handle giving everyone the information for the next set of classes if you need to get that," her assistant, Tina, said.

Heather forced a smile. "That's okay. I've got it."

But her mind was only half on her students as she wrapped things up and congratulated them on a job well done, letting them know she was available if they had any problems setting up their new businesses. Finishing up with a quick reminder about the big Bark in the Park fundraiser at the baseball stadium that coming Friday, and the silent auction the following Saturday night, she headed back to her office with Atlas, her Great Dane, close beside her.

Heather closed the door before pulling the phone back out and putting it on her desk. She wished she could just delete the message, but she knew from past experience that it would be smarter to find out what her father wanted.

*"Sweetheart, I was hoping I'd get you rather than your voice mail,"* he began, and she was amazed at just how strong his denial was. Didn't he realize she hadn't picked up a call from him in years? She rubbed her hands over her arms as he continued. *"I have a business trip to San Francisco next week and I'm thinking of bringing your mother with me.*

*It's been too long since we've seen our girl and we
both miss you."*

The skin on Heather's arms started to tingle, and
then burn. The sensation started at her wrists and
crept up across the pattern of crisscrossed scars that
went past her elbows and all around the back of her
arms. Nearly ten years later, the scars were faint
enough that she probably didn't need to wear long
sleeves all the time. But even though the cuts were
long since healed, every time she had to deal with
her father, she felt this phantom pain. It was almost
as if she were seventeen years old again and lock-
ing herself into her room to try to deal with her out-
of-control emotions. Back then, the only way she
could deal with the anxiety was by making small
cuts across the surface of her skin with a razor, and
then watching them bleed.

At the sound of her father's voice, Atlas hadn't
gone to his huge dog pillow in the corner. Instead,
he'd stuck right with her and put his big head in her
lap. She stopped rubbing her arms and stroked his
head instead.

*"Let me know your schedule so we can plan our
evening with you. Your mother sends her love."*

The message ended and she stared blankly at the
phone on her desk, her hand absentmindedly moving
over Atlas's short, soft fur. She couldn't believe how
long they'd been playing this game, the one where
her father acted as if everything was normal and they
had a perfect relationship. Especially when he knew
that she *knew* for a fact that everything wasn't per-

fect, that his "perfect" marriage to her mother and his "loving" relationship with his daughter was just a big, stupid lie.

A knock came at her door, jarring her out of her dark thoughts. "Come in."

Agnes Mackelroy, a pretty middle-aged woman whom Heather liked a great deal, poked her head in the door. "Good morning, Heather. I was hoping you had a few minutes." Despite Heather's smile, the woman seemed to sense something was wrong. "Is everything all right?"

Heather nodded quickly. "It's always so lovely to see you."

And it was true—she couldn't be happier to see Agnes and her dog, Joey, especially if it meant she didn't have to think about her father anymore.

Agnes had been one of Heather's first clients at Top Dog when the ink was still drying on her business cards. Over the past few years, she'd given dozens of referrals to Heather to work with her family's and friends' dogs.

Heather knelt to say hello to Agnes's chow chow. "Look at you with your fancy new knee," she said as she scratched the dog under his chin, right where he loved it. Atlas soon bumped her out of the way to say hello. "I take it he's been doing well since surgery?" she asked Agnes.

"Just splendidly! He's back to his old self, out digging up my garden morning, noon and night."

Heather had to laugh at that, even though stopping that behavior was something she'd worked on long and hard with Agnes and Joey last year. "Would you like me to drop by later this week to see if we can get him to celebrate in a different way?"

"No, I'm perfectly happy to let Joey have his fun. I didn't much care for the color of the begonias, anyway," Agnes said with a toss of her hand. "I'm actually here on behalf of a very good friend with a new puppy."

"Perfect timing. I've just finished up a group training class and have several new trainers who would love to get their feet wet. Why don't I give you a few of their numbers?"

"I was hoping," Agnes said, "that you might be available to help him personally."

Heather's business and dog-training staff had grown so much over the past three years that she spent most of her time managing the business. While she still loved to pop out of her office to play with the dogs that came in and out of her training campus, at this point she rarely took on one-on-one training clients. But she couldn't possibly say no to Agnes, who was responsible for so much of her early success.

Mentally reshuffling her busy schedule, Heather said, "What's your friend's name?"

"His name," Agnes said, "is Zach."

Something akin to a warning skittered down Heather's spine at the woman's almost-worshipful tone. Then again, she knew Agnes was happily married.

"I know how much he'd appreciate it if you could meet with him this morning at the garage where he works. He's dog-sitting for a couple of weeks, but I'm afraid the little Yorkie is running the poor man in circles."

Heather wrote down the address for Sullivan Autos, then gave both Agnes and her dog hugs as they said goodbye.

She couldn't imagine a mechanic's boss being too happy about a madcap puppy running around in an auto shop. Not to mention that it definitely wasn't the safest environment for an untrained dog.

"Ready to go play with a puppy?" she asked the huge dog lying at her feet.

Atlas's ears perked up at his favorite word. It had always amused her how much her two-hundred-pound Great Dane loved to play with puppies, even though they tended to nip at him with their sharp little teeth and use their nails to climb onto his broad back with no concern whatsoever for their own welfare.

She suspected the reason had something to do with the fact that the early part of his life hadn't been all that carefree. Once he became her dog things changed…a lot. Now he thrived on being around rambunctious puppies.

It was a warm day and Heather gathered her long hair up into a ponytail, then grabbed her training bag and headed to her car. Atlas bounded into the backseat, immediately sticking his head out of the window in anticipation of having the wind in his face, his tongue flying free.

Ten minutes later, Heather pulled up outside Sul-

livan Autos and slipped on Atlas's leash. She could
see a half dozen men on-site, and even though her
dog was worlds better around men than he had been
when she'd first taken him home four years ago, she
was concerned that so many big men in one place
might overwhelm him. She wasn't surprised when
he stuck close to her, the stiffness of his ears and tail
a telltale sign that he wasn't entirely relaxed.

"Everything's fine," she soothed him, rubbing
gently between his ears. "We're just going to play
with a puppy, remember?" His tongue plopped out at
that happy news and she grinned in response. "That's
right, we've got nothing to worry about at—"

*"Where the hell is that damned puppy!"*

# Two

The frustrated roar split apart the otherwise normal sounds of the sprawling auto garage, and both Heather and Atlas went on red alert. She immediately began to scope out the hiding places a puppy would be likely to go in a place like this…especially if it were afraid of its new owner.

Her Great Dane tugged her toward a hedge at the edge of the parking lot and she followed his lead. If anyone could find a lost and helpless little one, it was Atlas. He stopped in front of a thick hedge, sniffed at the bush, then whimpered and pawed at the dirt.

Heather dropped his leash to get down on her hands and knees to peer inside. Ah, yes, she could see black-brown fur between the leaves and branches.

"Hey there, cutie," she crooned softly. "Want to come out and meet a friend I've brought to play with you?"

Unfortunately, just then, the man yelled again. *"You'd better get your furry little butt back here!"*

Of course the puppy didn't move. And why would it, if all it had to look forward to was more yelling, or maybe even worse?

Hoping she wasn't going to end up with fierce little teeth clamped around her hand or ankle, she started to push in through the branches. The sharp tips scratched at the bare skin of her legs. For a brief moment she wished she had changed out of her shorts, but she was so intent on rescuing the puppy she paid no attention to the cuts and scrapes.

A large branch snagged on her long-sleeved T-shirt and she realized she couldn't go any farther. Breaking off a few branches, she finally managed to squat so she could get down on the puppy's level. Reaching into her pocket, she prayed she had a small crumble of a treat left over from the last time she'd worn these shorts.

Giving thanks that she hadn't actually remembered to do the wash last night, she pulled out a small piece of sausage.

"Mmm. Doesn't this smell yummy?"

She thought the puppy would have been trembling in the bushes, but now that she was closer, she realized it wasn't scared at all.

It was playing.

Its whole body was vibrating with glee, showing that the puppy thought her little predicament of being stuck in the bushes meant a whole lot of fun.

Despite her cramped position stuck among a bunch of sword-sharp sticks and branches, Heather had to agree that it was kind of funny.

At this point, knowing it was a matter of waiting for the little guy or girl to get tired of the game, she sat back on her heels and looked up through the branches and leaves. The clouds slowly changed shape above her in the blue sky. Huddled in a bush might not be the typical place for a breather from her hectic workday, but Heather found she was glad for a moment's respite.

Unfortunately, she could still hear the owner yelling for the dog and vowed to deal with him appropriately once she had the puppy.

"I wouldn't want to come out, either, if I were you," she told the puppy in a soft voice. "But don't worry, Atlas and I won't let anything happen to you."

She ran a training business, not a rescue, but if she found that an owner and a dog weren't compatible, she did anything and everything she could to take care of the dog.

"Doing okay out there, big guy?" she asked Atlas.

She heard the loud thump of his tail on the pavement in response.

"Quite the little adventure Agnes sent us on, isn't it?"

Which didn't make sense. How could the man who was yelling and cursing at the puppy be a close friend of a lovely woman like Agnes? Having seen her interact with her own beloved dog, Heather had trouble figuring out how her client even knew a guy like the brute who was still yelling at the top of his lungs.

Suddenly, a wet tongue pressed into Heather's

palm and she looked down to see the puppy trying to climb onto her lap as it munched on the treat.

"Well, hello there," she said to the very cute Yorkie.

Gently, she laid one hand on the puppy's back and a happy sound came from its throat as it tried to burrow closer to her fingertips. Heather spent a few moments massaging the incredibly soft fur, but with the owner still shouting for his dog, she knew they couldn't stay in here forever.

"How about we go find you a nice full water bowl?" *And a much nicer owner, too, while we're at it.*

She cradled the dog in her arms to shield it from the branches and slowly began the backward procession out of the brambles. She laughed as the puppy licked her chin, even though the scrapes on her legs were cutting deeper on the way out than they had when she'd dived into the bush.

Heather was still in the process of awkwardly crawling out of the dirt on her hands and knees while holding on to the wriggling puppy when she heard footsteps behind her, along with the renewed thumping of Atlas's tail.

Turning her head as far as she could to try to look over her shoulder, she spotted a pair of large brown boots on the pavement beside her dog.

"Did you find the little bugger?"

Gritting her teeth, she replied, "If you're talking about the puppy, yes, I found her stuck in this bush."

Okay, so maybe *stuck* wasn't precisely the truth, given that the dog had clearly been playing hide-

and-seek, but what the owner didn't know wouldn't hurt him. Besides, her allegiance was to the puppy in her arms, not to a man who clearly had no business owning it.

Heather continued to work on getting out of the bush, which, unfortunately, seemed intent on keeping her prisoner. Just a couple more feet and she'd be free to give the man in the brown boots a piece of her mind.

She felt a bead of sweat slide between her shoulder blades as she tried to lift her torso, but no matter how she tugged, she couldn't move more than an inch in any direction. Frustrated with being on her hands and knees in front of a stranger, with her scratched-up kneecaps stinging like crazy, she yanked herself back. But apart from her shirt ripping at the side of her ribs, she wasn't any closer to being free.

"Hold up, you're caught on a branch."

The man's voice, when he wasn't yelling at innocent puppies, had a rich, deep timbre that moved through her veins like potent red wine on an empty stomach.

She felt the stranger reach across her back to thread her T-shirt back through the branch that had taken hold of her. Did he mean for his fingertips to skim her spine? she wondered as she held her breath until he was done.

But whether he did or not had nothing to do with her reaction.

She shouldn't have felt as if a lover had just caressed her.

Heather waited for Atlas to growl at the man for daring to touch her, but instead, he just kept wagging his tail.

She couldn't believe it. After a lifetime of distrusting all men everywhere, Atlas hadn't decided to take an instant liking to this one, had he?

"All clear," the man finally said. "Here, reach back for my hand and I'll help you up."

He didn't give her time to agree or evade; he simply slid his calloused palm against her softer one and pulled her to her feet. Her legs had been cramped into the tight position for long enough that blood rushed too fast to her calves and feet. Unsteady, she swayed against him, her shoulder pressing against his chest.

Her hand still in his, he said, "I've got you," as he brought his other arm around her waist to keep her from tumbling with the dog in her arms.

She was shocked by how good it felt to have his arms around her. So stunned, in fact, that when he said, "I'll take her off your hands now," she almost let him take the puppy from her.

But despite how topsy-turvy her body was behaving, she hadn't forgotten the way he'd yelled for the puppy, or how angry he'd seemed.

Heather took a step back out of his arms, finally pulling her hand free to hold the dog closer to her chest to protect it. "No," she said as she finally looked up at his face, "I don't think that's a good id—"

*Oh, my God.*

She took another step back, but this time it had

nothing to do with the dog in her arms. Heather had never understood her friends who drooled over pictures of good-looking men, and she had always figured she wasn't particularly visually oriented.

Now she realized it was simply that her gaze hadn't landed on the right man.

Within five seconds of taking in his dark hair, his perfectly chiseled face, his blue eyes and broad shoulders, her heart started to pound too fast, her mouth dried out, her palms grew damp and her breath quickened. Not to mention the fact that she was growing hot and tingly all over.

Not once in twenty-seven years had she ever been struck with such a visceral, physical reaction to a man.

What was wrong with her?

Forcing her synapses to refire, she said, "Is this your puppy?"

He lowered his gaze to the puppy's cute face. "Unfortunately."

*Jerk.*

"I know you're interested in my dog-training services," she told him, "but I'm afraid—"

"You're a dog trainer?" he asked, cutting her off before she could tell him that not only was she not going to work with him, but she also thought it best that she find the puppy a new home right away. One that would appreciate the little dog in all her mischievous glory. "You're not one of the girls for the ad?"

He gestured over his shoulder and she looked to

see a half dozen women in bikinis standing around waiting for a photographer to finish setting up lights.

She blinked at him, unable to believe he could possibly have thought that. "God, no," she said, and then, "You asked Agnes Mackelroy to call me about some special dog-training sessions." She paused before asking, "Didn't you?"

He shook his head. "I always knew I loved that woman for more than just her killer Aston Martin collection." The smile he gave her was clearly intended to melt her into a puddle of lust at his feet. "Trust Agnes to also send the prettiest dog trainer on the planet my way."

Absolutely, positively refusing to melt for him, she arched her eyebrow. "Excuse me?"

Atlas reacted to the icy tone of her voice by letting out a low whine. She couldn't believe this man was talking to her like this, trying to flirt with her by suggesting she could be one of the models. Especially when she knew exactly what she looked like in her ripped, sweaty shirt, muddy shorts and skinned knees.

If only she'd trained Atlas to be an attack dog...

A man holding a large camera called out to them. "Hey, Zach, the models need to know how you want them on the cars?"

"Don't let us stop you from your important work. Atlas, let's go." Heather picked up his leash as her big dog rose to his feet beside her.

She was heading to her car when Zach said, "Hey, I thought you were going to stay to train me?"

How, she wondered, did he manage to make her job sound quite so *filthy?* Deciding not to dignify his obnoxious comment with a reply, she didn't even break stride.

At least until he said, "Forget something?"

Darn it. She'd been hoping to make a quick getaway while he was distracted by tiny bikinis and spray-on tans.

Steeling herself for the confrontation—and while reacting to him like a teenage girl hit with her first burst of hormones—Heather turned around slowly. "I heard you yelling earlier. We both know you're not interested in having a puppy." She looked down at the fluff in her arms, deceptively innocent as it snored softly. "Especially one that can be so playful."

He crossed the distance between them and she had to fight the urge to take a step back. "I'll get one of those crates for it for the next couple of weeks."

Heather didn't stop the snarl from erupting from her lips. "You use a crate for specific training purposes, not to imprison a dog all day." She should have just turned and walked away from him, but she had to know. "Why would you get a puppy if you don't even want one?"

"My seven-year-old niece-to-be dumped her on me this morning. I'm taking care of it while she's on vacation with her parents. She'll crucify me if anything happens to it." She was surprised to see a hint of fear hit his eyes. "I remember just how vicious my little sisters could be when I made them mad."

Even as she tried to steel herself against liking

anything about this man, she couldn't miss the deep affection in his voice as he spoke about the women in his life. She shouldn't care how good-looking he was, or how electric it had felt when he'd taken her hand or held her to keep her from falling.

And she certainly shouldn't care if he had a soft spot for seven-year-old girls and little sisters.

Still, it explained why he wasn't the least bit equipped to deal with a puppy. Heather sighed as she realized that perhaps walking away from him with his puppy in tow wasn't going to be quite as easy as she'd thought.

"Damn it," he said, his eyes darkening as he suddenly squatted down and ran one hand over her thigh.

She jumped back. "What are you doing?"

"You're bleeding." He looked incredibly pissed off by this fact. "What the hell were you doing crawling in there in shorts?"

"Saving the dog you lost," she shot back at him, even as a part way down deep inside warmed at the fact that he even cared about her bumps and bruises...not to mention the shockingly seductive feel of his hands on her skin.

She'd been taking care of herself for so long that she couldn't remember the last time someone had worried about her.

"Come inside the shop and I'll clean you up."

The thought of him touching her again had her swallowing hard. She'd always thought there was something so sexy about a mechanic's hands. The fact that they were so skilled at building and fixing things made it difficult not to wonder what else those hands were good at.

*No!*

She knew better than to wonder something like that about *this* mechanic. Talented hands did not make the man, unfortunately.

"You should get back to the models. I can take care of it myself."

But judging by the look on his face, for a moment she thought he was going to pick her up and carry her over to the garage against her will. Instead, he said, "You hurt yourself saving my dog. It's my fault you're bleeding. Let me take care of you—" He stopped, cursing softly. "You saved my dog and I don't even know your name."

"Heather."

"Heather." He held the seven letters on his tongue as if he was savoring them, and she was held spellbound despite herself. "That's a pretty name. I'm Zach."

It shouldn't have felt so intimate just to tell him her name. But when he'd repeated it in a low, husky tone, just hearing it fall from his gorgeous lips had been practically better than full-blown sex with any other man. And she definitely shouldn't want to savor his name on her tongue, too.

"What's the puppy's name?"

He winced, giving her another flash of normal that was so unexpected given the perfect package it was in. "Do you really need to know?"

"Trust me, I've heard a lot of crazy dog names

over the years." But something told her this one was going to take the cake. At least, she hoped it would. "And you know, she actually might have come back to you if you'd called for her by name instead of 'Dog.'"

A muscle jumped in his jaw right before he muttered, "Cuddles."

Heather pressed her lips together to try to keep her giggles from erupting, but she couldn't stop the silent laughter from shaking her shoulders.

There were half a dozen girls in bikinis waiting in his garage, but the woman laughing with his dog in her arms, wearing a long-sleeved T-shirt and muddy shorts, with a messy braid trailing down her back, put them all to shame.

He couldn't think of a time he'd ever seen eyes that color, brown with so many flecks of gold that he couldn't look away. And Jesus, that mouth of hers, rosy and full, made a man want to do crazy things... like grab the puppy and kiss it all over its drooly, disgusting little face for bringing Heather here today.

He'd been pissed off at Gabe and Summer for dumping the dog on him for two weeks. Now he realized he should thank them instead.

Unlike most women, however, he could tell Heather wanted nothing to do with him. Fortunately, her dog didn't seem to have any of the same qualms, especially when he sniffed the glazed sugar on Zach's fingers from the doughnut he'd been eating for breakfast.

"Hey, mutt," Zach said, thinking fast, "I left the rest of my doughnut on the counter inside. You want it?"

The huge dog's ears twitched as if he understood, but he didn't move. Instead, he looked up at Heather for approval.

Clearly, she was gearing up to refuse. But, man, that huge dog could play up the puppy-dog eyes when he wanted to. Zach was impressed. He'd have to remember how to do that in the future.

Her dog let out a low whine and Heather finally sighed and said, "Okay, fine. Go." When she let go of his leash the enormous dog loped off toward the garage and she followed him, still carrying Cuddles.

"I get that you weren't prepared for a puppy, but I can't leave her with you if you're going to put her in a crate all day. She needs to understand how to stay with you so she doesn't get hurt by something in the garage. You're going to need to work on training her to understand your commands. And you're going to have to do it without yelling at her." She shot him a hard look. "Ever again."

He would agree with whatever Heather said if she would stay long enough for him to convince her to give him a chance. He couldn't remember ever wanting a woman this bad, this fast.

"Hey, Chase," he told his brother, the photographer, "I've got to call off the shoot."

The models looked at Zach in confusion and Chase told them to take five before saying, "Chloe is going to have the baby any day now, and then I'm out of commission for a while. You sure you want to reschedule?"

Despite her ongoing protests that she was fine, Zach was already kneeling in front of Heather and gently wiping at the open skin on her knee with an antiseptic wipe from the first-aid kit.

"I've got to clear my schedule for puppy training."

"Seriously?" Heather blinked at him as if he were driving on three wheels. "That's why you're sending everyone home? Isn't your boss going to be mad?"

"Agnes didn't mention my last name, did she?"

Her eyes widened with disbelief as she looked from him to the sign on the wall, then back again. "You're the Sullivan in Sullivan Autos? This is your garage?"

"Don't worry, I know cars a lot better than I know dogs."

But he knew women best of all. And, he thought, as he slid a Band-Aid strip over her left knee, he couldn't wait to get his hands on more than Heather's knees. Because even as he cleaned and bandaged her cuts, her skin was so warm, so soft, so responsive to his touch.

After he slid another Band-Aid strip over her silky smooth skin, he held out his arms. "Now that the shoot's off, I'm all yours to train."

Most women would have been pleased by the sensual undertones in his words, or at least would have blushed, but she simply glared at him with icy cool eyes.

Cuddles yawned and curled closer into her chest. What Zach wouldn't do to be where the puppy was.

She shifted her legs out of his reach. "You can't cancel your photo shoot. You'll lose too much money." She stood up and grabbed her dog's leash again. "Atlas, it's time to go."

Damn it, she was going to leave. Panic gripped him, even though he'd only just met her. "Heather—"

She frowned as she looked down at where he was still kneeling on the cement floor. "Look, since you can't keep Cuddles here while you're—" she paused to look at the models chain-smoking and talking on their cell phones in the parking lot "—*working,* I'll take her to my office. When she wakes up, she can play with Atlas until you get there for our first session."

She told him the address, then made a clicking sound that had her huge dog following her out of the garage with an adoring look on his face.

Zach understood exactly how the dog felt. One sign from her and he'd happily do the same thing.

Chase came over beside him and, together, they watched Heather leave, her long braid swinging behind her, her legs strong and tanned in her shorts.

"Who's that?"

Zach grinned. "My new dog trainer."

And, hopefully, a hell of a lot more than that real soon.

# *Three*

The afternoon sun was streaming in through Heather's office window as she finally hung up her phone. Rubbing the back of her neck with both hands, she stretched the tight muscles. If she'd known it was going to be this much work to head up the fundraising committee for the San Francisco animal shelter, or just how hard it would be to convince potential donors to give to their worthy cause…

Well, she would have signed up for the job, anyway. But at least she might have been better prepared for it. Fortunately, both the big fundraising events were this weekend. When they were over she could lie in a bath with her eyes closed, sipping a very big glass of wine for as long as she wanted.

But for right now, coffee would make everything better. And maybe a couple of those chocolate truffles she had told her assistant, Tina, to throw away.

She got up from behind her computer and Atlas and Cuddles both yawned as she walked past. "Don't let me interrupt your naps," she told them.

They'd played together all day and she was impressed that Zach's dog had only a couple of accidents, more from the excitement of playing with a big dog than anything else.

Atlas immediately plopped his big head back on his huge dog pillow and she shot him a mock scowl as she opened the door. "Keep rubbing it in how awesome your relaxed schedule is and next time I'll send *you* out to deal with every one of those companies I just called."

Her final words landed in a thud against a hard, male wall. "Talking to the dogs, huh?"

Heat seared her hands as she pressed them against the chest of the ridiculously gorgeous man whose low voice had just rumbled through her.

"Zach."

"Heather."

He smiled down at her, his dark eyes full of so much sensuality that she almost felt singed by nothing more than his gaze. One that seemed to promise more pleasure than she'd ever imagined.

Seriously, what was wrong with her? She took a much-needed step back. And why was it so difficult to pull her mind back from the gutter's edge around this man?

She'd never had a problem keeping her guard up around men before. For all his good looks, Zach Sullivan shouldn't be any different. Especially when he was as charming as they came.

*Charming* had never been a point in any man's

favor where Heather was concerned. Not when her father had given the trait such a bad rap.

"How's the puppy doing?"

She moved to the side so that he could see Cuddles licking Atlas's muzzle with the kind of great enthusiasm that only a puppy could exhibit.

"She seems to have him under her spell."

"She sure does."

She realized Zach was staring at her, or more specifically, her hair. She'd had it back in a braid earlier but had tugged it free as the afternoon wore on.

"You have beautiful hair." His mouth moved up into a ridiculously sexy smile. "Makes a guy want to run his hand through it to see if it's as silky as it looks."

Since she foolishly found herself wanting the same thing, she reached into her pocket for a hair band, then pulled it back into a ponytail. She'd put on a new shirt upon her return to the office, but she still had on her muddy shorts.

Pointedly ignoring the compliment about her hair, while telling herself she didn't care if she still looked like a grubby mess, she said, "Are you ready to get started with the training?"

Her voice was brisk and professional, but Zach only relaxed even more against her doorjamb.

"You didn't tell me you owned this place. Very impressive."

"Heather, I'm back from the bank drop-off and they wanted to know if—" Tina's mouth fell open, then snapped shut. "Hi," she said, recovering herself.

"Hello," Zach said to her attractive blonde employee. "I'm Zach Sullivan."

Her assistant's eyes widened and all she said again was a breathy "Hi."

Tina was brilliant not only with dogs, but also with their owners. She was an organizational whiz. And she had a very serious boyfriend.

Still, one look at Zach was clearly all it took for her brain cells to liquefy on the spot. It was a small comfort to Heather to know that she wasn't the only one who had had that reaction today.

Good thing she was over it.

Completely, 100 percent over his square jaw, and his broad shoulders, the way his mouth—

*Yikes.* Really, her brain needed to stop doing that.

"Tina," she said in a scrupulously professional manner, "Zach is the new client I mentioned earlier. He has come by for some one-on-one training with Cuddles."

"She's such a cute puppy," Tina gushed. "And I just love her name. Most guys wouldn't be confident enough to name their dog Cuddles." She beamed at Zach.

*Ugh.* Heather didn't think she could stomach either coffee or chocolate anymore. The sooner she got Zach out of her office and out into training, the sooner he'd leave.

And then everything would go back to normal.

Like her heart rate, for one.

"Atlas, heel." Her dog carefully extracted himself

from beneath the tiny puppy and moved to her side. "Okay, let's go."

Five o'clock was precisely the time each day when the majority of her day-care clients came in to pick up their dogs. Unfortunately, today, just the walk across the large indoor space out to the fenced-off grass behind the building was enough for Zach to attract a shocking amount of female attention. Women she'd known for years, whether single or happily married— including the grandmothers—couldn't keep their eyes off him as he followed Heather and Atlas with Cuddles tucked under his arm. The last thing a guy like Zach Sullivan needed was a puppy to make him a magnet for even more female attention.

When they finally managed to get outside, he put the dog down on the grass. Cuddles immediately started running in circles, chasing her tail and looking over at Atlas, who clearly wanted to play, as well. But Atlas was too well trained to leave Heather's side unless invited to do so.

Heather took a few minutes to say goodbye to her customers and then she turned to Zach. "How long did your brother have Cuddles before he asked you to watch her?"

"A couple of days."

She was glad to hear the slate was fairly clean, at least. "The first few days with a puppy are really important. They can be so cute that even when you want to keep to the rules, you end up breaking them. But that would be a big mistake with her."

"She weighs three pounds," he said as Cuddles

began to roll on the grass. "How much trouble can she really get into given a little freedom?"

Heather knew far too well the price of freedom. Not just for dogs who felt lost and afraid in a world without boundaries, but for women who fell for the charms of men like Zach Sullivan. Men who wanted what they wanted, when they wanted it, without regard for anyone else.

"Freedom is overrated," she told him in a hard voice. When he raised an eyebrow at her tone, she moderated it before saying, "Don't forget, she's recently been taken away from her mother and littermates and she has no clue whatsoever how to navigate our world. Just like this morning at your garage, anything could happen to her. It's your job to watch over her and to teach her how to stay safe."

"This isn't just a business for you," Zach commented. "You really care about dogs, don't you?"

Surprised that he had any insight whatsoever into her, she put her hand on Atlas's back and said, "Someone has to."

Zach looked down at her big dog. "What happened to him?"

Atlas's ears perked up when he realized they were talking about him.

Once more, she was stunned by how closely Zach was paying attention to her subtle cues. She'd assumed he would be more interested in admiring his reflection in the window to notice anything else in the world around him.

"I found Atlas at a puppy mill."

"A puppy mill?"

"It's where unscrupulous breeders crank out as many pedigreed dogs as they can sell for big bucks. His left ear flopped to the side just enough that no one wanted to buy him. Once they realized that, they stopped feeding him or letting him out of his crate."

Zach got down on the grass. "Rough start, huh?" Atlas not only let the big man rub his ears, but he practically started purring. "Lucky you, getting to go home with Heather."

She rolled her eyes, positively thrilled that Zach had capped off his too-sweet reaction to Atlas's story with a blatantly sexual quip. She could tell that he genuinely liked her dog, and she would have been more afraid of it getting to her if he hadn't been so busy trolling out the overused—and underwhelming—pickup lines.

"Okay, let's get started. I'll demonstrate with Atlas how to do things, and then we'll begin the process of teaching Cuddles how to obey your commands. Sound good?"

Zach stood up and nodded. "Sure. I'm great at giving commands."

Intent on ignoring the sexual undertones he seemed to include in every phrase out of his mouth, she said, "There are five basic commands we'll want Cuddles to understand. *Come, sit, stay, down* and *heel.* But for the first day, the most important is *come.*"

Thankfully he didn't jump on any double entendres with that command as she picked up a dog toy and threw it across the lawn. "Atlas, fetch."

Her dog loped off with the puppy hot on his heels, almost as if they didn't want to be separated for even a second. When he was halfway to the toy, she called out, "Atlas, come!"

He skidded on his huge paws and did a quick about-face, all but hurling himself toward her, the toy instantly forgotten. Still, he was careful not to step on the puppy.

"Good boy."

As she gave him the signal to sit and then held out a treat, Cuddles finally reached the toy, falling onto it and causing a faint squeak. Atlas's ears went up, but he didn't move from where he was sitting in front of Heather.

"Your turn," she said to Zach, knowing just how badly this was going to go with such a rambunctious puppy and a temporary owner who she very much doubted was taking any of this seriously. She handed him a tiny doggy treat. "If she comes, give her this."

He raised his eyebrows at her use of the word *if*. Without her telling him what to do, he knelt on the grass, held his arms out wide and said in a firm voice, "Cuddles, come!"

Hearing Zach's command, the rambunctious puppy looked up from the oversize plastic toy she'd been trying to gnaw on and flew across the grass as if she'd been merely trying to find a way to kill time.

"Good girl," he said as he stroked her fur and fed her the small dog treat. He looked up at Heather. "How was that?"

Grudgingly, she admitted, "Good."

*Really good.*

And the worst part of it all was that she knew exactly why the puppy had come running. Zach wasn't just a magnet for women.

It seemed he was able to exert a near gravitational pull over all living things.

She refused to let herself be charmed, though. Especially when every second she was around Zach she had to force herself to get a grip on her self-control to keep from smiling at one of his lines…or from being overly impressed at how good he was with both his puppy and Atlas.

"Walk with me to the other side of the grass and we'll do it again."

For the next fifteen minutes, Zach Sullivan demonstrated a surprising affinity for commanding the attention of the puppy. Heather knew she should be happy about the fact that Zach was a natural. Rather, it grated on her, and at the end of their session, instead of praising Zach, she gathered up the puppy and kissed its soft nose.

"Great work, Cuddles. Did you have fun in class today?"

The dog licked her, then wriggled until she set her back down to continue tormenting a happily bothered Atlas.

"We're done already?" Zach sounded disappointed.

"Puppies tire easily." When he pointedly looked down at Cuddles, who was now trying to dig a hole to China in the grass, she clarified, "What I mean is that they don't have very long attention spans. Fifteen minutes is long enough for them to learn a little more each day without either of you getting frustrated. In any case, today was a great start. And hopefully, if she does manage to run off again, now you'll be able to get her to come back on your own."

"We're both really glad you were there to find her in the bushes this morning." He looked down at Heather's legs and she almost shivered as she remembered the feel of his big, warm hands on her skin. "How are your knees?"

"They're fine," she said briskly, wanting to turn his attention back to his dog. But, in truth, it was her attention she was really worried about—she was all too aware of how good he smelled, and she had to work to keep her gaze from straying to his big, strong hands or from getting lost in his far-too-mesmerizing eyes. "Tonight is going to be really important," she lectured. "You should set up a small room or section of a room to be hers for the next two weeks. Put paper on the floor and put her food, water bowl and bed in one corner. Put her toys throughout the area. And, whatever you do, unless she's sleeping, I don't recommend leaving her alone outside of the gated area for more than fifteen minutes at a time."

He frowned. "What if I have plans?"

She could quite easily guess the kind of "plans" he had. "You'll have to break them, unless you can bring her along and pay close attention to her the entire time." She smiled at his disconcerted expression. "Would you like to schedule another fifteen-minute training session for tomorrow?"

"When are you free?"

She shook her head. "I only met with you today as a favor to Agnes. Now that I can see you'll do fine with proper instruction, you can work with any of my trainers."

"I don't want anyone else, Heather." He made sure she was looking back at him as he said, "I only want you."

He might as well have pulled her against him and kissed her senselessly. The effect of his words on her had Heather quickly realizing that, after a few minutes with Zach Sullivan, she was already too close to the edge of wanting something she could never make the mistake of letting herself have.

Until she turned seventeen, she'd believed in love. She'd thought her parents had the most wonderful marriage, had prayed she'd find a man to love her the way her father so clearly loved her mother. And then she'd found out the truth...that her father had been cheating on her mother for virtually their entire marriage. All that time, he'd been lying to her mother...and to her. Every time he came home from one of his business trips saying how much he loved them, how much he'd missed them, how they meant everything to him—it had all been a lie.

Heather slipped a finger beneath the sleeve of her long-sleeved shirt and traced over the fine lines of her old scars. They were from cuts she'd put there herself, night after night, when she hadn't known how to deal with her swirling, dark emotions. When all she'd wanted was to feel control over something. Over anything at all.

She hadn't known at the time just how many teenage girls and boys cut themselves like that. It wasn't until later—when she went away to college—that she met a nurse at the student medical center who helped her turn her life around. The nurse had seen the cuts during a gyno exam when Heather was wearing a cloth gown. After the exam the nurse had given her a pamphlet on cutting. She'd already begun to get past it by then, but knowing she wasn't the only girl in the world doing it did help some. Still, even though she hadn't cut herself in nearly ten years, the scars had never quite disappeared, both inside and out.

Fortunately, she wasn't that lost girl anymore. She was a strong, capable woman who enjoyed channeling her energy into work, friends and dogs. She was happy. She had everything she wanted.

A man like Zach was exactly who she didn't need to get tangled up with. Not when he was too charismatic for his own good…and hers, too.

Heeding the warning bells going off throughout her brain and her body, she held her ground and told him, "You can't have me."

It wasn't until she saw determination flare in his eyes that she realized she'd just issued a challenge—a really big one—to the wrong man.

"Another trainer will be waiting here for you tomorrow at 5:00 p.m." And she'd make certain it was a completely heterosexual male trainer who Zach couldn't sweet-talk into doing whatever he wanted.

The most important thing was that she put an end to their connection. "It was nice meeting you."

She doubted the wisdom of holding out her hand to shake his, but it was the only way to make sure he knew they were done, that whatever sparks had been jumping between them were officially going to be extinguished in about one nanosecond.

He moved nearer and wrapped his fingers around hers. "I owe you for saving Cuddles today."

"No," she said, shaking her head as his warmth enveloped her head to toe, "you don't owe me anything."

"We both know I do. And I always pay my debts."

Oh, God, why couldn't she breathe?

She wasn't a virgin; she wasn't some young girl easily dazzled by a man just because he looked in her direction. On the contrary, she was a pragmatic woman who knew only too well just how false a pretty facade could be.

"Take good care of Cuddles." She slid her hand from his. "That's all the thanks you owe me."

Before she could walk away, however, her stomach growled and she muttered, "Agnes's call came just as I was about to grab something to eat."

Again, unable to think quickly around him, she realized, too late, she had played right into his hands. "Let me make it up to you by buying you dinner. Somewhere we can sit outside so the dogs can play."

Did he think she'd just fallen off a turnip truck? She knew exactly how he expected a *make it up to you* dinner would play out. He'd ply her with a few glasses of wine and then the next thing she knew, she'd be flat on her back, begging for him to take her.

It wasn't that she was a prude. On the contrary, just because Heather had always carefully guarded her heart with men didn't mean she'd foolishly given up the pleasure of being a woman. She'd just always made sure that her partners weren't any more interested in her heart than she was in theirs, and that there was no chance of anything ever going deeper than the physical.

But with Zach…

Daring to give in to the shockingly strong urge to kiss him would be the stupidest thing she ever did. Even from a distance, being near him made her feel completely out of control. If he were to put his mouth, his hands, on her naked skin—

Just the thought of that had her senses reeling.

She took another step back from him. "I'm still playing catch-up from being pulled out of the office for so long this morning, so I'll have to pass on dinner."

She told herself she wasn't being a coward, that she was being smart, protecting herself from exactly the kind of man who could destroy her.

"Remember what I said about tonight," she told him before he could press her on dinner again. "Don't make the mistake of letting Cuddles get away with anything because she's cute. You'll only confuse her."

"What if I've got a thing for cute?"

This time, he very clearly wasn't talking about

the dog. Evidently, she hadn't been direct enough with him thus far. It was long past time to put him in his place.

"Then you'd better get over it real fast. Atlas, time to say goodbye to your friend."

Heather made a low clicking sound, then turned her back on Zach and walked away from temptation.

# *Four*

Zach wanted Heather with a hunger he'd never felt before. His fascination with girls had started early and he'd been kissing in school hallways way back in middle school, going a heck of a lot further than that by high school. But for all the playing he'd done during his thirty years, he'd never felt such a strong need, especially so quickly.

Had this been the way his father had felt about his mother when he'd met her?

Suddenly realizing the crazy direction his brain was going, he almost lost his hold on Cuddles. She gave a little squeak as he tightened his grip on her.

What was wrong with him, thinking about Heather that way?

Ever since he was seven and his father had died unexpectedly of an aneurysm, leaving his mother behind to mourn him while raising eight kids on her own, Zach had known that he could never let himself form a bond that strong with a woman. He was too much like his father. Looked like him, acted like him, had all the same interests. He even got the same headaches his father used to get, ones that would come on like a bullet train one minute and be gone the next. They'd been so much alike that Zach's uncles had barely been able to be around him after his father's death because he reminded them too much of Jack Sullivan. Even now, whenever he saw his father's brothers, he could tell how hard it was for them.

All his life, Zach had been careful to keep the boundaries clear with women. He was all for great sex until they made the mistake of trying to stick emotions on it, at which point he always got the heck out. He couldn't stand the thought of a woman falling in love with him, planning her life around him, only to have him checking out on her way too early, the way his father had his mother.

*Like father, like son.* It was why Zach had always gone for speed. Cars. Women. *Life.* He wanted to experience as much of it as he could before it ended early. Because he knew he was too much like his father for it to go any other way.

Damn it, he needed to stop wasting time analyzing this thing with Heather. She was hot. Smart. And sex with her was going to be great.

That was, if he could convince her to give him a go.

Finally, he smiled. Because if there was one thing Zach knew how to do better than any guy on earth, it was convincing women to give him a go.

A half hour later, when he knew her employees had all gone home, he dialed Heather's cell phone. "Pizza delivery out front."

"I didn't order any pizza."

He hung up on her and waited by the locked front door. When she saw him through the long window at the side of the door, he thought he caught a flash of a small smile before she replaced it with a scowl.

"Why are you here again? And how did you get my cell number?"

"Cuddles couldn't stop worrying about you missing meals because of us." He leaned against the door-jamb. "And Agnes checked in a little while ago to make sure we were doing all right. I told her we were, but only because of you. She thought it best if I had your direct line just in case I have another puppy emergency."

Again, it looked as though her lips wanted to curve upward, but from the way she always worked to keep her beautiful face so serious, he knew she was bound and determined to resist him.

Lord knew he'd like to have her bound and begging instead....

Knowing there was a good chance she'd simply take the pizza from him, then lock him out on the sidewalk, he held Cuddles out so that Atlas could see his new friend from the office. The Great Dane immediately started whining.

"Really, Atlas?" Heather asked in an exasperated voice. "You're going to pull this *now?*"

Her dog happily wagged his enormous tail and

Zach used the opportunity to put the puppy inside, knowing she wouldn't leave him out on the front step if she had his dog inside.

Yup, he now officially loved the annoying little ball of fur, even if she had tried to use his T-shirt to sharpen her tug-of-war skills on the way back from the pizza place.

"I'm guessing you want to share the pizza." She looked impossibly grumpy at the thought of his joining her for the dinner he'd brought over.

"I'm one of eight. We learned to eat fast as kids or go hungry. If *you* want some, you'd better start now."

Her eyes grew big. "Eight? Please tell me you're the worst of the bunch."

He grinned. "Easily. Except for maybe my sister Lori. We call her Naughty."

She was shaking her head at the news of his big family as she headed for a table and chairs off in the corner. As she washed her hands at a nearby sink, she gave him ample time to appreciate the view of her gorgeous legs in her shorts and the way her long hair nearly brushed her hips, even in the ponytail. He couldn't wait to find out how soft it was when his hands were tangled in it and—

The loud screech of a chair over linoleum yanked him from his hot daydream. Heather's face looked like thunder as she sat down. "Stop looking at me like that."

He washed his hands, then sat down across from her. "How am I looking at you?"

She narrowed her eyes at him. "Don't ask me a

stupid question when you know exactly what you're doing."

This wasn't usually the way it played out, with both sides flirting while no one said what they really meant. But Zach was perfectly happy to give up the game. Really happy about it, in fact, given that the game had been getting pretty old lately.

He shrugged. "Sorry, but it's going to be pretty much impossible for me to stop looking at you like that." He let his eyes move over her face. "You're gorgeous, you know."

She looked shocked by his completely honest compliment, and he knew he'd gotten one up on her. Finally. Feeling good about things, he flipped open the large cardboard box, grabbed a piece of pizza and put it on one of the paper plates he'd picked up at the restaurant. She looked down at the slice, then back up at him.

"You like egg on your pizza?"

"Never order one without it," he lied.

He put the slice in front of her, then picked one up for himself, taking a large bite of it, egg and all. Little did Heather know her assistant had been only too happy to tell him what her favorite pizza toppings were. He had been prepared to suck it up regardless of how bad it tasted, but it was actually pretty good.

"No one likes egg on their pizza but me and people from France. You're the first."

"Your first, huh?"

She shook her head and sighed. "I can't believe I have to spell this out to you, but I obviously do." She looked around the building as if to make absolutely certain they were the only two people in it before saying, "I'm not going to sleep with you."

Well, then. Now they were *way* off the normal track.

"Why not?"

"You really want me to tell you why I find the thought of sleeping with you completely abhorrent?"

Sexy as hell *and* a good vocabulary. He was going to give Agnes a freebie on her tune-up next time he saw her as thanks for this introduction.

"Sure, lay it on me." It would help a great deal, actually, if he knew why she was resisting him. Because then he could break down each of her reasons, one by one. He nodded at her pizza. "But eat first. It's getting cold and I know you're starved."

When her stomach grumbled again in agreement, she finally took a bite. He handed her a cold soda to wash it down, and as he watched her take a large gulp of the sweet, fizzy drink, Zach wanted her more with every passing second. Gorgeous, smart and, as a bonus, she ate and drank like a woman who enjoyed food, versus the kind of women he normally had sex with, who barely picked at it.

Lord, what he wouldn't give to feed her pizza in bed, to have her naked and using his stomach as a plate, her tongue licking up the oil from between his abs, and then lower down....

"You're doing it again," she said when she caught the way he was looking at her, but her chastisement was milder this time.

He resisted the urge to do a fist pump in the air after finally making some headway. "Already told you, I can't help myself. You're too pretty."

She reached for another piece of pizza. "That's one big reason, right there. You're way too quick with the lines."

"It's not a line. It's true."

"See?" She picked a piece of egg off the pizza and popped it into her mouth. "Way too quick."

"Okay, I've got it. I won't talk when we're in bed."

"I should be surprised that you just made a comment like that," she said almost more to herself than to him, "but I'm not."

She ran her finger over the rim of her drink and sucked the sweetness off, creating a huge ache in him. Fortunately, his groin was well hidden under the table.

"I'm also not interested in being your flavor of the week. Or night, as the case probably is."

"Forget about a night or a week," he told her. "A month will work just fine." Although right now, even if he had thirty days with Heather tied to his bedposts, her long, silky hair spread all around her, it wouldn't be long enough.

She let out a long, irritated sigh as she turned to watch the dogs drinking from the big water bowl across the room. "You should have been a politician instead of a mechanic."

He didn't correct her by telling her he was more than a mechanic, that he owned forty Sullivan Autos franchises up and down the West Coast.

"And just to be clear," she added, "you're not my type."

Now it was his turn to say, "Good thing you're a dog trainer and not a politician. You're a terrible liar, Heather."

She scooted her chair back and he could tell she was angry as she chucked the rest of her pizza into the trash. "What, you think you're so irresistible that you believe there isn't a woman alive who doesn't want to be with you?"

"I'm sure there is," he said in an easy voice as he stood up, "but you're not her." Before she could throw something at his head, he said, "Cuddles, come!"

His smart little puppy raced over into his open arms and the two of them got the hell out of there.

# Five

*"Help! I'm having another puppy emergency."*

Heather held the phone to her ear as she rolled over in bed and blearily looked at the clock. 5:30 a.m. It wouldn't be so bad if she'd gotten more sleep, but all night long she'd watched the clock tick over from 11:00 p.m. to midnight to 1:00 a.m. and then 2:00 a.m. before her brain finally gave up and shut down.

Damn Zach Sullivan for not only waking her up… but for being the reason she hadn't been able to sleep in the first place.

"It's five-thirty in the morning."

"Cuddles doesn't care what time it is," he growled into her ear.

Yesterday, she would have been in a panic over the tone of his voice, would have assumed he was going to do something horrible to the puppy. But after spending part of the evening with him, while she'd confirmed that he was full of himself, she also felt confident that he was good with animals.

Even naughty little puppies.

"That's life with a puppy," she informed him around a yawn as she leaned back against her pillow and watched the sun start to rise outside her bedroom window.

Strange that it should seem so easy and natural to be talking on the phone with Zach when she'd just met him. And yet, it was.

"Just clean up whatever mess she made, tell her you love her, anyway, and be sure to show up for your training session this evening."

"Cuddles!" he roared.

She heard something crash to the floor, and then a muffled string of curses, before they were disconnected.

She closed her eyes, but already she knew it was pointless. She shouldn't go running whenever he called, especially not to a man like Zach Sullivan, who would only see it as confirmation that he was king of the world. But at the same time, she knew she'd only be distracted all day wondering if he and Cuddles were going to make it to 5:00 p.m. in one piece.

She dragged herself into the shower and ran it a bit colder than usual to try to wake herself up—and to cool down from the very sexy dream she'd been having about the exact person she shouldn't have been dreaming about. After she dried off, she pulled up his number on her cell phone and left him a message saying she would be coming to help, after all.

It was far more tempting than it should have been

to blow-dry her hair and throw on some makeup. It was bad enough she was heading to his house this morning after nothing but a phone call. If she actually dressed up for him, all chance of retaining her self-respect would disappear.

She slid on a pair of jeans and put on one of a dozen long-sleeved T-shirts in her closet. Then she braided her hair to keep it out of the way while she was dealing with whatever puppy mayhem had descended at Zach's house. By that time he'd texted her with his address.

She let Atlas out into the backyard and fed him before they set out. "Guess what? We're going to see your new best friend Cuddles."

At the sound of the puppy's name, her dog happily thumped his tail.

"I'm glad at least one of us is happy about this," she muttered as she drove toward Potrero Hill, one of the most exclusive districts in San Francisco, with views to forever. Who knew auto mechanics did this well?

The thought hit her again as she pulled up to the enormous house, along with the question of how Zach could possibly afford it. But when everything inside sounded ominously quiet as she stood on the front step and knocked on the door, worry about what had happened between him and the puppy made that question disappear.

Because even though she had a sense that Zach probably lived to do things like wake people up out of a sound sleep at five-thirty in the morning, she now had a feeling the real reason he'd called her was out of actual desperation.

Hoping she wasn't too late, she knocked on the door again, more loudly. Zach opened the door, saying, "Shhh."

He looked like hell. Still far too gorgeous for a mere mortal, but definitely not his best.

Without a doubt, even she'd managed more sleep than he'd had last night. And from the looks of his half-shaven face, and the jeans pulled up over his hips, the real damage had started to go down when he was in the shower.

Okay, she firmly told herself as the muscles on his shirtless chest rippled in front of her, she could handle a nice set of abs. Heck, she'd casually dated a professional athlete for a while, so it wasn't as if she hadn't seen a good body before.

Fortunately, Zach was so distraught by whatever Cuddles had done that he didn't seem to notice her drooling over his bare chest. The last thing she needed was for him to know just how hard a time she was having resisting him.

He pointed down to her dog and ordered, "Don't wake the puppy up."

Atlas's ears flattened and Heather rolled her eyes. Men were such babies. Zach was behaving as if waking up Cuddles would bring on the end of the world. He slowly opened the door, wincing at every creak in the hinges.

Heather's mouth fell open. "Oh. My. God." She looked at Zach in shock, then back at his living room.

"I can't believe Cuddles could possibly have done all this by herself."

A muscle jumped in his clenched jaw. "Believe it. She's the devil in a puppy disguise."

Normally, Heather would have taken offense at such a comment about a helpless, sweet puppy, but she was stunned by the destruction to Zach's living room.

The puppy had not only ripped open every pillow on his couch, she had also gone to town on what Heather guessed was a really expensive rug. There were scratch marks up and down one side of the kitchen island and a half dozen dark stain spots on the exposed parts of the hardwood floor.

Even Atlas looked alarmed by the state of the apartment as he stood beside her inside the front door looking more like a statue of a Great Dane than the real thing.

"Where is she?" Heather asked in a hushed tone.

He pointed to a pile of feathers beside the couch. Heather had to look closely to see Cuddles curled up in the center of it, sleeping the sleep of the truly exhausted.

"I'm going to kill my brother," he said in a low voice that told her he meant every single word.

She didn't blame him for feeling that way. He was a bachelor who'd had a rambunctious puppy dumped on him. In truth, none of this was Zach's fault. He was just doing the best he could. Unfortunately, it seemed he was way out of his element with this particular puppy.

Heather had worked with hundreds of dogs over the years, and she'd been able to tell right away that this one was a handful. The smart, playful ones always were.

"What happened?"

"She wouldn't stop crying last night when I put her to bed behind her gate."

Heather rolled her eyes. "What did I tell you yesterday about sticking to the rules?"

"Neither one of us was going to get any sleep unless I let her come into the bed." He gave her a rueful look. "She fell right to sleep as soon as I put her on one of my pillows, and I figured we were good to go until morning." He ran his hand over his face. "I know, I'm an idiot, but I didn't think three pounds of fluff could do this kind of damage. I can't believe I forgot about the teeth. And the bladder. And the nails."

"How long do you think she was up by herself?"

"I don't know. I thought she had burrowed under a pillow and I assumed she was still in the bed when I got up to shave and get in the shower." He grimaced. "That was when I heard the crash. A lamp shattered, fortunately not on her. She knocked over another one right after I called you. Swear to God, I look away for three seconds and she's like the freaking Tasmanian Devil."

Heather gave Atlas the signal to stay by the door before she moved toward the pile of feathers and puppy. "Is she hurt?"

"She's fine. I checked her over before I let her sack out."

The truth was that, by this point, most people would have been angry enough to at least give the puppy a smack on its rump. Funny, wasn't it, that she could so easily imagine Zach's large hands moving gently over Cuddles's legs and soft belly as he made sure the puppy was okay.

Taking pity on him, she said, "I'll help you clean up. Go ahead and finish your shower."

He looked pathetically grateful as he showed her where the garbage bags were.

"Thank you, Heather."

*Oh, boy.* She hadn't prepared for a smile like that, one completely devoid of seduction or wicked intent. It was one thing to guard her heart against a lothario with no moral fiber…it was another entirely to remain cold and distant with a flesh-and-blood man who she was afraid might be just as human as the rest of them.

He was halfway across the living room when he turned and said, "If it weren't for the puppy of mass destruction over there, I'd invite you to join me."

Ah, there was the man she had no trouble fighting her attraction to.

"If it weren't for her, I wouldn't be here."

She turned her back on him as she stuffed feathers and ceramic shards into the trash. When she heard Zach turn the shower on, she let out the breath she'd been holding. Rocking back on her heels, she looked at Atlas, who was watching over Cuddles from his spot by the door.

"What have we gotten ourselves into, Atlas?"

He raised his dark eyebrows at her question, but he didn't look away from the puppy. She didn't blame him for being completely wrapped up in the cute, but very naughty, little dog.

Lord knew she couldn't seem to pull her thoughts away from Cuddles's equally cute and naughty temporary owner.

# *Six*

Zach still couldn't believe the way the puppy had gone to town on every piece of furniture in his house, but it was worth it. Because Heather was here.

After the way she'd tried to blow him off last night, he doubted anything else could have gotten her to agree to come over as quickly.

His sisters, Lori and Sophie, had been itching to redecorate his place for a while, anyway. Lord knew they'd probably never stop laughing when they heard what had happened. His siblings were going to *love* this. Chase had probably already spread the news about Heather to everyone after yesterday's photo shoot.

Zach put on jeans and a T-shirt to head into the living room to help Heather clean up. He stopped at the end of the hall in surprise. "You're done already?"

She smiled at him from the open kitchen at the other side of the living room. "I've participated in more than my fair share of puppy cleanups. It looked worse than it was. Although your couch is definitely a goner."

He sniffed the air. "Are you cooking something?"

She flushed slightly. "I didn't get a chance to eat breakfast and I figured you must be hungry, too. I hope you don't mind that I helped myself to your fridge."

With a kitchen towel tucked into the waistband of her jeans and her hair starting to come out of her braid as the sun rose in the kitchen window behind her, she was hands down the most beautiful woman he'd ever seen in his life. His chest clenched as he watched her stirring eggs and buttering toast.

Apart from his mother, no woman had ever made him breakfast before. Many had wanted to, but he'd never let them, had never wanted to share anything so intimate just in case they got the wrong idea. If someone had told him he'd welcome a woman in his kitchen, and that he'd be trying to find even more reasons to get her to stay with him awhile longer, he'd have told them they needed psychiatric help.

The thing was, he wanted Heather bad enough that he was willing to break a few rules for her. Not the big one, of course. He wasn't going to fall in love with her or anything.

But breakfast, and wanting to spend more time with her than he usually did with a woman, wasn't that big a deal.

She looked over at him from around an open cupboard door, clearly surprised to see that he was still standing in the same place. "I can't find your whisk."

He finally got his feet moving, but when he got to the kitchen, he stood there and stared at the cabinets.

"You don't have a clue where it is, do you?" He could tell she was laughing at him, which he'd take any day over her shutting him down the way she had last night.

"I don't even know what a whisk looks like."

When she started to laugh out loud, he leaped to cover her mouth with his hand. At her alarmed expression at his manhandling, he whispered, "Cuddles might wake up!"

Heather nodded her understanding, then covered his hand with hers to pull it off, but not before he felt how soft her lips were against his palm.

And not before he noted the way her eyes darkened as her hand covered his to slide it away from her mouth and cheeks.

He'd wanted her from the second he'd seen her stuck in the bush at his garage. And there was no stopping the kiss from happening anymore. Not when she was in his kitchen, and she was so close and warm and soft against him.

Her eyes went soft as he lowered his head to hers. One kiss wouldn't be nearly enough to take the edge off his desire, not when she was all he could think ab—

A high-pitched series of barks had her jumping out of his arms.

Cuddles had picked one hell of a time to wake up.

Zach and Heather turned to watch the puppy dash across the room to make a flying leap onto Atlas. The big dog remained still as the puppy rubbed and wriggled against him, but Zach could see how happy he was about the affection.

Quickly turning to action, rather than letting them get close again, Heather grabbed two plates and ladled on scrambled eggs.

"I can't believe how fast those two bonded. It's like they were always meant to be together and were just waiting until they could finally meet."

Zach tried to ignore the way his chest clenched again at her words. It was just that she was so damn sexy as she sat down at his dining table, kicking off her flip-flops and tucking one leg under her.

"It's really amazing how good she always is around Atlas," Heather commented. "It's almost like she wants to impress him."

"In that case, you guys should move in for the next two weeks." Purposefully ignoring her *as if* look, he sat down and took a bite of the eggs. "These are so good, you could cook for me every morning, too."

"Really? Could I?" Sarcasm dripped from every word.

"Sure thing," he responded with a grin.

She shook her head, but he could see her fighting the urge to grin back at him. If only he'd been able to sneak in that kiss in the kitchen, he wouldn't have to work so hard for her now or keep moving so slowly.

He thought about how long it took him to rebuild a classic car from the engine out, and how satisfying it was, not just getting the final product, but loving every minute he spent fine-tuning the intake manifold or working under the rear end.

Could it be that rushing things with Heather wasn't the way to go, either?

"Oh, I almost forgot," she said, getting up from the table to hand him a photo. "I found this under a pillow on the sofa. The frame is broken, but I don't think Cuddles did any damage to the picture."

It was an old black-and-white photo, one of the only ones he had with his father in it. His mom and dad had their arms around each other and Marcus, Smith, Chase, Ryan and Zach were doing their best to hold still for the photographer. His mother was holding Gabe in her arms and she had been pregnant with the twins at the time.

"If I didn't know better, I would have thought the man in the picture was you."

"It's what everyone says. I'm the carbon copy of my father. When I was a kid, we would spend hours under the hood of some junky car he was trying to put back together."

"How old were you here?"

"Four."

His father had died only three years after that picture had been taken. Three years and two weeks. The anniversary of Jack Sullivan's death was never a good day. Zach's crew at work had learned to steer clear of his shitty mood once a year.

"In that picture you look like you're dying to rip off that bow tie," Heather said with a small smile. A smile that told him more about the way she felt about him than she'd revealed so far.

"You know the way the living room just looked?" He grinned, remembering. "Multiply that carnage by six 'cause after this picture was taken we were let loose."

He loved the sound of her laughter, the way it pushed away the dark clouds that came from thinking about his father.

"I wouldn't think a woman as beautiful as your mother could deal with so many boys," Heather commented.

"Even when she was yelling at us, you could have sold a picture of her to a magazine." He smiled down at the black and white, keeping his focus on his mother rather than his father this time. "Even now, after everything we've put her through, she's still a great-looking broad."

He looked up to see Heather staring at him as if she'd never seen him until this very moment. Damn it, he'd never had a problem with flapping his lips around women before. It was usually the other way around, when they couldn't stop telling him how excited they were to be with him, how much they were hoping to meet his famous brothers.

"I thought there were eight of you?"

"Mom was pregnant with Lori and Sophie in this picture." He decided to break the ice and pointed at the faces in the photo. "Smith is that one. And there's Ryan."

She looked at the picture again. "Who are the other two?"

He frowned. Didn't she care that Smith was one of the biggest movie stars in the world and Ryan was the star pitcher for the Hawks?

"Marcus and Chase." He studied her face carefully to make sure she wasn't putting him on. Sure, if she wasn't a sports fan she might not know who Ryan was, but she'd have to live under a rock to not know who Smith was. "You watch movies, right?"

"Of course I do." She got up, picked up their empty plates and took them over to the sink. "Seen anything good lately?"

Atlas pawed at the screen door and Zach got up to let the Great Dane go take care of business. Of course Cuddles went with him. He hoped she'd learn something about using the grass rather than his hardwood floor in the near future.

"You really don't care that Smith Sullivan is my brother?"

He didn't know why he was pushing her so hard on it. But he didn't want to be disappointed later when it turned out she'd been secretly angling for an invitation all along.

She paused with a plate in one hand and a sponge in the other. "He is?" She laughed at herself. "I should have put two and two together earlier, shouldn't I? I've been so busy with my business this past year that I guess I don't get out as much as I used to." She shot him a look as if she was afraid she'd offended him by not caring about Smith's fame. "But I hear your brother has been really great in his recent movies. Is there one I should see?"

He joined her at the sink, drying the dishes she'd just washed. "Seen one, you've seen 'em all."

"I can tell from the way you talk about all of them how much your family means to you," she said softly.

"I'd take a bullet for any one of them."

"You would?"

He didn't have to think about it. "We're family."

"Family." She was silent for a long moment. "They're lucky to have you."

Wanting to erase the shadows that didn't belong in her pretty eyes, he said, "That's what I'm always telling them."

She shook her head. "Go check on the dogs, would you? I think we should get away from the scene of the crime for a bit to do more training. I'll finish up in here."

He was heading out of the kitchen when he realized he'd forgotten something important. He walked back to where she was standing on her tippy-toes to put the clean plates back in his cupboard.

Before she realized what he was doing, he kissed her on the cheek.

"Thanks for breakfast, Heather. And for coming to help with Cuddles. I'd have been completely lost without you."

Her skin was so soft, and she smelled so good, he wanted to do so much more than kiss her cheek. Instead, he forced himself to step away and head toward the backyard. He hadn't given up his quest to get her into his bed, but just then it didn't seem right to try to seduce her the way he normally would have.

As he walked away, he couldn't stop himself from turning to look back at her.

She was standing in front of the cupboards, her hand on her cheek where he'd kissed her…looking just as shell-shocked as he felt.

# *Seven*

Heather wasn't used to people surprising her. It had taken her a while to learn how to read people, how to separate the honest from the deceitful, the real from the fake, but ever since the age of seventeen, she'd made sure not to let anyone slip through her filter.

She'd thought she had Zach Sullivan pinned from the first time she'd met him. But the way he'd looked at the black-and-white photo and talked about his family with such deep love and affection…it made her wonder if she'd been wrong about her first impressions.

On the surface, a man like Zach didn't seem to need anyone else. Not when he looked so perfect, so untouchable. It was obvious he'd spent his whole life with strangers falling all over themselves to please him just for the barest scrap of his attention.

But in the end, it was the simple kiss he'd given her on her cheek that had taken her aback.

Standing that close to him in the kitchen, with the

heat of his palm across her lips, had her on the verge
of begging him to kiss her. No doubt she would probably have done just that and more had it not been for
Cuddles's very well-timed barking.

She actually found herself wishing Zach would
stick to his original game and be the charmer with
only one thing on his mind. Because more than anything, she needed to shut her emotions down before
things went any further inside her.

She couldn't risk feeling anything for the charming man with the adorable puppy...not when she already knew how it would all end up. The lie that
played out between her mother and father in her
childhood home for seventeen years was evidence
enough that "charming" was dangerous.

Wanting to change gears and focus on the dogs,
Heather told Zach about a good park with an off-
leash area for dogs that was only a couple of blocks
from his house. It was close enough to walk to and
the dogs would enjoy running around. Of course,
that short walk was plenty of time for at least half a
dozen complete strangers to waylay them with ex-
clamations over the amazingly cute puppy or, more
accurately, the puppy and her owner.

If she heard the words *so cute* and *adorable* one
more time she was going to make Cuddles and Zach
wear masks the next time they went out in public
together.

Not, of course, that she was planning on any future public outings. These were extenuating circum-

stances, after all, not the beginning of any kind of foursome around town.

Poor Atlas, she thought as he nudged Cuddles with his nose and the puppy let out a happy bark. He was going to be heartbroken when she found another trainer for his new friend.

Then again, for the sake of the dogs, if she could be tough enough and trust herself enough around Zach, then she could make some additional concessions to her daily schedule and continue working with them directly. Surely she had enough self-control to keep their relationship on a professional level for the next two weeks. Didn't she?

When they found an empty patch of grass, she put down her bag of training gear and said, "We're going to work on positive reinforcement today."

Zach raised his eyebrows. "You want me to reward the little punk after what she pulled this morning?"

She gave Atlas a subtle signal and he stopped panting after the squirrel climbing up the tree to train his full attention on her instead. "Good boy." She smiled at him. "Down."

She reached into the pouch she'd strapped onto her belt loop and squatted down to hand him a treat. She scratched between his ears and looked up at Zach. "Why do you think Atlas wants to please me?"

His eyes sizzled. "Who wouldn't want to please you?"

She swallowed hard, not sure how their conversations—even those about totally unsexy things like dog training—always managed to veer off into forbidden territory so quickly.

No, that wasn't precisely the truth. She knew exactly how it happened.

Zach Sullivan was walking, living, breathing sex. And she was a sensual woman who couldn't help but respond. At least on a physical level.

Continuing as if he hadn't just set the blood racing through her veins, she said, "It's comforting for him to know that I'm in charge, and that I'll always give him clear cues as to when I'm happy or upset with him."

Zach frowned at the puppy in his arms. She didn't think he was aware of it, but even though he still claimed to be angry with Cuddles, he held her gently against his chest, her little head resting against his heartbeat. "Seems to me yelling is a pretty clear cue."

She had to smile at what an adorably cute pair they were, shaking her head at the fact that she was acting just as pathetically as all the women they'd come across during their walk.

"Honestly, all the yelling does is make her more anxious. Which makes her act out more, especially when she doesn't know the proper behaviors to replace the naughty ones with."

"And here I used to think I liked my girls naughty."

She groaned. "You're incorrigible."

She should be a whole lot more upset about it, but the truth was, she kind of liked his sense of humor.

"Incorrigible enough to tell you how hot it is when you use big words?"

She should have known better. If she gave him an inch, he'd take a mile. Suppressing a grin, she said, "Try irritating instead." She took Cuddles from him, then handed him the bag of dog treats. "Go over to that tree and let's work on the *come* command a few times first."

She held her breath, waiting for him to make some off-color play on the command they were working on, but he simply stuck to the program and headed over to the tree. Not, of course, that she was disappointed he hadn't grabbed the opportunity for a double entendre, or that she was starting to enjoy the constant spark of being with such a magnetic man.

But, oh, as she watched his lean, muscled body move in the sunlight, she couldn't hold in a sigh of pure female appreciation. Zach Sullivan might have been irritating and incorrigible on the inside, but on the outside he really was a work of art.

After a few minutes of Cuddles running into Zach's arms at his command, the puppy's tongue was hanging out.

"Bring her over here and you can give her some water."

She put a small bowl on the grass and handed Zach a water bottle. Cuddles immediately plopped her muzzle into the bowl. Before Heather told him what she wanted him to do, Zach started petting the puppy and telling her how smart she was. Her tail wagged all the while and Heather knew there was no point in trying to fight her smile as she watched them together.

Okay, so Zach had made a terrible first impression on her, but he just might turn out to be her best student yet.

When Cuddles had her fill of water, Heather turned to Atlas, who had been waiting patiently by her heels. She pulled a multicolored rope out of her bag and tossed it a few feet away.

"Go ahead and play, Atlas." Cuddles bounded through the bowl of water in her hurry to go play, too.

"That mutt of yours worships you."

"He's a purebred Great Dane, not a mutt," she informed Zach, and then said, "I think he's pretty great, too."

It was so tempting to relax with Zach and to pretend they were sharing a morning in the park together with their dogs. Too tempting.

Clearly, she needed to work harder to remember what they were together: dog trainer and puppy owner. Nothing more.

"Now we'll work on positive reinforcement. What I'd like you to do is call out Cuddles's name a few times while they're playing. You don't need to tell her to come, but every time she looks at you, give her a treat or pet her or tell her how great she is."

Zach nodded, then turned his focus to the puppy. "Cuddles."

The puppy looked up at him, still holding the tattered rope in her mouth, to see what her temporary owner wanted. He was immediately there with a treat and a hug. What a lucky pup she was to be the recipient of so much of Zach's focused attention.

He stepped back. "How'd I do?"

"You're a glutton for praise, aren't you?"

He moved to brush a strand of hair out of her eyes, his fingertips making the barest contact with her skin. "That good, huh?"

Oh, God, she thought, as thrill bumps rose across the surface of her body at his gentle touch, *good* didn't even begin to cover it.

"Do it again," she said, her words coming out far too breathy for anything outside of a bedroom.

His eyes darkened as he slid his fingers against her hair again, this time brushing the pad of his thumb across her cheekbone. "With pleasure."

She got so lost in sweet sensation, in the sinful promise of pleasure in his eyes, that it took her far longer than it should have to step back from his heat.

"Not that. Say the puppy's name again."

For a moment, she thought he was going to ignore her and pull her against him instead. Her eyes dropped to his mouth of their own volition. What, she couldn't stop wondering, would it be like to feel them press against hers? Not one of those soft kisses he'd given her against her cheek in the kitchen, but a raw, demanding kiss that left her no room to hide exactly how he made her feel?

Abruptly, he turned and called for the puppy. Again, Cuddles responded immediately and he showered her with praise and affection.

Heather could feel her cheeks flaming at the embarrassing way she kept losing herself over him, especially after the way she'd mentally derided so many other women for doing the exact same thing. Tightening her resolve to keep her wits about her, she turned her entire focus back to the training session.

When Cuddles had responded to Zach saying her name a good dozen times, she said, "I think that's good enough for her to start to associate pleasure with you."

"Pleasure?"

Oh, no, what had she just said?

She forced herself to continue as if it were what she would have said to any other client. "The more she associates treats and affection with you, the less likely it is that she'll get her jollies from shredding your couch apart. Especially once she learns that you don't approve of that behavior."

"I thought you said yelling was out."

"You won't need to yell at her anymore. Because if you catch her pulling feathers out of a pillow and don't smile and pet her and tell her how wonderful she is, she'll be disappointed."

"I wonder if the same thing would work with my staff at the garage?"

She had to laugh at the idea of him dealing with the big men she'd seen working in his garages the way he just had with the puppy.

A young couple walked past, their hands linked, their mouths fused to each other's faces. It wouldn't have been so bad if they hadn't stopped just then to paw at each other and murmur adoring words against each other's lips.

Zach caught Heather's grimace. "You don't approve of the loving couple?"

"I could have lived without seeing them clean each other's tonsils, but other than that, I'm happy for them for as long as it lasts."

"As long as it lasts?" He looked confused. "I thought all women believed in forever?"

*Just the stupid ones.* "Nope, not all of us."

Helping her pack up her bag, he asked, "Why not?"

Their conversation had crossed the line again, from professional to personal. Clearly, Zach wasn't big on boundaries. So instead of answering him, she just shrugged and said, "What about you?" even though she was certain she could easily guess the answer.

"I'm not a forever kind of guy," he said, as if that explained everything. And then, "Some guy you were dating broke your heart, didn't he?"

Any warmth she might have been letting herself feel toward him immediately cooled. "My heart is perfectly intact, thank you."

He snapped his fingers. "I've got it. Your parents split up and you've never gotten over it."

She had to unclench her teeth to say, "Wrong again. My parents are still together. Not," she added pointedly, "that it's any of your business."

And not that their *intact* marriage had given her one single good thing to believe about love and marriage—

or any hope whatsoever in a beautiful forever. In fact, whenever she thought about her parents' relationship, about the way her father had cheated on her mother probably from the first day they'd met, and the fact that her mother stayed with him, like a dog begging for scraps regardless of the way he treated her, it just enforced Heather's view that there was no such thing as forever.

Wanting to leave, Heather picked up her bag and called for Atlas. She never should have come over to Zach's house this morning or had breakfast with him, let alone agreed to a second one-on-one training session. She couldn't wait to get back to her office. Back to her normal life. Back to the way things had been before thoughts of Zach Sullivan—and what his kisses might feel like—had started to crowd out all her good sense.

But instead of getting the message that she was done talking about why she didn't believe in love, as Cuddles came sprinting up behind Atlas, Zach said, "There's got to be a reason."

Professional had gone out the window so long ago she didn't even try to get back there this time. Instead, she said exactly what was on her mind. "Let me make sure I have this straight. A guy cannot look for love because it'll complicate his easy life. But a woman is different? She is expected to fall in love, forever, just like that?"

Even the nauseating couple stopped licking each other's faces to take in their heated discussion. Well, heated on her side, anyway, because Zach looked completely unrepentant. Worse, he seemed amused with her reaction.

"That sounds about right."

She threw the bag of doggy treats straight at his heart. "Why don't you fall in love with this?"

Beautiful women fell at his feet; they didn't chuck things at him. And they definitely never said they didn't believe in forever.

Was Heather perfect, or what?

Hot damn, he couldn't wait to get her into bed and keep her there. Especially now that he knew she wasn't secretly looking for the big commitment.

The fun they were going to have once she finally came around…

The dogs threw themselves on the doggy treats that had spilled out of the bag when it bounced off his chest.

"Was that part of your lesson on positive reinforcement?" he teased her.

He tried not to laugh when she growled at him as she bent to pick up the bag and shoo the dogs away from the food. He was bending down to help her when he looked up to see a teenager on an out-of-control skateboard barreling down the hill straight toward them.

The kid was yelling for them to get out of the way and Zach quickly scooped Cuddles up in one hand and slid his arm around Heather's waist with the other. "Atlas, come!" he ordered as he rolled quickly to the side.

The edge of the skateboard clipped Zach's calf hard enough to make him grunt in pain, but all that mattered was that he had Heather safe and sound beneath him, the puppy cradled in the crook of one arm and Atlas beside his beautiful owner.

They were out of the path of danger now, and he should have let Heather go. But how could he when she was so soft, so warm…and was looking up at him with those big eyes that had turned his heart over in his chest from the first moment he'd seen them.

He'd wanted her from that first moment, but strangely, he wasn't thinking about sex now. Not entirely, anyway.

"Did you really have to do that?" she asked in a voice that trembled slightly.

He brushed her hair away from her forehead, letting his hand linger in the soft strands that had come loose from her braid.

"Yes."

He wanted to press his lips to her forehead, wanted to reassure himself that no harm had—or would—come to her.

He leaned closer and brushed his mouth to her skin before saying, "It would have really pissed me off if you'd been obliterated by a pimply fourteen-year-old and his skateboard."

"I was all set to stay irritated with you," she whispered, sounding aroused and breathless and anything but irritated. "Say something cocky, please."

Strange, but for the first time he could remember, he didn't want to use one of his usual comebacks.

This was the perfect chance to take that kiss he knew she wanted to give him. And it would be more than just brushing lips against her cheek.

He'd just saved her and she was grateful—he could feel her heart beating against his as her breath came too quickly. Lord knew she'd been driving him crazy with her curves, her pretty smiles, her expressive eyes, all morning long.

*Damn it.*

He couldn't do it...all because he *liked* her?

This was too much. What the hell was happening to him?

Zach rolled onto his back on the grass and stared up at the blue sky, biting back a string of curses at his stupidity in willingly giving up his chance to finally seduce Heather.

Once the puppy was set free again, Cuddles immediately scampered onto his chest and started licking first him, then Heather, long enough that the puppy got them both laughing as they tried to roll out of the way. And when Heather's fingers accidentally slid against his, it was the most natural thing in the world to fit his against hers so that he could lift her hand to his lips and press a kiss to her palm.

His phone rang at the same moment hers did and he felt her fingers stiffen in his. And even though it turned out that lying there, fully clothed beside each other, was better than any time he'd ever spent naked with another woman, he made himself let go of her hand as she moved to get back on her feet.

Neither of them said a word as they checked their

messages and then walked back to his house, and as she and Atlas got in her car and drove away, Cuddles whined in his arms as if her heart had just been split in two.

# *Eight*

Heather didn't believe in backing down from a challenge. It was how she'd been able to build Top Dog from a one-on-one training business into a full-service training center and doggy day care. She wasn't afraid of standing up for herself or facing down difficult situations.

But she hadn't gotten to where she was by being stupid, either.

And that was what spending any more time with Zach Sullivan would be. *Stupid.* To the nth degree.

It wasn't even the two almost-kisses that worried her. Kissing, even sex, was something she knew how to compartmentalize. Just because she wasn't looking for a happily-ever-after didn't mean she was a nun.

But that moment when she and Zach had been laughing together and his hand had found hers... She scrunched her eyes shut to try to shake away those feelings of warmth. Of contentment.

Of sweet connection.

Of forever.

Only, no matter how hard she'd tried since that morning to block Zach out—to pretend he hadn't made her feel something deep and true, to try to ignore how he lit up every time he spoke about his family, and that he'd *take a bullet* for them—every time she thought about him she'd ended up right back in the same spot. Not just stuck in desire, but longing for something she didn't even think she knew how to believe in.

The clock was ticking ever closer to 5:00 p.m. and Zach would be appearing with Cuddles any minute now. But she'd be busy meeting with her advisory board members to discuss the pros and cons of a possible expansion into a wholesale dog-treat business. Luckily, everyone had been available when she'd called them earlier in the day.

Heather was leading the last of her board members to the conference room when she felt the air in the building shift. She didn't need to turn around to know that Zach was there. And not just because she could have sensed his presence in the middle of a hurricane. Not even because Atlas was vibrating with the need to greet his tiny little friend.

But because the combination of the beautiful man and Cuddles always elicited an overwhelming chorus of cooing and giggling.

She tried to get the conference-room door closed, but before she could, Jerry Caldwell, a leading organic-dog-food manufacturer, spotted Zach and called out his name.

The man she was working so hard to avoid pinned her with an intense look that had her breath coming too fast before he walked over to shake Jerry's hand.

"I've got a 1958 Austin-Healey coming in with your name on it, Jerry." Zach's gaze shifted to Heather as he added, "She's a real beauty, with gorgeous lines and curves. You don't have a chance of resisting her."

She felt herself flush and knew the only chance she had of covering her reaction to him was to focus on the puppy in his arms instead. Atlas and the puppy were already sniffing and licking each other with pure happiness. Clearly, she wasn't the only one who'd been waiting for 5:00 p.m. to roll around.

Only one of them had been dreading it, though.

But, oh, what a liar she was. Because the truth of it was that she had been anticipating seeing Zach again even more than Atlas had dreamed of seeing the puppy.

"How did Cuddles do today at your garage?" she asked Zach.

Jerry laughed out loud at the name. "You've got a puppy?" He shook his head. "And you named her Cuddles? I've got to admit, Sullivan, I didn't see this coming. Not in a million years."

She waited for Zach to make an excuse about his niece and how it wasn't his dog or his name, but instead his gaze shifted to her for a split second before he replied, "I didn't see it coming, either."

Fortunately, Jerry didn't pick up on any of the strange undertones in the conversation as he said, "Dogs will do that to you. But it's worth it. Best friend you'll ever have." He shook Zach's hand again. "I'll drop by the shop early next week to check out the Austin-Healey."

After Jerry had walked over to the coffee dispenser, she informed Zach, "This evening David is going to be working with you and Cuddles out back." She didn't have to make excuses to him since he already knew she'd planned to pass him off to another trainer, but still she said, "I've got a meeting with my advisory board tonight."

"Sounds important."

"It is." The heat of his body drew her toward him and she forced herself to take a step back. "Have a good training session."

Atlas's ears were down as he followed her inside the conference room and watched the puppy he adored head to the back with Zach.

God help her…she felt the same way.

An hour later, Heather sat at her computer to type up her meeting notes. But for the first time in a very long time, she couldn't concentrate on the work she needed to get done. Atlas pawed the door and she walked outside with him to let him take care of business. He sniffed every inch of the lawn and she knew he was searching for a sign that Cuddles was still there. But both the puppy and her owner had left.

Was it only twenty-four hours ago that Zach had

been standing outside the front door holding a pizza box, acting as if he owned the rest of the world and he wanted her to become another one of his many possessions?

Atlas finally gave up on Cuddles and watered a bush in the corner, but he didn't look all that relieved. Heather knew she probably looked the same way. Irritated and lost.

She needed something to take her mind off Zach. Knowing more work wasn't going to do it, she texted her best friend. Up for a movie tonight?

Brenda texted back in the affirmative and that she'd pick up tickets to a sweeping historical drama she'd wanted to see for a while. She would meet Heather at the theater in time for the 7:00 p.m. show. Heather had just enough time to drop Atlas off at home before heading out.

At the theater, she hugged her friend, careful not to knock the huge container of popcorn onto the floor. "I'm so glad you could come."

Brenda grinned and linked their arms together. "Me, too. It's so much better to drool over Smith Sullivan with you, rather than trying to sit there with my husband and pretend that I'm not getting hot all over."

Heather stiffened from head to toe. "We're watching a Smith Sullivan movie?"

Her friend picked out seats right in the middle of the theater and people started to fill in all around them, trapping Heather.

"Even better, I hear he has his shirt off for half of it. My husband is so going to get lucky tonight."

Oh, God. Heather had needed a night out at the movies to take her away from Zach Sullivan…and not be reminded—for two straight hours—that the star of the film was none other than the brother of the man she was trying so desperately to forget.

"So," her friend asked, right on cue, "have you been seeing anyone new lately?"

Heather choked on the popcorn and reached for the red Slushie Brenda had bought for her, sucking it down so fast she got nailed with brain freeze.

"No," she said, although Brant, a guy she'd casually dated for the past few months, had called and left her a message today about wanting to see her. She liked him well enough, but if she agreed to meet him for dinner she knew what he'd expect. And right now, she couldn't imagine getting naked with anyone except—

Her groan of self-disgust was cut off by the start of the previews. Heather sank down in her seat and gritted her teeth. Somehow she'd make it through the movie. After all, how similar could Zach and his famous brother be?

*Really freaking similar.*

Brenda was still wiping away her tears as the lights came up in the theater. "Wasn't that an amazing love story? To have a man like that want you so badly…I can't even imagine."

Heather pressed her lips together. She was going to keep her mouth shut. She wasn't going to say—

"I know his brother."

Shoot, what was wrong with her?

Heather slung her purse over her shoulder and tried to stand up, but Brenda clamped her hand on her arm, holding her in place in her seat. "Whose brother?"

They were the only two people left in the theater and the cleanup crew was coming in with their garbage bags.

"Smith Sullivan's brother."

Brenda squealed so loud that Heather winced. "Oh, my God! When were you going to tell me?"

*Never* had been the plan, because Zach wasn't supposed to play any kind of important—or long-term—role in her life. At all.

"Zach is one of my new dog-training clients."

"Does he look like Smith Sullivan?"

Heather felt her cheeks turning pink at the way her friend said his name as if they were kids out on the playground and he was the popular boy they all had a crush on.

"Actually," she admitted, "he's even better looking."

Her friend pinned her with a look she couldn't escape. Brenda was the only one who knew all about Heather's family. She'd met her father and mother and had seen their icky dynamic—the charmer and the charmed, the liar and the enabler—firsthand.

"Is he really just a client?"

Brenda's voice had softened, and Heather knew the question didn't have anything to do with her one degree of separation from a movie star, but was more about the fact that her friend genuinely wished for Heather to find true love one day, despite everything.

"Yes." She stood up and went to throw away the empty popcorn box. "Seriously, I wouldn't have mentioned him if we'd seen another movie."

Brenda blocked her way out of the theater. "What does Zach do? He's not the baseball player, is he? Or the winery owner?"

Heather narrowed her eyes. "Why do you know so much about Smith Sullivan's life?"

"I'm a fan," Brenda said without the slightest hint of defensiveness. "So, which one is he?"

With a sigh, Heather said, "He's the mechanic."

Brenda's eyes went wide. "You're kidding, right? He's not just a mechanic. He's a mogul!"

"A mogul?" Heather shook her head. "He owns an auto shop, not GM."

Her friend almost looked disappointed in her. "I know you've been really busy with your business lately, but even you should know more about one of the most famous families in San Francisco. Your new client owns a zillion auto shops. They've made him filthy, stinking rich." Her friend was practically drooling. "Talk about an eligible bachelor."

Well, that explained the big house in the pricey neighborhood, at least. Funny, though, even with all the money she now knew he had, he certainly hadn't tried to woo her with it, the way her father had always worked to buy her and her mother's love with lavish gifts and trips.

In fact, she found herself thinking, with a small smile she couldn't contain, even if Zach didn't have money, she was certain he'd be just as irritatingly sure of himself.

"Please sleep with him and tell me how it is."

Heather had to smile. Only two people who'd known each other since college could say things like that to each other with a straight face.

"Sorry. I don't think it's going to happen."

"But he wants to, doesn't he? And don't deny it—I can tell by the way you've been blushing this whole time that he's more than just a client."

Heather couldn't lie to her best friend. "You're right. I think he wants to. But I've already shut him down."

"Why would you do that when you have the chance to sleep with a Sullivan?"

That one was easy. Because if keeping the walls up around her heart with Zach while they were fully clothed and training the dogs was hard…well, it would be downright impossible if she were naked in his arms.

But all she said was "It wouldn't be a good idea."

Heather could tell Brenda wanted to say something more, but she simply put her arm around Heather and said, "Let's do this again soon, okay? Maybe make it a double date?"

Heather shook her head. "Ever the hopeful one, aren't you?"

"For true love?" her friend replied. "I'm always hopeful."

# Nine

The next morning when Heather got to work, feeling cranky and tired, Tina was obviously excited about something. "A package came for you a few minutes ago."

The sugar from last night's Slushie had given Heather a headache, which was exacerbated by the fact that every time she closed her eyes, she saw Zach and herself dressed in the period clothes from the movie acting out the scene where he pulled her into his arms and kissed her as if he'd been waiting his whole life for her love.

She stopped at the threshold of her office when she saw the big red rectangular box sitting on her desk. Atlas immediately ran to it and started sniffing, his tail wagging fast.

No one ever sent her gifts.

She had her hand over her pounding heart as she moved close enough to pick it up. Even though her assistant was dying to know what it was, thankfully

Tina respected Heather's privacy enough to give her some space.

She looked for a card, but there wasn't anything but a huge red bow on the outside of the box. Slowly lifting the cover, she had to blink a couple of times to make sure she was seeing things right.

She couldn't contain her smile as she lifted the huge dog bone from the soft velvet fabric it had been sitting on.

"Looks like you have a secret admirer," she told Atlas as he sat like the very good dog he was and looked longingly at the bone. She held it out to him and he gently took it from her before trotting to his pillow bed in the corner.

That was when she saw the small card almost buried in the thick folds of red velvet.

Atlas,
I missed you yesterday. Training wasn't the same without you. I wanted to play with you afterward. I hope I'll see you tonight.
Your friend,
Cuddles

Heather's heart turned over in her chest as she carefully put the note back inside the box. She felt funny, right in the region of her chest. Her eyes felt strange, too, as if they had something in them.

"You just got your first love note, Atlas," she said in a voice made raw with unwanted emotion.

Her dog's ears perked up at his name, but he was

too focused on his bone to pay much attention to his owner.

Which was a very good thing, because right then Heather didn't want anyone to look too carefully at her reaction to the gift.

Not even her dog.

Zach nearly smashed his phone a half dozen times throughout the day. Everyone on the goddamned planet had called him.

Except for the one person he'd wanted to hear from.

He'd been so sure the dog bone would thaw Heather's resistance to him. He was convinced she'd call him, laughing at the note, picking up where they'd left off in the park when they were laughing together on the grass.

But nothing.

Not a goddamned thing.

Rather than keep her distance due to his foul mood, Cuddles had truly lived up to her name all day long. Every time he turned around, she was rubbing up against his leg or begging to be picked up. The guys at the garage had gotten so used to seeing him haul her around with him that they'd pretty much stopped making sarcastic comments.

The puppy burrowed onto his lap as he drove over to Top Dog, and he was surprised to realize he didn't hate having a warm bundle of fur attached to him as much as he thought he would. For a couple of weeks, he supposed it wouldn't be so bad having the fur ball around.

When they turned the corner and Cuddles saw Heather's building, she stood up and pawed excitedly at the window. "Don't worry," he told her in a grim voice filled with purpose, "we won't leave until you've had some quality time with your friend tonight."

If Heather tried to hide from his 5:00 p.m. training session with a meeting or some other lame excuse, he was going to wait her out and force her to face the attraction simmering between them, no matter how long it took or what she was in the middle of.

Damn it, he wanted her. And he knew she wanted him, too. Not acting on their mutual desire was just plain stupid.

He headed straight for Heather's office, and when she looked up and saw him, he could have sworn her eyes flashed with a mixture of happiness and attraction.

Of course, she didn't act on either of those. Instead, she pointedly looked at Cuddles in his arms and said, "She has legs, you know."

He held the puppy closer to his chest as he walked into Heather's office. "She likes it up here."

Heather muttered something he couldn't quite make out, but he didn't need to hear it to know it wasn't flattering. Atlas nearly tackled him trying to get to the puppy. Cuddles leaped out of his arms and practically landed on the Great Dane's back.

Heather watched the two dogs tangle with each

other in horror. "Please don't tell anyone you just saw my dog do that."

"What will you trade me for my silence?"

Because he'd sure like that kiss sooner rather than later. It was making him cranky, all this waiting. Especially when he wasn't used to waiting for a woman.

Hell, he'd never waited for anything in his life before Heather.

She pinned him with a look that told him he wasn't going to corner her into a kiss that easily. "I'm here tonight to work with you and Cuddles, aren't I?"

"What changed your mind?"

She looked surprised by his question. Frankly, he was a little surprised himself.

Zach wasn't one to spend a lot of time trying to figure women out. Apart from his sisters, whom he could barely make heads or tails of, and his mother, he hadn't had any long-running relationships with women. He hadn't wanted one.

And even though he was still committed to the idea of never making wedding vows, or sticking a ring on someone's finger, he wanted to know her answer, anyway.

In lieu of answering, she looked over at the dogs. When he followed her gaze, he saw that Atlas and Cuddles were playing a hilariously off-balance game of tug-of-war with a rope. Atlas was patiently holding the wet, frayed rope in his mouth and Cuddles was losing her furry mind trying to shred it. Suddenly, the big dog tugged on the rope and the puppy went sprawling in a slobbery heap on the floor.

Heather's laughter warmed him in places he hadn't realized had been cold.

"How could I resist the *Huge and Tiny* show?"

She ran her fingers over the red dog-bone box he'd sent and he wished she were touching him like that. Soon, damn it, she would be. He wouldn't rest until he figured out how to get her to come around.

"Besides, no one has ever sent Atlas a gift before."

"So it was the bone that threw you over the edge?" he said, letting himself savor the victory of a great idea perfectly executed.

She shrugged. "Plus the fact that all of my other trainers were busy tonight."

Her timing with the slam was so perfect that he had to laugh, even though it was at his expense.

She motioned for Atlas to follow them out back to the training area. Of course, Cuddles followed right beside her big friend. She was all business as they began with the *come* command again, then began to work on *sit.*

As if he knew he had to make up for his earlier outburst of excitement, Atlas was the perfect example of a well-trained dog. No matter how Cuddles tried to distract him, he kept his eyes on Heather.

Zach couldn't pull his eyes from her, either. She was shockingly beautiful, even in a sweatshirt and faded jeans, her braid trailing down her back with wisps of hair framing her face.

He wished he had an excuse to touch her, to feel the warmth of her skin beneath his fingertips, her softness against his lips.

She directed him to begin using the *sit* command, but for the first time, Cuddles didn't immediately pick up on what they were trying to learn.

After a few failed attempts, Heather said, "You've got to focus on your dog to let her know how important it is to you that she does what you're asking her to do. She can tell if you're distracted by something else."

"You're right," he admitted. "I am distracted." In all seriousness, if he didn't get that kiss from her soon, he was going to lose his mind.

"All she needs is fifteen minutes of your focused attention. Surely," she challenged him, "you can pull that off."

"Do you know what Cuddles did all day long?" Without waiting for her to reply, he told her, "She pined for your mutt, hoping he'd be here tonight. I'm pretty sure a training session is the last thing on her mind when all she wants to do is play with her friend."

"I told you, Atlas is not a mutt," she said automatically, and then, "And you're exaggerating about the pining."

"Swear to God," he said, "I showed her a picture of a Great Dane on my phone and she went wild."

He could see her fighting a grin as she worked to keep to just business. "Our time is almost up and I'd hate for you to leave tonight without making headway with Cuddles."

"How about this," he negotiated. "I'll get both of

us on track for the rest of the session if you'll agree to let them play while we eat dinner afterward?"

Her mouth tightened. "After breakfast at your house and what happened at the park—" Another flush told him she hadn't forgotten how perfectly their bodies had fit together when he'd saved her from the skateboarder. "I know it seems like the lines have gotten blurred, but I haven't changed my mind about things. About us. I'm happy to support your training with Cuddles to make things better for the both of you while you're taking care of her, but I'm not interested in anything else."

"Are you seeing anyone?"

She blinked at him. "Did you hear what I just said?"

He grinned. "So that's a no."

Her lips lifted from her teeth in that snarl he found so sexy. "I've never met anyone like you before."

"Thank you." He couldn't stop grinning.

"It isn't a compliment," she snapped.

"One date."

She began to pack up her training bag. "No dates. I think we're officially done here. And I can't work with you on Thursday or Friday."

"Cuddles and I don't want to work with another trainer."

"It's nothing personal," she said. "I just can't do it."

Zach hated the fact that it actually didn't sound personal. But why? Women loved him. Why didn't this one? And, more to the point, why couldn't he just let it go and move on to the next easy—*boring*—conquest?

"What could possibly be more important than Cuddles?" *And me?*

"Bark in the Park."

It took his brain a beat too long to figure out what she was talking about. Finally, it hit him. "The dog day at the ballpark?"

"I chaired the committee and I have a lot of loose ends to tie up before the game starts Friday night."

"Sounds like a lot of work."

"It is," she agreed, and he finally noticed how tired she looked.

"I can help."

"No!" She flushed again. "What I mean is that I've got a great team of people who have been working with me and we're in the homestretch now. But thanks for the offer." She looked at her watch. "We should call it a night."

Like hell if he was giving up that easily.

"If Cuddles sits on command, have dinner with me."

She looked as if she was going to refuse, but then she glanced over at Cuddles, who was on her back, working on a good deep back scratch in the grass.

"Okay, but when she doesn't, you have to agree not to ask me out again."

He couldn't believe the whole thing was up to the puppy. "Deal."

"Cuddles!" The puppy looked at him from where

she was sprawled out on the grass and he gave the hand command a split second before saying, "Come!"

She immediately hopped up and sped over to him.

"That one doesn't count," Heather told him.

He shot her a look that said he already knew that. He paused, sent up a silent prayer, then said, "Cuddles, sit!"

The puppy blinked up at him for several seconds and he thought it was all over...until her little ears went back and she plopped her rear down on the grass as if she'd been waiting her whole short life for him to tell her to sit.

He reached into the treat bag on Heather's belt— taking any excuse to touch her—and handed one to the puppy while telling her what a good girl she was.

"How was that?" he asked Heather.

She shot him a suspicious glance. "You played me." She looked at Cuddles's innocent face and then his less-innocent one. "You were practicing before tonight, weren't you?"

"We wanted to impress you." Which was true. "Still, you've got to admit it was pretty close there for a while."

She sighed and said, "I know a great Indian place with a patio that allows dogs."

# *Ten*

They settled into their seats with the dogs contentedly chewing on the Mylar bones she'd brought for them. Heather took a sip of her cold beer and couldn't repress a sigh of pleasure. She and Zach hadn't talked much as they'd walked the three blocks from her business to the restaurant, apart from her trying to convince him that Cuddles could manage the trip on her little paws, while he made one excuse after another for why he "needed" to carry her.

She'd never seen anyone get attached to a dog so fast, and frankly, she was worried about how he was going to deal with giving the puppy back to his brother. She'd actually taken a few minutes that afternoon to scan her list of Yorkie breeders to see if any of them had a new litter coming soon, but she was very much afraid Cuddles was irreplaceable.

The mischievous but loving puppy fit perfectly with the mischievous but loving man who was holding her in his arms.

*Loving?*

Ugh. She took another gulp from her glass, while sternly reminding herself that even though this was practically a script of her vision of a perfect night out, it wasn't a date. And she had no business thinking of Zach as *loving*...not even if he was currently looking at her with more affection than desire.

His eyes darkened as she stared into them and she amended that thought to *slightly more.*

Just as the waiter came to their table, Zach's phone went off. "Sorry, it's my brother." He gestured to the menu. "Go nuts with the meal. I trust you." He stood up to take the call away from the other diners.

Even after she'd ordered, the buzz was still going through her from his last casually tossed-off words. *I trust you.*

What would it be like to be able to say that to someone without a second thought, to give her trust to someone she'd met less than a week ago?

She tried not to stare at Zach standing on the sidewalk talking with his brother, but when he laughed and his gorgeous face lit up, she realized she wasn't the only one who couldn't take her eyes off him. Every other woman on the patio was staring, too.

Amazingly, he didn't seem to notice or care that he was the center of attention. Instead of soaking up the public's adoration like the vain man she'd once thought he was, he was utterly focused on what his brother was saying.

"Is everything okay?" she asked when he sat back down.

"Chase's wife, Chloe, is a couple of days past her due date. I left him a message earlier to make sure everything was okay. She's fine, but antsy."

Yet again she was amazed by how close he was to his family, especially given his outwardly footloose-and-fancy-free personality. Amazingly, the fact that he clearly wasn't looking for a wife of his own didn't stop him from appreciating—and worrying about— his siblings' wives.

She couldn't put the puzzle of Zach Sullivan together...and it only added to her worries where he was concerned. If only it were more black-and-white, then she would know exactly where to shelve him in her head, rather than having the very real concern that he was creeping into her heart by bits and pieces every time they were together.

"How many nephews and nieces do you have?"

His excited smile made her go warm all over. "This will be the first."

A man who loved puppies *and* babies was hard to resist. Almost impossible, actually.

But she needed to keep doing just that, darn it....

"Do they know if they're having a boy or a girl?"

"If they do, they haven't told any of us." He grinned at her. "We've actually got a betting pool going."

"Your family is betting over the sex of your brother's child?"

He refilled her glass as he said, "It was my mother's idea."

She laughed out loud at that, the feel of that spontaneous joy bubbling up from her chest surprising her the same way it always did when she was with Zach.

"She really does sound like a remarkable woman. Stunning, raised eight kids and now has her first grandchild on the way." She shook her head. "A gambler, too, from the sounds of it." She thought about the gorgeous man in the black-and-white photo who looked so much like Zach. "I'm assuming your father encourages all the Sullivan family madness?"

The laughter left his eyes. "He died when I was seven. Just a couple of weeks before my eighth birthday."

She gripped the stem of her glass tighter. He hadn't said anything during breakfast at his house when they'd been looking at the photo.

"I'm sorry. I just assumed—" She tried to clamp her mouth shut, but still the words "That must have been so hard on you" slipped out. He'd said before how much like his father he was, that he got his love of cars from him. A young boy who clearly worshipped his father had to have been devastated by his death.

He shrugged, but she could almost see the weight on his shoulders as he forced the movement. "We pulled together, all looked out for each other."

She did some quick math from the picture she'd seen and realized he'd been right there in the middle as the fifth child out of eight, not the oldest, not the youngest. She knew how easy it was to get lost in a family, even when you were the only child.

Had that happened to Zach?

"How did it happen?"

"He had an aneurysm at the office. We found out he was dead when we got home from school. He was only forty-eight." He lifted his eyes to hers and what she saw in them tore at her heart. "It will be twenty-three years next week."

She had to reach for Zach's hand. Even though it had been more than two decades since his father's death, she could see that it still hurt him. Deeply.

"I'm sorry," she said again.

Every time they'd been together, he'd tried to touch her. But now that she was the one who'd reached for him, he pulled away and reached for his beer, gulping it down before putting the empty glass back on the table.

"Shit happens," he said. "Sucks, but what can you do?"

It wasn't hard to guess that the flippancy came from trying to cover how bad he felt. And, really, who was she to question people's coping mechanisms? After all, when she found out that her beloved father was a two-faced bastard, she'd turned into a seventeen-year-old cutter.

Still, she felt there was more Zach wasn't saying and was absolutely certain that his father's death had affected him on some deeper level than what he would be sharing with her over Indian food tonight. No matter how much she tried to remind herself that it was dangerous to let him get too close, his unexpected vulnerability struck right at the heart of her.

After the waiter delivered steaming platters of

naan bread, tandoori chicken and curry, Zach looked up at her and said, "Your parents are still together. What else should I know about you?"

Most men barely listened when a woman talked about herself. Trust Zach to remember every freaking word, no matter how casually tossed off it had been during an impromptu training session in the park.

She broke off a piece of the flat bread and took a bite of it, even though it suddenly tasted like sawdust. When she'd washed it down with a sip of beer, she said, "There's not much else to tell."

But he wasn't that easily daunted. "Where did you grow up?"

"Washington, D.C." She stared down at a plate full of food she no longer had the desire to eat.

"You're a long way from home," he commented.

Yes, she was. On purpose. She'd wanted to get as far away from her parents as possible. "I like the West Coast."

He raised an eyebrow at her curt words and she realized she wasn't playing it nearly cool enough as he said, "Any siblings?"

"No."

Atlas looked up at the tone of her voice and moved to put his head on her lap as if to comfort her.

"What did they do to you, Heather?"

She sighed, knowing that if Zach had been that persistent about getting her to have dinner with him, there was no way he was going to leave this one alone without eventually getting her to tell him what he wanted to know.

And maybe it would help him understand her reluctance to date him if he knew more.

"Everyone loves my father," she told him. "It's what always made him such a good salesperson. People can't help but be charmed by him."

"Selling what?"

"Used to be chemicals. Now it's cell-phone towers all over the country."

"How much time did he spend on the road when you lived at home?"

"About half the year."

"That's got to be hard on a kid."

She liked how he made it sound as if they were talking about someone else. "My mother worked overtime to keep us busy when he was gone so she and I wouldn't have time to think about being lonely or missing him. And it was always a big celebration when he returned. He got me great presents from the road to make up for being gone." Presents she'd wanted to smash into a zillion little pieces when she'd found out the truth.

"Did it work?"

She met Zach's gaze. "No." She reached down to stroke Atlas's head as if to steel herself for what was coming next. "But it was worse when I found out he'd been cheating on my mother for years. For their whole marriage, actually."

Zach cursed. "That sucks."

"You want to know what was even worse than

that?" She couldn't wait for him to reply, not when the words were suddenly tripping over one another to get out of her mouth. "She knew about it." Heather pushed her plate away. "All those years, even now, she knows he's cheating on her, but she stays with him, anyway."

She'd never told a man this before, hadn't even come close to letting someone in enough to speak about family secrets. If someone had told her a week ago she'd be spilling her guts to the cocky man who owned the auto shop, she never would have believed it.

"Why do you think she stays?"

It was the question she'd asked herself a thousand times over the years. "He always makes sure to tell her how much he loves her. Even though we all know it's a big fat lie."

Zach Sullivan was pissed off. Beyond angry. If her father wasn't twenty-five hundred miles away, Zach would be hunting him down to pound him into a wall.

No wonder Heather wouldn't take a chance on being with him, even in the short term, if all she knew were "charming" men who lied through their teeth to her and her mother. It killed him to think of her as a young girl stuck in the middle of all that.

Seeing the virtually untouched food on their table, the waiter came over with a worried expression. "Does everything taste okay?"

Zach watched Heather pin on a false smile.

"It's great, thanks." She slid her fork into a chunk of chicken, but she didn't put it in her mouth, just pushed it around on her plate, her mind clearly elsewhere.

Thinking about what a dick her father was, he guessed. And why her mother didn't have a backbone.

He'd hugged his sisters' tears away a hundred times over the years, had listened to Summer pour out her feelings about a boy she liked in second grade who liked to pull her pigtails. But he'd never been tempted to comfort a woman who wasn't part of his family.

Zach knew it was dangerous to feel this way about Heather. He was breaking all his rules for her, ones that had never been in danger of cracking apart before.

But how could he possibly leave her like this, with shadows in her eyes?

The thing was, he knew Heather didn't want his shoulder to cry on, that it would only wound her pride. Fortunately, he'd sat through one of Summer's "shows" only a few weeks earlier, and all the bad seven-year-old jokes were still firmly lodged in his brain.

Although he'd never felt less like making a joke, he also knew he'd never needed to make one more. "What do you call frozen dog poo?"

Heather's eyebrow rose as she looked up from her mutilated chicken chunk. "What did you just say?"

"A poopsicle."

Her eyes widened as she realized he was telling her a joke.

"I'm going to pretend you didn't just make that horrible joke."

"What happened when the dog went to the flea circus?"

"Please, don't make me guess."

"He stole the show!"

She groaned and put her hands over her ears. "Someone, anyone, please make it stop."

"What do you say to a dog before he eats?"

Relief swept through him when she played along by scrunching her eyes shut and whispering, "Bone appetit."

For the rest of their dinner they each worked to see who could tell the worst joke while they polished off every last bit of the Indian dishes. Zach was pretty sure he won by a landslide, but even if he hadn't, he'd memorize the contents of every bad joke book in the world if it meant putting a smile on Heather's face.

He hadn't just broken the rules tonight—he'd smashed them to smithereens. But for a couple of hours, he decided he didn't care.

Besides, there was a big difference between laughing with Heather and falling in love with her. He'd wanted to sleep with her from the start. It was no hardship to add laughter—and comfort—to the mix.

Love still didn't have to play into the equation.

Hell, after what he'd just found out about her father, it was no wonder she wasn't looking for forever. Yet again, the two of them were well matched.

When the dishes were cleared away and the waiter mentioned dessert, she put her hands over her stomach. "I wish I could." She reached for her wallet, but Zach had already handed the waiter plenty of cash.

"Thanks for dinner," she said, a soft smile on her beautiful face. "I had fun." She looked faintly surprised as she added, "A lot of fun."

So had he. More fun than he could ever remember having with a woman.

Whether she'd liked it or not, they'd just had their first date.

And it had been a good one.

As if she'd just realized that, she tensed. "I've got to get a really early start tomorrow. David will take good care of you and Cuddles on Thursday and Friday. I'll check my schedule to see if Monday evening will work for me to check on your progress."

Even though they'd just spent the past few hours together, Zach wasn't ready for her to go yet. Plus, with the way the spicy food had made her lips a little redder, a little plumper than they usually were, all he could think about was kissing her. He stood and reached for her hand to help her up from her seat. She looked at it for a moment before putting her hand in his.

Before he could make his move, Heather made hers. Her mouth soft on his cheek, she whispered, "Good night, Zach," a warm breath against his ear before she patted Cuddles on the head and walked away with Atlas following beside her.

With any other woman he would have assumed she was teasing him, taunting him by coming close but not nearly close enough, purposefully testing his patience as some sort of sensual dance.

But from Heather, that kiss on the cheek had been something completely different. Not a tease, but the beginning of trust that he guessed she rarely, if ever, gave a man.

By the time he'd picked up Cuddles and had headed up the street to get his car from Heather's parking lot, she was long gone. Which was just as well, because he had an important phone call he needed to make. One he didn't want her to hear.

Pulling his cell phone out of his pocket, he dialed his brother Ryan, who would be pitching for the Hawks on Friday during Bark in the Park.

"Hey, Ry, I need you to do something for me."

Unlike Heather's father, Zach had never cheated on a woman. But that didn't mean he wasn't willing to play a few games if necessary. Because he sure as hell wasn't willing to wait until the following Monday for the chance to get on Heather's calendar again…or to have their first real kiss.

# *Eleven*

$F$riday evening, Heather walked up to the will-call window at the baseball stadium with Atlas on his leash. He was sticking extra close to her side because of the crowds of men.

"Hi, I got a call from the front office to say that they've upgraded my ticket for the game tonight."

She gave the man behind the glass her name and he whistled when he pulled out her ticket. "This is one of the best seats in the stadium."

She grinned as she thanked him for the ticket and headed into the stadium. It had been a really nice surprise when she'd found out she was being upgraded to a better seat as a thank-you for her help with the fundraising event. She didn't get out to the ballpark much, but she never missed the one day each season when dogs and their owners were invited to enjoy the afternoon together.

It was a perfect day, full of bright sunshine and

blue skies with soft clouds moving slowly overhead. Even better, dogs were absolutely everywhere. How could she not have a good time?

She sighed as she scanned the signs looking for the section her seat was in. For the past couple of days she'd been dragging. Sleep was hard-won and even her favorite chocolate truffles had lost their appeal. She'd been putting in double time between the office and the finishing touches on the fundraisers, but her output wasn't even close to being half as good as it had been the week before.

Maybe she was coming down with a summer flu. Or maybe her friends were right and she was working too hard.

*Liar, liar, pants on fire.*

Another sigh followed the first as the childish phrase played on repeat in her head. She knew exactly why she was bummed out.

She missed him.

Somehow, Zach Sullivan had wormed his way into her head. She didn't regret giving her time to the animal shelter, but on Thursday at 5:00 p.m. when she'd been down at their headquarters working out the final details for tonight's event and Saturday night's auction and party, there was somewhere else she had wanted to be.

Joking with Zach. Laughing with Zach. Being impressed by how well he worked with his temporary puppy.

Finally finding the right section, she and Atlas

navigated their way down the stairs past the other dogs. There were six empty seats in her row, and as she took hers, she looked up and realized she really did have the best seat in the house—right behind home plate.

Firmly reminding herself that this was her chance to relax and enjoy herself for a few hours, she closed her eyes to lean back in her seat and soak up some sun, when Atlas started quaking and shivering. Not the bad kind where he was scared, but with pure excitement.

It was the way he acted whenever Cuddles was—

"Great night for a baseball game, isn't it?"

As the low voice she hadn't been able to get out of her dreams rolled over her, through her, finally settling deep down in her fluttering belly, Cuddles and Atlas had an ecstatic reunion before beginning to happily root around on the cement for remnants of smashed hot dogs and popcorn.

In a millisecond she went from dragging and tired to abundantly alive. At the same time, her unstoppable pleasure at seeing Zach made her mad.

Mad at herself for not having any self-control, even though she knew better. And mad at him for outmaneuvering her time and time again. Because all the things that hadn't made sense about her ticket upgrade suddenly did.

"I can't believe I forgot—your brother plays for the Hawks, doesn't he?"

Zach settled into the seat next to her. Too close.

Close enough that she could feel the heat of his thigh against hers. Why had she worn shorts instead of jeans?

"I'll introduce you to Ryan after the game."

She ignored the offer. "You switched my ticket, didn't you?"

He grinned at her. He actually had the nerve to look proud of himself as he leaned closer and lowered his voice, his breath warm and far too seductive in her ear as he said, "You're welcome."

She rolled her eyes. "Most people wait to hear the words *thank you* first."

Just then, a beautiful pregnant woman stopped at their row and said, "Zach, what are you doing here?"

Damn it, thought Zach, his sister Sophie had told him they were planning on skipping this game because they had to deal with one of Jake's out-of-town pubs.

Sophie's husband, Jake, quickly zeroed in on Heather before looking back at Zach with a clearly amused expression on his face. "Isn't this the day of one of the biggest NASCAR races of the year? Never thought you'd miss one of those."

Jake was right, but Zach had barely given it a second thought. Sullivan Autos sponsored one of the racers, but his staff would handle the event.

"Heather, this is my sister Sophie. And Jake."

His old friend pulled Sophie closer and clarified in a possessive voice, "I'm Sophie's husband."

Heather stood up to say, "It's so nice to meet you," but as she reached out to shake their hands, Atlas decided to make his move on a popcorn seller who was almost within reach.

Sophie gasped as Heather's feet were yanked out from under her by her oversize mutt. All three of them reached for her, but Zach got to her first, pulling her down onto his lap before she could hit the cement.

Pleasure shot through him as she instinctively wound her arms around his neck and breathlessly gazed into his eyes. "You keep saving me," she said softly enough that he was the only one who could hear.

Eighty thousand people and their dogs ceased to exist as her warm curves shifted against him. He was stunned all over again at how beautiful she was with her hair falling out of her braid, in a long-sleeved T-shirt and shorts that shouldn't have done anything to showcase her figure, but managed to all the same.

"You're welcome."

This time, instead of forcing herself to remain irritated with him, she let herself give in to a smile.

It was the most beautiful thing he'd ever seen.

"Thank you." She gave him another small smile before she frowned. "I don't know what's come over Atlas lately. Maybe it's the puppy energy rubbing off on him."

Hell, thought Zach, forget her dog. What had come over *him?* It was one thing to enjoy the feel of her curves pressing against him because she was a beautiful woman. But it was another thing entirely to want to hold her *just because*.

Unfortunately, Heather obviously remembered that they had an audience as she quickly pushed out of his lap. He was impressed with how well she played off what could have been an awkward moment by joking with Sophie and Jake about the dangers of owning a dog who was twice as big as she was.

Zach almost groaned at the fact that he and Heather were going to be on display for the next two and a half hours. Sure, his siblings were used to seeing him with women. Lots of women. What they weren't used to, however, was seeing him with a woman like Heather.

As soon as they realized the two of them weren't sleeping together yet, there were going to be questions.

And if they realized that he actually *liked* her, the questions might never run out.

He'd never told his brothers or sisters about the way he felt about his father's death, or the impact it had made on his life and his beliefs about his future.

He didn't want to start having to explain now.

Fortunately, his sister and her new husband were pretty wrapped up in each other. Just as long as only one of the twins came today, he'd live through—

"Yay, it's a party! Scoot over."

*Damn it.* Lori had come, too.

It was turning into a Sullivan family reunion at the baseball stadium.

He scowled at the new arrival. "Aren't you supposed to be on tour with Nicola right now?"

His other little sister gave him an evil smile, the one she'd patented by the time she could speak her first word. Clearly, she'd not only seen Heather sprawled across his lap as she walked into the stadium…but she'd likely seen the way he'd been looking at her, too.

"We're on break for a few days and I haven't caught one of Ryan's games yet this season." She leaned over him and held out her hand to Heather. "Hi, I'm Zach's other sister. It is *so nice* to meet you."

"Great to meet you, too," Heather said as she shook his sister's hand. "I'm Heather. And this is Atlas."

Lori's eyes lit up as she cooed over Heather's huge dog. "Oh, my God, he's *gorgeous!*"

Atlas shoved past Zach to get to Lori, with Cuddles only a beat behind.

"I think the feeling is mutual," Heather said, laughing as Lori encouraged both dogs to jump up on her lap at the same time.

His hopes that the dogs would save him from his sister's prying were dashed when she simultaneously patted them and asked, "So, how do you two know each other?"

"I'm working with your brother to train Cuddles."

"Boy, that must be a pain in the butt, huh?"

Heather frowned. "No. Of course not. Cuddles is incredibly smart and receptive to positive reinforcement."

Lori laughed. "I'm not talking about Summer's puppy. I'm talking about Zach."

Heather's eyes widened for a moment before she threw her head back and laughed. "You have no idea. No idea at all."

# *Twelve*

Heather spent more time watching Zach interact with his sisters than she did following the game. She loved seeing him on the wrong foot for once, even if it was just from his momentary surprise at seeing them there.

At the same time, however, he was as enamored of them as he was annoyed by the way they poked and prodded at him as all good little sisters must. Through it all, she could feel his protectiveness toward them simmering just beneath the surface.

Just as he'd said, he would take a bullet for his family without blinking an eye. He kept asking Sophie, who was pregnant with twins, how she was feeling. Finally, his sister had snapped, "Next time I see the doctor, I'm going to send you her report so you'll believe I'm fine."

Zach had actually looked serious as he'd said, "That'd be great, Soph."

Sophie's husband muttered, "That's never going to happen."

No wonder Zach was so confident. It wasn't just his looks—it was all that unconditional love from his family.

A family who actually understood what love was.

Envy stole through her as she imagined what it must have been like to grow up in a family like his. She hoped he knew how lucky he was.

After the fourth inning, Lori called out for popcorn for everyone. Zach grumbled and reached for his wallet when Lori said, "This one's on me."

He raised an eyebrow in surprise. "Feeling generous today, Naughty?"

Heather had to grin at the nickname. It definitely seemed to fit the sister sitting beside him.

"I just figured I should get some celebrating done early," Lori said.

"What are we celebrating, Ryan's impending shutout?" Sophie asked as she took a bag of hot popcorn.

Lori pinned Zach with a knowing glance and a wicked grin. "Zach knows what we're celebrating, don't you, big brother? See, when you guys got married, we made this bet about who would be the first to fall—"

Zach abruptly stood up and grabbed the dogs' leashes. "The dogs need to take care of business. You coming?" he asked Heather.

"I think you've got this one," she told him. "Oh, and don't forget these." She handed him a couple of blue plastic bags.

He looked at the bags with disgust before taking them with a scowl, scooping up Cuddles and drag-

ging Atlas up the stairs. After Jake got up to join
Zach and the dogs, Lori scooted over onto Zach's
seat beside Heather.

"How long have you and Zach been dating?"

Heather choked on the piece of popcorn she'd just
swallowed and had to quickly take a sip of lukewarm
lemonade to wash it down. "We're not dating. I'm
just helping him train Cuddles."

Lori looked terribly disappointed. So, Heather
noticed, did her twin.

"Seriously? You're not together?"

Why hadn't she gone with Zach to take the dogs
outside?

And what was with these Sullivans, who always
said the first thing that popped into their heads?

"No, we're not," she told Zach's sister, but she
flushed as she thought about all of his double entendres, the way he'd kissed her cheek, her hand. And
how much fun she had with him, the way he made
her laugh even when she should have been scowling.

"Darn it. You're beyond perfect for him, isn't she,
Soph?"

"Lori, stop embarrassing her." Sophie shot her a
sympathetic look. "Sorry about my sister. I wish I
could say this is an aberration, but the truth is, she's
always like this."

Heather hoped they could move on to another subject, like Sophie's pregnancy, but those hopes were
quickly dashed as Sophie added, "Although it would
be really fantastic if you two did start dating."

Heather felt as if she were back in high school,

getting grilled on her secret crush, as Lori said, "I've never seen him look at anyone the way he looks at you."

Heather barely restrained herself from asking, *How does he look at me?*

"He's just happy I agreed to work with him and Cuddles." She shook her head, remembering the way she'd found the two of them that first day at his garage. "I'm afraid the puppy was way too much for him to handle at first. But he's done really well with her."

Sophie smiled. "He's always been great with animals and kids. Even when he tries to act like he can't be bothered with them, they all adore him the instant they meet him."

"Funny you should say that," Heather found herself telling Zach's sisters. "Atlas doesn't trust men very often, especially big ones, but he was never afraid of Zach. Not for one instant."

Lori clapped her hands together with glee. "You *do* think he's great! I can't wait for you to meet everyone," she said as if it were now a done deal.

"I can't date Zach!" Heather's words came out too loud, too fast, too impassioned.

God, she was making such a fool of herself. As soon as Zach had shown up with Cuddles, she and Atlas should have hightailed it out of the ballpark. But she'd been so happy to see him. Had felt so incredibly, wonderfully alive just at the sound of his voice.

She'd thought she was strong enough not to be

tempted by him. But not only had he succeeded in tempting her…he'd done it so fast it made her head spin. He was slipping in under her walls, and the armor she wore around her heart, too fast. Too frequently. It seemed that no matter how much energy she expended to try to push him away—when she remembered to push him away and wasn't laughing with him or wanting him—she wasn't even close to succeeding.

The problem was that while Zach was fun and blatantly sexual, he also came with a core of something *real* beneath the devil-may-care sarcasm. And that was precisely what scared her: the real man beneath the jokes and the sexual innuendos.

She could fight her reaction to the charming Zach, but the sweet, loving, genuine Zach was a whole different story.

Still, she knew she needed to keep fighting. Because if she made the mistake of letting him in, and then he ended up hurting her, she'd never forgive herself.

Of course, she hadn't meant to insult the older brother Sophie and Lori clearly worshipped, so she said, "Zach is a nice guy. I'm sure he'll find someone great one day."

"I hope so," Lori said with a sigh. "I know he acts like he doesn't need anyone, but I've never bought it. Then again, maybe it's because he's my brother and I love him and I don't want him to be alone forever."

"He loves you, too. All of you." She'd known that ever since the first time he'd spoken of his family, before she'd ever met them. "He has pictures of you all over his house."

Lori shot Sophie a look before saying, "You've been to his house?"

Heather clarified, "He had a bit of an emergency with Cuddles the first night they spent together. We had an emergency training session."

One that ended with her hand in his and his lips on her cheek.

Strangely, Lori picked that moment to stop torturing Heather. Instead, she leaned back in her seat, popped a handful of popcorn into her mouth and said around it, "Sophie's right. I shouldn't have said all that stuff to you. I was just so caught up in a fantasy of having someone like you as a sister-in-law instead of one of the awful girls he usually hooks up with." She sighed. "It figures you'd be too smart to want anything to do with him."

Jealousy hit Heather at the same moment as the urge to defend Zach did. Clearly, he could have—and regularly did have—any woman he wanted. Heck, as they'd been watching the game hadn't every woman in their section been drooling over Zach, with Sophie's good-looking husband coming in a close second?

"Trust me," Lori continued, "I totally get why you don't want to date Zach, but I have a couple of other great brothers who are single. Smith and Ryan are total catches, if you ask me."

Heather was flattered but couldn't imagine being with a movie star or a professional athlete. "Thanks, but I'm not looking for a relationship right now." Or ever.

Before Lori could get in one more word about her brothers and what great catches they all were, Heather turned to Sophie and asked about her pregnancy. Heather loved kids as much as she loved dogs, and as she edged closer to thirty, she was thinking more and more about when she was going to try to have them. She was beyond glad that there were so many options for a single woman, between in vitro and adoption.

"Are you excited about having twins?"

Sophie lit up. "Yes. When I'm not terrified about having them." Her face went all dreamy. "Jake is going to be a great father."

Lori made a puking sound. "It's bad enough that you're all over each other like Saran Wrap. Save us from the *love is perfect* soundtrack, would you?"

Even though she silently agreed with Lori on the whole love thing, Heather was amazed that Sophie didn't look the least bit insulted. Instead, she started singing, "Love is perfect, oh, so perfect," to the tune of "I Feel Pretty."

Lori covered her ears and started singing "Love Bites" in a perfect imitation of Def Leppard's singer until the three of them collapsed into giggles.

Suddenly, Heather actually wished she *could* date Zach. Not just because her hormones wouldn't leave her alone, but because there was no doubt in her mind about how fun it would be to be a part of the Sullivan family.

But even as she let herself envision that for a brief moment, she knew the reality was nothing like the fantasy. Regardless of how well things might start for her and Zach, no matter how much he seemed to like her and want her in the present, she knew with utter certainty that he wasn't the kind of man who would ever commit to one woman forever.

So if a part of her was at all envious at the way Jake had continually kissed his pretty wife, if she secretly longed at all for a man to look at her with such complete adoration, all she had to do was remember the vow she'd made to herself when she was seventeen and had found out the truth about the extent of her father's lies.

*Never.* She would never put herself in a position to be treated like that. Because she would never make the mistake of letting herself fall in love.

"Heather's a pretty girl."

Zach tugged Atlas away from the lamppost he was admiring and directed him toward a bush. "Pretty? Are you blind? She's gorgeous."

Jake nodded his agreement just as Cuddles got into a position that had Zach groaning. The blue bags were burning a hole in his pocket and he really wanted to keep it that way. It was one thing to clean up after the puppy in his backyard...

He muttered a curse that perfectly described not only what the puppy was doing, but Heather's huge dog, as well. Jake hadn't stopped laughing at him since they'd left their seats and he only laughed harder now.

"So Heather's just training the puppy?"

Zach wasn't going to admit to his closest friend that he'd struck out with Heather a half dozen times already and that the only way he'd gotten her here today was by tricking her into it.

"She's one hell of a dog trainer." And one hell of a woman, too.

Lord knew she had him wrapped so tightly around her little finger that he barely knew which way was up anymore. He only knew he wanted her more with every passing second…even as she tried to push him further away.

Jake nodded in the direction of the dogs, both of whom were frisky now that they'd taken care of their important business. "Looks like you've got some cleanup to take care of."

Zach still wasn't completely okay with the fact that Jake had gotten his little sister pregnant on the sly. Which was why he shoved a blue bag in his friend's hand and headed for Cuddles's pile. In the name of payback, Jake could deal with Atlas's mess.

# *Thirteen*

The second Zach sat back down, he could tell something was different. It was as if Lori, Sophie and Heather had gone from being strangers to becoming friends.

Who knew what his little sisters had told her? All he needed was for some of his crazier exploits to get back to Heather and she'd grab her dog and start running.

"Everything go okay with Huge and Tiny?" Atlas had already plopped down across their feet and closed his eyes. Cuddles was curled up against his chest, quite clearly the pup's favorite place on earth, considering how much time she spent there.

"Those blue bags came in handy."

He loved her smile and soft laughter. "Good," she said, still chuckling. "Thanks for taking Atlas with you." She looked at him almost shyly. "And thanks for changing my seat, too. I've really loved getting to know your sisters."

Her sweet words landed straight in the center of his chest. He leaned closer, close enough that he could have easily taken her mouth with his.

"Whatever they've told you, it's all lies."

He expected more laughter, but her eyes were dark instead of filled with humor, and her breath was coming faster, her gaze trained on his lips.

"I hope not" fell from her lips, and he would have kissed her right then and there, his lookee-loo family be damned, if she hadn't jerked back sharply.

She focused her entire attention on the game after that, and the second it finished, she stood up. "That was fun. So nice to meet you all, but I should really be going—"

Lori cut her off. "Wait, you have to meet Ryan." Before Heather could protest, his sister shoved past Zach, picked up Atlas's leash and slipped an arm through Heather's. "You're going to love him." She winked over her shoulder at him before saying, "He isn't anything like Zach."

Okay, so Zach had been irritated with his sister earlier, but now he recognized Lori for the jewel she really was for not letting Heather run from him so fast.

Heather was frowning and he overheard her say, "Actually, I'm not sure it's such a great idea if I go back where the rest of the team is."

Lori brushed off her concern without asking for a reason. "Are you kidding? All those hot, sweaty guys taking off their clothes make it a *fabulous* idea."

As if Ryan would ever let Lori date one of the

guys on his team in this lifetime. Fortunately, the players on the Hawks had always understood just how off-limits the Sullivan twins were. Unlike, he thought with a scowl in Jake's direction, his own friend. Of course, given the way Sophie and Jake were always giving each other gooey looks just the way they were doing right then, he supposed it had all worked out in the end.

Walking behind Heather, Zach couldn't take his eyes off her gorgeous legs in her shorts, the sweet curve of her hips, the way her dark, shiny hair swung over her back in its usual braid. Frankly, the last thing he was worried about right now was his little sister. Because if Ryan—or any of his teammates— looked at Heather the wrong way, he was going to have to kill them.

Heather hadn't been in the locker room before, even though she'd been invited more than once. If she'd taken the guy she dated occasionally up on his invitation, it would have made their casual relationship seem like more than it was.

Which was why she shouldn't be freaking out right now. Just because she and—

"Heather?"

Brant Johnston, the first baseman for the Hawks, grinned when she walked in with Lori.

She felt herself flush, but it wasn't because of Brant. It was the knowledge that Zach had moved beside her in a flash, every muscle in his body tense as if he was about to spring.

She was just flustered enough that, before she could stop him, Brant pulled her against him for a hug. "You look gorgeous, as always."

For a professional athlete, Brant was actually quite sweet. And there was no question that he was good-looking, with his golden hair, blue eyes and athletic build. But she had never even been tempted to take things beyond dinner and sex. It had been a few months since she'd last seen him, even though he'd called a couple of times to see if she wanted to get together. She just hadn't been all that interested.

Quickly stepping out of his arms, she planted a smile on her face that she hoped looked genuine. "Great game."

Out of the corner of her eye, she could see that Zach's face looked like thunder. Lori, Sophie and Jake were watching the scene play out with something akin to glee on their faces.

"If I'd known you were coming today, I would have made sure you had a great seat." He finally noticed her dog. "Hey, how's it going, Antler?"

She thought she heard Zach growl just as his brother Ryan found them. Atlas wasn't particularly comfortable with so many big men around, but she could tell Zach's presence made him feel much more secure than usual.

"Ryan," Zach said, putting a rather possessive hand on the small of her back, "this is Heather and her dog, Atlas."

She knew the special emphasis on her dog's name and his hand on her were both for Brant's benefit, but even while something warmed up inside of her at the crazy thought of actually belonging to Zach, she couldn't stand being the bone that two men were fighting over.

Stepping out of Zach's reach, she shook Ryan's hand. "It's so nice to meet you."

She could feel Ryan working to size up the situation between her and Brant and Zach. Atlas hadn't much cared for Brant the couple of times he'd met him, but just as he'd been with Zach, he practically turned into a squirming puppy when Ryan scratched his head. Yes, indeed, there was no doubt that the Sullivan men had quite a potent effect on all living, breathing things.

Somewhere in there Brant had moved closer to her. "It's been too long, Heather. Why don't we celebrate the game together tonight?"

A month ago, she might have gone. After all, she was a sensual woman and sex with a good-looking guy wasn't a terrible way to end a Friday night.

But even though she didn't have any other plans, and certainly wasn't in a relationship with anyone else, the idea of casually seeing Brant didn't seem like a very good one anymore. Actually, it seemed like a *terrible* idea.

She opened her mouth to say "no, thank you" when Zach reached out and slid a lock of hair that had escaped her braid behind her ear.

"You didn't mention you knew Brant this morning when you were making breakfast for us."

At his gentle touch, she simultaneously wanted

him more than she'd ever wanted another man… and, at the same time, she could have punched him for behaving like such a caveman with the false insinuations of why she'd been making breakfast at his house.

Purposefully turning her back on Zach, she told Brant, "It's been a pretty big day already and it will be an even bigger one tomorrow." She glanced down at her dog, who looked as if he'd run a marathon instead of gobbling up stray pieces of popcorn and playing with his best puppy friend all afternoon. "I've got to get home."

She was turning to Zach's family to say her goodbyes when Brant surprised her by pulling her against him for another hug. An even longer one this time. "I'll call you soon."

She barely stopped herself from rolling her eyes as she stepped out of his arms and turned to tell Lori, Sophie, Ryan and Jake, "It was so nice meeting all of you."

"It was *totally* our pleasure." Lori hugged Heather. "I hope we'll see you again really soon."

Heather didn't know what to say to that. She was Zach's dog trainer, not his girlfriend. What reason would she have to run into his family ever again unless they all got dogs?

She pulled up the slack on Atlas's leash and headed for the door. When she realized Zach was right beside her every step, she said, "I know the way out."

Of course, he didn't back off, but just stayed right beside her as she walked out of the park.

"How many times have you been with him?"

She picked up her pace. "That's none of your business."

"Why didn't you go with him tonight?"

That wasn't any of his business, either, but she said, "I'm tired. My dog is tired. I'm ready to go home."

She pushed out a side exit into an alley that led to the parking lot. The truth was, even the thought of kissing Brant again had her entire body recoiling. Not because he hadn't been an okay lover, but because, suddenly, there was only one man she could imagine kissing.

"What if he calls you when you're not so damned tired?"

Fury at herself for her continued lack of control where Zach was concerned had her spitting out, "Right now I'm not feeling it, but maybe on a different day, if I'm in the mood, why not?"

Zach grabbed her arm and pulled her into him. "Here's why not."

His mouth came down on hers in a kiss that had everything simmering between them finally exploding.

# Fourteen

Heather had fought this kiss for nearly a week. She'd lied to both of them about not wanting it, even as fantasies about what it would be like kept her distracted during the day and tossing and turning at night.

But none of her fantasies had done justice to their first kiss. There was no way she could have ever imagined it taking place in a deserted alley, with Zach's strong muscles pressing her into a cement wall, his hips against hers, his large hands sliding into her hair.

And, oh, God, the feel of his lips on hers, the way his tongue slipped and slid against hers… She was lost to sensation, to the insatiable greed to take more of the forbidden fruit she'd been craving body and soul.

*"Heather."* He groaned her name against her lips, then began to alternately nip at her lower lip, then lave over the small bites, as if a simple kiss wasn't enough when what he really wanted was to devour her.

She knew she should be pushing him away, that she should keep fighting their connection out of sheer self-preservation, but her body simply refused to follow that intelligent dictate.

Instead, she was wrapping her arms around his broad shoulders. She wanted him closer, needed *more.* She'd never felt like this with anyone else— completely out of control, already way out on the edge from nothing more than one incredibly potent kiss.

Yes, she knew she should stop, that she should be pushing him away and telling him it could never happen. Only, in a moment of more perfect connection with Zach than she'd ever imagined having with a man, she found herself deepening the kiss instead.

Leaving one hand in her hair, he began to run the other slowly down the side of her body. She nearly cried out into his mouth when he slid over—and past—the curve of her breast on the way to cup her hip with his palm. He didn't stop until he had curved his palm around her thigh, bare beneath the hem of her shorts.

God, the feel of his hand on her skin was shockingly good. And she was even more shocked when he lifted her leg up around his hip, but not shocked enough that she thought to stop him from taking that leverage to move in closer to the heated V between her legs.

Heather had always enjoyed the purely physical release of sex, but it had never been intense enough for her to forget herself, to lose track of what she believed in. Anyone could come out the side door and find them here like this, practically having sex against the wall. They were still fully clothed, but even so, she felt as if Zach had already stripped her bare.

She tried to pull herself out of the abyss, oh, how she tried, but when he started to rain kisses down across her jaw and found that supersensitive spot just at the underside of her chin, how could she do anything but let her head fall back against the wall and drink in every exquisite sensation of his mouth on her skin? His rough stubble scraped at her in the most delicious way and she used her leg hooked over his hip to pull him in even closer.

Any and all protests she might have given him— or herself—had flown out the window, and she was threading her fingers into his dark hair when something pulled at her wrist once, then twice, hard enough the third time to finally jolt her.

"The dogs," she managed in a breathless voice as she tried to catch hold of her racing heart. While she and Zach had been lost in their kiss, the dogs' leashes had tangled up around each other and their owners, too. "We need to untangle them."

Zach very reluctantly let go of her leg before snapping, "Cuddles, quit moving!" in a frustrated voice as he bent down to unclip the leash and scoop the puppy up in his arms.

"It's not her fault," she told him as she worked to pull the leashes apart with shaky hands. "We shouldn't have been doing that here." As if the location were the only problem with their kiss. "We shouldn't have been doing that anywhere at all," she quickly clarified.

Only, the truth was that if the dogs hadn't been there with them, Zach probably would have stripped her clothes off while he kissed her up against the wall. And instead of trying to stop him, she would have been begging him to hurry so she could get closer.

So she could have *more*.

"It's exactly what we should have been doing," he snapped at her.

His frustration shook the breathlessness right out of her. After all, as she reminded herself yet again, she wasn't a teenager who couldn't control her raging hormones.

"This isn't even about me," she snapped back. "You just want me because I'm a challenge."

"Wrong," he shot back. "I want you because I want you. From the first second I saw you, I've wanted you, Heather."

How did he manage to turn her insides to goo? First with his kiss, then with his words.

Still, she had to hold her ground. "You and Brant were fighting over me like I was that bone you sent Atlas."

"I was fighting for you because you're *mine*."

Her eyes widened at his possessive declaration. "I'll never belong to a man."

For the first time, he didn't launch back at her

with a quick retort. Instead, she felt him stop. Look. Assess.

"What," he said in a suddenly soft voice, "are you afraid of? Is it me? Or is it you?"

It was the very last thing she'd expected him to say. And even as her brain flooded with answers ranging from *falling for you* to *everything,* she said, "I'm not afraid."

He raised an eyebrow but didn't call her on her fib. Instead, he said, "Prove it."

She lifted her chin. "I know what you're doing. I know that whatever way you want me to prove it to you is going to be for your good and your good only."

He actually had the nerve to reach for her again, to slide the pad of his thumb across her lower lip. And fool that she was, she craved his touch enough to let him.

"It'll be good for both of us. I can promise you that." He trailed the back of his hand over her cheek in a lover's caress. "I'm not looking for love any more than you are. We're the perfect match, Heather. Don't worry, this is going to make us both happy. Really, really happy."

*Oh.*

She should be cheering, should be glad that he'd just spelled things out so clearly. But even though he'd just given her precisely what she'd always said she wanted, his words felt like a knife shoved straight through her chest…as if some stupid, reckless part of her heart had secretly been wishing he would fall in love with her.

Even though she wouldn't have trusted his professions of love if they had come.

It was yet another reason she should have been walking away from him, hauling Atlas out of the stadium, getting both of them away from the man who was more potent than any she'd ever known.

Only, she'd lost hold of her self-control at the first brush of his mouth against hers, and knowing how good it felt to have his body pressed into hers, warm and solid, had her desperate for another taste. A longer one this time, with no barriers between them, and no one and nothing interrupting the natural flow of their passion.

But at the same time that she could feel herself sinking deeper beneath the sensual spell he wound around her, Heather had run her life for too long to let a man—especially one as confident and charming as Zach Sullivan—lead her down a dark path.

If she were going to head into the darkness, she'd go of her own free will, damn it.

"Just sex," she said in a steady voice. Wanting to be absolutely sure she was clear with him—and herself, too—she added, "That's all this is ever going to be."

A flash of pure male victory moved through his eyes as he immediately threaded his fingers into hers and tugged her closer.

"Kiss me to seal the deal."

Her breath came even faster at his softly spoken command. She hadn't realized how much she craved

Zach's brand of sensual dominance until today. She'd loved the way he'd stolen the kiss from her, had been beyond excited by the sinful feeling of wantonness as he took what he wanted from her up against the wall. And now, even as she should have been annoyed at his demand that she kiss him to finalize their arrangement, she was more turned on than she'd ever been.

She knew what he expected her to do—either give him a peck on the lips out of annoyance or let him control the kiss again.

But now that she'd made the decision to enjoy being physical with Zach, she not only wasn't going to deny herself whatever pleasures were in store... she was also going to make darn sure he realized he wasn't any less affected by her than she was by him.

This time she was the one reaching for his jaw, feathering out her fingers across the supersexy dusting of stubble that shadowed his tanned skin. Desire flared in his eyes as she moved onto her tippy-toes to get closer. She slid her hand into his hair and pulled his face down to hers.

Her lips touched his a split second before he growled and slammed his mouth against hers. It was the perfect kiss to seal the deal for their newly negotiated affair, a wonderful indication of the incredibly passionate, no-holds-barred sex they were going to have with each other.

And nothing more.

* * *

Zach had never lost control with a woman before. Not even close.

Not until Heather.

When they both finally came up for air with the puppy squirming between them, he couldn't bear the thought of letting her go. Giving Cuddles room to breathe while still holding her close, he asked, "Do you need anything from your place for Atlas?"

Her beautiful eyes were hazy with pleasure from their kiss as she blinked up at him and nodded.

He wanted her in his bed. It was where she belonged, where he'd needed her from the first second he set eyes on her curves as she coaxed his puppy out of the bushes at his garage.

Lord, he couldn't wait to hear more of those little gasps of pleasure she'd been making when he'd been kissing her…and to watch her expression as she came apart beneath him.

Desperation to get her naked ASAP had him taking her hand in his, her dog's leash in his other hand, and pulling all four of them out toward the parking lot.

"I'll follow you over to your place and help you grab what you need."

He felt her hand stiffen in his. "It's just one night, Zach. We're not moving in with you. It's just going to be sex," she reminded him in a firm voice.

She was too firm. Too controlled. Even after their second kiss.

Oh, yes, he was going to enjoy making her lose control. In fact, that was going to be his sole mission for the foreseeable future.

Atlas's ears had perked up as if he'd just realized he was going to get to spend the night with his best friend. The Great Dane nuzzled the puppy and Zach grinned. Heather could fight the pull between them all she wanted, but he was counting on her having a hell of a time breaking up their dogs.

Using the dogs to keep her close to him wasn't playing fair.

Then again, when had a Sullivan ever played by the rules?

# *Fifteen*

Heather worked to slow down the overly fast pounding of her heart. Now, more than ever, there shouldn't be anything to be nervous about. Not after she and Zach had just clearly laid out the terms of their sex-only relationship.

And yet, now that the deal had been made, she was still more than a little amazed to find herself in his bedroom. Back at the baseball stadium, she'd thought she knew what she was getting herself into.

She suddenly realized how far from the truth that really was.

Zach Sullivan was a force of nature. Not just because of his stunning male good looks, but because of his strong, yet sweet, personality. The first time she'd ever looked at him, of course she'd thought of sex. There wasn't a woman alive who wouldn't, not with a face and body like his.

Oh, but if he knew how nervous she was, she could only imagine what he'd do. Laugh at her, probably. Tease her mercilessly from here on out. And consider himself the victor.

That knowledge was what had her resorting to the act she'd perfected as a seventeen-year-old, the one that said she didn't care what anyone thought of her...even if she desperately did.

"So, this is the legendary bedroom." She deliberately kept her body language loose and easy, hooking a thumb into the pocket of her shorts as she raised an eyebrow to scan the room.

Zach, who was standing in the doorway, said, "Legendary, huh?"

Darn it, that had been exactly the wrong word to use on a guy with an ego like Zach Sullivan's. But she knew better than to try to backtrack. Instead, she pulled her sweatshirt off, tossing it over the leather chair in one corner.

"So," she said when she slowly turned back to him, "are you ready to do this, or what?"

His dark gaze heated up, causing ripples of electricity to move across her skin with nothing more than one look. "There somewhere you need to be?"

God, no, she wasn't planning on leaving anytime soon. Heck, she could barely remember the rest of the world existed when she was with him. But boy, would there be trouble if he ever realized that.

His beautiful mouth moved up into a small grin just before he added, "Or are you just in that much of a hurry to finally have me?"

"I'm just ready to be impressed with your patented moves before my next birthday rolls around."

Any other man would have acted as if she'd just called his entire masculinity into question, but not Zach. Instead, he simply continued to grin that way-too-gorgeous grin.

"Box number two it is," he said as he made a small check mark in the air. "You can't wait another second to have me."

Heather would have made it a point to contradict that ridiculously arrogant—and pathetically true—assumption had it not been for the soft click of Zach closing his door to keep the dogs out of the bedroom. The bedroom lights went off a beat later.

She heard her swift intake of breath as his bedroom went immediately dark. Despite the large windows, the moon was hidden behind a thick layer of fog tonight and her heartbeat ratcheted up even higher.

She'd never much cared for the dark, had never seen the romance, the sexiness, in having the control of her eyesight taken away. Not when it felt as though it took away her choices, too. One of her lovers a few years back had wanted to blindfold her, but she hadn't been even the slightest bit interested.

She worked to fight back her innate panic as she said, "What are you doing?"

Heather couldn't see Zach in his bedroom, but she could hear him moving slowly toward her from the doorway.

"Getting ready to impress you."

Why did his voice sound even deeper than usual

in the dark…and why couldn't she stop herself from holding her breath as he came closer and closer?

She'd spent so long in control that even the few moments of standing in an unfamiliar room waiting for Zach to kiss her, touch her, were too long.

She couldn't keep the slight tremble out of her voice as she said, "Zach, I don—"

Before she could finish admitting to weakness, he was there with his hands on either side of her face, touching her so gently she could hardly believe it was the same man who'd practically been born with a wrench in his hands.

The pads of his thumbs stroked over her lips, whisper soft, and she instinctively opened for him to lick at the tip of one finger. His low groan rumbled through the room, the only sound apart from her breathing.

She was panting even though she was standing perfectly still, but there didn't seem to be any way to get her breath back when Zach was sliding his hands slowly down from her cheekbones to her neck. She wanted to arch into his hands, but even though his touch was barely skimming the surface of her skin, it was as if he was holding her completely captive.

"Such soft skin," he murmured, and she wanted to feel the almost-reverent words against her lips, wanted desperately for him to kiss her.

She'd always been an equal opportunity lover, never believed in waiting for a man to make the first move, never hoped for the chance of pleasure if she could act to take it for herself. But that was sex.

This was seduction.

One she'd never seen coming.

Because how could she have predicted the feel of his calloused hands lighting every inch of her skin on fire so slowly, so sweetly, that she was barely aware of them working on the few small buttons at the top of her long-sleeved shirt so that he could more easily pull it over her head?

And how could she have known that he'd smell even better up close in the dark, a clean all-male scent that had her senses racing to drink it in?

"From the way you talk about the lines and curves of your cars—"

He made his way from one button to the next without so much as grazing her breasts. She'd known he loved to tease, but she hadn't realized that trait would transfer over to the bedroom, too.

"—I thought you'd want to see everything."

It was too dark for her to see more than the faint outline of his shape, but she swore she could feel his smile. "You're right. I do like looking at pretty things," he confirmed softly as he moved to the hem of her shirt and pulled it up over her head to let it fall to the ground behind her. "Good thing I have great night vision."

"I can barely drive in the dark," she said, knowing she was babbling now, but standing there in only her bra and shorts had her nerves bubbling up all over again.

This time she didn't have to guess if he was smiling—she could hear it in his low chuckle. The warmth of his laughter washed over her the way it always did and helped settle her down some.

For all the times he had irritated or frustrated her, the truth was she'd always liked being with him. More than she could ever remember enjoying being with a man, which was precisely why she'd made sure they didn't end up in his bedroom before now. Not without a list of rules and regulations about what was allowable.

Great sex was obviously on the menu. Emotional entanglement wasn't.

Where, she had to wonder, did seduction fall?

But, as Zach's hands spanned her waist before moving to stroke over the taut muscles of her back, she couldn't hold on to the question.

All she could do was feel.

And, oh, how wonderful it was to have strong hands on her, working deep to relax parts of her that had been tight for so long she hadn't even been aware they were tense.

"You feel so good, Heather. Just the way I knew you would."

She could hear the honest appreciation in his voice, knew it didn't matter if he'd said the same things to a hundred women before her. All that mattered was that he was saying it to *her* now.

He moved his hands up to her shoulder blades and found a knot that had her almost whimpering as he pressed into it with absolutely zero mercy.

"You don't take good enough care of yourself," he admonished in that low voice that made her insides turn to liquid. "You work too hard. And that big mutt of yours is always yanking you around." He gently spun her around so that her back was to his front and he could dig harder into her shoulders. "He needs to be more careful with you."

Despite the fact that his massage was turning her to mush, she had to remind him again, "He's not a mutt."

"Funny," Zach said as he slid her hair over one shoulder, close enough now that she could feel his warm breath on her exposed neck, "he always answers to 'mutt.' You sure his papers weren't forged?"

She still couldn't believe the way her dog had taken to Zach, considering his basic distrust of all men. Then again, animals had a gift for seeing beneath the surface to people's true natures. They knew how to read a false smile for evil, a seemingly innocuous touch as a dangerous threat…or, conversely, they knew that a man who acted like an island was capable of such warmth and enough sweetness to take her breath away again and again.

Before she realized it, he had the clasp of her bra undone and was working it off her shoulders so that it was falling to the floor to join her shirt. Even in the dark, she wanted to cover up, wanted to lift her hands over her breasts, though she'd already consented to sleep with Zach.

"Am I making you nervous?" he asked, his lips nearly at her earlobe now as he moved closer still to her now-half-naked body.

"No." And it was true. She wasn't scared.

She was excited.

*Beyond* excited.

At long last, he pressed his mouth to her skin, brushing his lips against her earlobe, his tongue barely making contact before he asked, "Then why are you trembling?"

"I have sensitive ears," she told him.

"Good to know." He pressed another soft kiss just below her earlobe this time before saying, "Anywhere else I should know about that's sensitive?"

*Oh, God.*

Until now, she'd felt as if she'd been able to pit herself against Zach Sullivan as an equal. But that was before they'd entered his bedroom…where she quite clearly didn't stand a chance of being anything but putty in his big, strong, all-knowing hands.

Still, she had to keep trying to stay toe-to-toe with him, didn't she? Otherwise, how would she possibly be able to respect herself in the morning?

"Maybe we should turn the lights back on and I'll draw you a map."

"Such a sassy mouth," he murmured. "Makes me think I should put it to better use."

It should have been enough warning for her to brace herself for his kiss, but when he slid one hand into her hair and turned her face so that he could reach her mouth with his, she couldn't do anything but gasp at the extreme pleasure of having his mouth on hers again.

For how gentle his hands had been—and still

were—the wildness of his kiss told her a different story.

He wanted her. Badly. And as his tongue thrust against hers, she was glad to be able to finally unleash all the passion, the desire, she'd been holding in check since the first moment she'd met him.

She tried to turn into his arms, wanted to press her bare chest up against his, wanted to know if he was as hard, as hot, as she'd dreamed he would be. But instead of letting her move against him, he slid one hand around her waist and held her against him like that, back to front. And, strangely, instead of wanting to fight his hold, instead of feeling as if he was controlling her, she felt the exact opposite.

Heather felt the comfort, the safety of knowing he wasn't going to let her fall, and accepted, in this one instance at least, that he knew precisely how to lead them both straight to pure pleasure.

Her shorts were falling to her feet before she even realized he'd undone the button and zipper. Shocked by how easy it was to get lost in his kisses, she pulled her mouth from his.

As if he could guess at her skittishness, rather than claiming her lips again, he ran soft kisses over her cheek and then her neck and shoulders. Her skin came alive inch by inch—a path of sensation, of pleasure.

And yet, she still couldn't let go of that hit of fear, the worry that she was allowing herself to get lost in someone else, until Zach's voice broke through.

"Are you sensitive here?" He brushed his thumb

up along the top of her spine until it reached her hairline, and she shivered in response. "I'll take that as a yes," he said softly as he followed that same path with his tongue. "What about this spot?" His fingers found the small of her back, and the next thing she knew, he was kneeling behind her, his mouth barely a beat behind as his tongue licked over the incredibly sensitive skin.

When she couldn't stop the breath from whooshing from her lungs, he said, "Definitely, yes."

And then, just as she was trying to process the startling fact that he was indeed making a map of the sensitive places on her body, she felt his large hands come around either side of her rib cage, just beneath the lower swell of her breasts.

"I'm going to take a guess that this one is going to be a yes, too," he said against her left side as his tongue traced between two ribs and she shuddered against him, her knees nearly buckling at the sweet pleasure of being touched like this.

As if she was all that mattered.

As if he actually thought she was precious and worth the time it would take to explore her pleasure, to learn where it hid and what would make it come to life.

He mirrored his actions on the other side of her body and she tried to hold still and not beg for more, but the small, desperate sound that came from her throat gave her away.

Zach pressed his lips to the small of her back. "All in good time."

A moment later, still kneeling behind her in the dark, he hooked one finger into each side of her panties and held there. She swallowed hard, a loud sound in the dark silence.

"Do you know how long I've been waiting for this moment?"

Each word came more ragged than the one before it. Just as his wild kiss had been, the raw statement was testament to how badly he wanted her, despite his slow, teasing seduction.

Somehow she managed to ask, "How long?"

He slid her panties down just enough to press a kiss to the top of one cheek, groaning as he gave equal measure to the soft flesh on the other side.

"Forever, Heather. It feels like I've been waiting forever for you."

And then, just after the most shocking words in the world had been spoken, her panties were off, lying in a puddle of cotton at her feet.

She waited, holding her breath, for Zach to touch her again, to kiss her—*please, please, please don't leave me like this*—but he was as still as she was, his breath on her skin all that was touching her.

"I love the way you smell." His words went from raw to guttural as he inhaled. "I love the way you feel." His hands moved to her hips, and she felt small and intensely feminine as he gently caressed her. "And I love the way you taste." He rained small nips and kisses at her backside, then down her thighs, until he finally reached the backs of her knees.

It shouldn't have been an erogenous zone. She

should have been laughing, not softly moaning, as his tongue moved across the skin at the backs of her legs.

"I think we've found a whole set of other sensitive spots," he confirmed for her as she trembled so hard that his hands on her hips were the only things holding her up. "But I bet there's more." He paused and her breath caught as he said, "A whole lot more."

The next thing she knew, he was back on his feet and lifting her in his arms.

"Zach, what are you doing?"

No man had ever picked her up like this before and carried her over to a bed. It felt too romantic for what they were to each other, for what they'd agreed on.

"Heather, I'm carrying you over to the bed!" he teased, mimicking her shocked tone.

How could she do anything but laugh, even though she was more aroused than she'd ever been in her life? Laughter and sex had never been connected for her before.

Then again, she'd never been with a lover like Zach before, had she?

# *Sixteen*

Zach Sullivan should have been in his element. Giving women pleasure was what he did best.

It didn't make sense, then, that he felt so far off his game, so totally lost in Heather that every other sexual experience had fallen away—leaving him to figure it all out with one kiss, one touch, at a time.

He'd turned off the lights to make sure that he stayed in control of the evening. Only, the darkness was doing a number on him, too.

Her scent was everywhere, sweet and aroused. Her skin was impossibly soft. And when she trembled as he kissed her, when she gasped with pleasure as sensation took her over, his chest clenched tight.

"Your arms are going to get tired soon if you don't put me down."

He lowered his mouth to hers again but stopped just short of making contact. "Questioning my stamina, are you?" Without waiting for her sure-to-be-sassy reply, he covered her lips with his own and kissed the breath from her lungs.

Both of them were panting by the time he finally laid her down in the center of his bed, then quickly took off his clothes.

He hadn't been exaggerating when he'd told her he had great night vision. My God, she was beautiful. He just wanted to look at her, wanted to memorize every soft curve, every hollow laid out before him.

"Zach?"

She reached out into the darkness and he captured her hands in his. "I'm right here. Just enjoying the view."

She made a sound of surprise at the knowledge that he really could see her in the dark, even as her fingers threaded through his. Coming palm to palm with her was yet another moment of connection he hadn't expected. One more to add to all the rest that he had experienced.

Zach didn't hold women's hands. But he didn't want to let go of Heather, so he moved onto the bed with her, straddling her thighs with his own to keep her right where he wanted her.

"You really can see me?"

Well enough to see the panic on her face at finally being naked with him on the bed. Of course, he greatly enjoyed throwing her off-kilter, especially when she tried so hard to be the steadiest woman on the planet.

"Sure can."

She made a frustrated little sound that he had to cover with another kiss, a soft one this time. Not letting go of her hands in his, he put them on either side of the pillow and took his time exploring her sweet mouth.

God, he'd wanted to kiss her like this for so damn long, desire eating him up more with every second he spent with her. He loved the way she didn't hold anything back, that she wasn't trying to tease him or turn him on. She kissed the same way she did everything else, with sweet focus.

Zach had planned on seducing her, but as her tongue stroked against his, as her fingers tightened against his, and she lifted her hips up to try to find the release he was drawing out, he had to wonder if it was really the other way around…and Heather was the one seducing *him*.

He pulled back from her mouth on the crazy thought, determined to get back on track. The one where he was the one holding the cards, not the woman he hadn't been able to resist from the first moment he'd set eyes on her.

Staring down at Heather in the shadowed room, he marveled again at just how beautiful she was. Other women with bodies like hers would have done whatever they could to showcase it to the world, not cover it up with faded shirts and shorts.

Only, hadn't he been going crazier day by day, wondering exactly what was hiding beneath those shapeless clothes? Almost as if by not simply showing him her assets, she'd amped up his anticipation of the moment he finally got to see all of her.

"So?"

He could hear the bravado covering the insecurity,

*Bella Andre*

and the fact that she had any worries at all about her worth made that twinge come back in his chest again.

Knowing he wasn't the kind of man who had words for moments like this, he decided to show her how beautiful she was in a way that she couldn't possibly misunderstand.

He lowered his mouth to the tip of one breast and tugged it between his lips. Heather arched up into his hands and gasped out his name, but he was so focused on the sweet taste and feel of her aroused flesh against his tongue that he barely heard her. He swirled his tongue around the taut peak before letting it go to taste the other.

Using his hands on hers and his thighs on either side of her hips, Zach held Heather still as she tried to writhe against him while he loved her perfect breasts, one to the other, again and again, until she was begging.

"Please, Zach, I need—"

He lightly scraped his teeth over the tip of one breast and her gasp of pleasure swallowed up the rest of her plea. He didn't need her to tell him what she needed because he needed it, too, needed to taste every inch of her skin, needed to know the feel, the scent, of her all over.

He moved up from her breasts to her shoulders, then to the soft underside of one arm. But instead of turning even more into liquid, she stiffened as his lips and tongue trailed toward her elbow.

Of course, that only made him more intent on making her feel good. On helping her to forget anything but how good it was to finally be together like this.

His mouth found her softness again, only this time he realized the skin was slightly raised. When he tasted the crook of her elbow and then the underside of her forearm, each time he found more of the same. Slightly raised skin that came as a total surprise against the perfect smoothness of the rest of her.

"Heather," he asked, his gut twisting at the pain she must have felt to have such scars now, "how did you get hurt?"

Even as he asked, he was trailing his fingers over her other arm, finding the same scars. They were faint, completely healed, but he couldn't have missed them. Not in the dark when there was nothing to distract his senses from her.

And not when nothing seemed to matter more than Heather.

"They're old scars," she said softly. "From an accident—when I was a teenager."

Her voice had broken on those last words and he hated the way she'd gone from being so sensual, so open to him, to suddenly still. Stiff. As if she was scared...and regretting what they were doing.

"I'm glad they've healed," he told her before pressing another kiss to first one arm, then the other.

Her breath hitched as if she might cry. But then she said, "I am, too."

He had to kiss her again, needed to turn their lovemaking back around, back to where it had been before he found the scars and she'd gotten upset. He didn't know how long they kissed, but he loved the way she threaded her fingers back through his, as if she needed him just as much as he needed her.

And Lord, how he needed her. Needed to taste more of her, needed to know if the scent of her arousal would be as sweet on his tongue.

Pulling her hands down with him, not willing to relinquish that connection with her for even a second, he lifted his mouth from hers to move lower, down over her stomach, and then lower still to the damp curls that drew him like a magnet.

He'd practically lost control earlier when he'd been kneeling behind her. It was even worse now, this desire to take her, to make her his.

And to keep her.

Zach barely managed to remind himself that he didn't keep women. He didn't even consider it. Sex was for pleasure. Only pleasure.

Sweet Lord, what pleasure it was to be with Heather.

Loving the way she instinctively opened her legs for him as he came closer to her core, he swept over her with a broad stroke of his tongue. He had planned to tease, to taste her slowly, but the way she arched up into his mouth, those sweet little sounds she made as he drove her higher and higher, made him lose hold of his control.

Next time he'd make her wait, next time he'd tease her mercilessly until she was begging and pleading for release.

Zach needed to claim her as his right this very second. He needed to know that she was as out of control as he was, that he wasn't the only one out on the edge of passion.

Like a man possessed, he licked and sucked at her aroused flesh. Already, he knew he'd never get enough. He was already addicted to the taste of her.

And then, a moment later, her hands clamped down so hard on his that her nails bit into his skin as she shattered against his mouth.

# *Seventeen*

None of her other lovers had ever noticed the scars on her arms, not even with the lights on.

Heather knew why, knew that it was because none of the men she'd been with before Zach had cared enough about her to take the time to learn her secrets.

Sex had never been all about her before.

But, as she was surprised to realize yet again, Zach was different. He noticed everything, things that other men would never have paid any attention to. He'd lingered over her scarred skin with his mouth, and he'd given her such soft healing kisses she'd hardly be surprised if the scars were completely gone in the morning.

Heather had never felt anything like this, such all-encompassing pleasure. She'd always been the one to know her body best, usually having more success with battery-operated devices than any of the men she'd been with.

But none of them had been Zach Sullivan.

The things he could do with his lips. With his tongue. She'd never come that hard, that long, that good, before. Even now that she was starting to come down from the incredibly high peak, Zach didn't seem to be done, wasn't climbing over her to finish what he'd started and get what was coming to him.

Instead, he licked over her slowly, soothing the sensitive area after the riotous explosion of pleasure he'd just put it through, while seeming to savor her at the same time.

Finally, he lifted his head and said, "I love the way you taste when you come," before lowering his mouth back between her thighs and pressing a kiss to her. "You know how greedy I am," he murmured against her incredibly sensitive flesh. "I want more of your sweetness, Heather. Right now."

She shouldn't have been so easily aroused again, not by a couple of bossy sentences, but even before he treated her to more focused attention from his brilliant tongue, just knowing how much he was enjoying being with her had Heather going from zero to a hundred again in a matter of seconds.

Gently, he slid one of his hands from hers and ran it down over her hips. She shivered at his touch, and then she was losing control of her body again, needing that beautiful release that only Zach could give her. Again and again she bucked into his hand, his mouth, wanting, begging, needing, gasping.

And then there it was, a kaleidoscope of colors, as she burst apart again, crying out his name, needing to feel it on her tongue as she rose to impossible heights, then fell down, down, down into the darkness.

Heather had never known that she could be pure sensation. Every inch of her skin felt hyperaware. Every cell inside her was ready, waiting, for *more*.

She should have been exhausted, shouldn't have been able to crave anything more, but when Zach began the long, slow climb up her body, his mouth pressing kisses to the insides of her thighs, her hip bones, her rib cage, she couldn't wait another second.

He had never let go of his grip on her right hand, and as he slid the fingers of his left over hers, connecting them again, she used all her might to pull him toward her, over her. She couldn't see his face in the dark, but that didn't matter. She didn't need to see him anymore.

Just knowing he was there with her was enough.

*"Zach."*

"You're so beautiful," he said as he took her lips with his, her hands back up on either side of her head.

He might act as though life was just for fun, but here, in bed, she sensed who he truly was. A man to whom everything mattered deeply.

She didn't want to feel anything for him beyond annoyance and laughter and arousal. But she knew why she had started to fall for him. Not just because of his ridiculously good looks…but because she sensed what he tried to keep so deeply hidden from them all.

A surprisingly big, beautiful heart.

Still blurry after her orgasms, and from the emotions she couldn't seem to fight back in this one perfect moment, she reached out to put her hands on his chest, on his breastbone, beneath which his heart beat hard. Steady.

She leaned forward, pressing a kiss to the hairs that dusted over his skin.

He stilled after her kiss landed on his chest. She wanted to make a joke, wanted to say something to lighten the mood, to make it clear to him that what they were doing was just sex.

Instead, she found herself whispering, "You are, too." *So incredibly beautiful.*

Suddenly, he was slipping his hands from hers and she felt the bed shift. For a split second, she worried that he'd seen the truth beneath her kiss over his heart—a truth she couldn't even admit to herself—and was planning to get the heck out of the bed before she could make the mistake of pairing any more emotion with the great sex they were having.

But before she could find a way to string any words together that would make sense, to make it clear to him that she wasn't going to make that mistake, she could hear the ripping of paper.

Thank God, she thought, he was putting on a condom. And then she was pressed down against the mattress again and he was over her, her fingers threaded through his again, his thighs pushing hers open, wider, then wider still until she was wrapping them around his waist to take him into her.

*"Mine."*

The one word penetrated the darkness and her

heart was nearly pounding out of her chest as she waited, poised on the edge of dangerous anticipation.

"I've been waiting for you for so long, Heather. I'm finally going to make you mine."

"Yes," she said, the one word raw and more desperate than she'd ever heard from her own lips. And for all that she was trying to stop herself from saying something she'd regret in the morning, the words "Make me yours, Zach" couldn't be stopped.

When he surged inside her, so fiercely that her head would have hit his headboard if he hadn't been holding her so firmly in place, her breath whooshed out of her.

She'd never been with a man this big or this strong. And she'd certainly never known one with such sweet knowledge of a woman's pleasure. Because as he continued to take her hard, fast, deep, she knew that this was what she wanted, was exactly what she'd been yearning for.

Not only to find someone who could help her lose herself. But to find a man who would possess her body in the darkness, then make her laugh in the light.

Zach's power over her was extraordinary. She felt it inside of her; she felt it as the sweat from his chest mixed with her own. She wanted to touch him, wanted to run her hands over all those muscles, the unwavering strength. But at the same time, how she loved holding his hands…and being held right back.

Her hips moved with his, rising to meet each powerful thrust, falling as he pulled back before coming into her again, seemingly deeper every time. She could feel her body tightening, inner muscles not used to such exquisite pleasure, almost aching with how sensitive her aroused flesh now was.

"Again," he gritted out, she was sure from between clenched teeth, as he worked to hold on to his own control. "Come for me, Heather. I need to feel you around me." He plunged in harder, deeper. "Now."

She was the one who gave the orders, the one always in control. Even as far flown as she was into the sensual spell he'd wound around her with kisses, and caresses, and mysterious darkness, her brain tried to send out a warning. A warning to hold something back. A warning to be the one dictating pleasure for herself, rather than having it given to her as a gift.

But even as flashes of sense came at her through a thick fog of desire, how could she do anything but obey Zach's order? Especially when he was only telling her to do what her body so desperately wanted?

Yes, she thought as she released her remaining hold over herself and let the plunge and pull of Zach's body take her careening over the edge one more time, this was exactly what *she* wanted. To allow herself a pleasure she'd never been able to find with anyone else.

She would heed the warnings, she would guard her heart, but she wouldn't deny herself any of the primal need, the elemental desire for this man. For as long as it lasted, she would take all he had to give.

"Sweet Jesus," he groaned as her inner muscles

gripped him and she ground her hips up against his to prolong the pleasure, "why did I wait so long to take you?"

She should have been insulted by the way he spoke about *taking* her and maybe she would be later, but she knew the truth.

Until this very moment, he'd been *giving* to her, everything she needed, everything she wanted. All he'd cared about was her pleasure. Yes, her pleasure pleased him, but that wasn't why he'd touched her, kissed her, loved her the way he had.

He'd done it all for her, had been minutely attuned to every breath, to every heartbeat, to her scars, and then to every gasp of pleasure. Only now that he knew she was completely satisfied did he let himself take.

Heather knew the precise moment their lovemaking went from being all about her to being for him. The tenor changed as he let go of her hands and slid his palms over her breasts, cupping her, squeezing her before moving his hands lower, to cup the curve of her hips in his hands.

It was perfect, the shift from her pleasure to his. It was just how it should be, just how she wanted it. They were equal partners in each other's pleasure. She wanted to give Zach what he'd given her.

Complete freedom to fall apart, with no repercussions waiting afterward.

As he gripped her hips tighter and tighter, she could feel him growing even bigger, even harder, with each powerful thrust. His focus might not be entirely on her pleasure anymore, but even so, she could feel herself on the verge of flying again.

Finally able to touch him, she reached up, ran her hands over his chest, then over to his upper arms. His muscles and tendons flexed beneath her fingertips and she marveled at his strength even as she used her own to hold on to him with her hands on his sweat-slickened skin, her legs tightly wrapped around his hips as she met him thrust for thrust.

She wanted to focus only on him now, needed to make sure he felt as good as she did, but she couldn't stop her body from responding to how good it felt. Only, she didn't want to go there alone this time.

"Zach." She tried to warn him, but it was too late—she was already falling. "Please," she heard herself beg through a fog, knowing he wouldn't understand what she wanted, that he would just think she was pleading for him to prolong her next climax. Still, she said it again, the only two words she could form. "Please, Zach."

It didn't take more than a split second for Heather to realize she'd underestimated him yet again. Somewhere in the back of her mind, it occurred to her that he understood her desires, that he quite likely knew her body, her sensual needs, better than she ever had herself.

In the next sweet, perfect moment, Zach's name fell from her lips like a benediction as he stilled above her, then pulsed long and hard with his own powerful release.

And, oh, how she loved the way he threaded his

hands into her hair, then covered her mouth in a kiss that told her just how much she pleased him. At least as much as he'd pleased her.

Finally, he came down over her, breathing hard, his weight heavy over hers as he pressed her even deeper into his mattress. She didn't mind his weight or the dampness that stuck between them, not when she could wrap her arms around his back and simply hold him.

# *Eighteen*

Heather woke up a few hours later in the circle of Zach's strong arms. Instinctively, she snuggled into his naked body, but the warnings that hadn't been able to pierce through the arousal clouding her brain before now rushed in with unrelenting fury.

Here lay danger, feeling soft and warm and safe with Zach Sullivan.

She was a woman, so she would allow herself a little softness. Warmth couldn't be helped, either. Not when Zach was a walking, breathing heating unit.

But safety?

Only a complete fool would let herself believe she was safe with him.

Besides, their agreement in the ballpark's alley had been perfectly clear. Their relationship was all about sex.

Nothing else.

Oh, God, how could she already be in so far over her head with this man? She'd thought she was tough enough to make a pleasure-only deal with him...but if she'd known the way he was going to make love to her last night, that it would feel as if he was giving his heart and soul to her, too, she never would have been so stupidly arrogant as to think that she could be the one woman on the planet not to lose her heart to Zach Sullivan. Adding in the way he'd found her scars and asked how she'd been hurt, as if it broke his heart to even think of anything happening to her— not to mention the way she'd completely lied to him about how the scars had come to be—had a shiver of warning skittering up her spine.

And yet, even had she known all of that, would she have been able to turn her back on the chance to feel his arms around her, his lips pressing against hers, his hands rough and sure on her skin?

No, she honestly didn't think she would.

Beyond irritated with herself for having neither self-control nor a big enough sense of self-preservation where he was concerned, she began to lift his arm from where he was holding her tightly to him.

Zach's arm tightened around her waist. "I've been waiting for you to wake up."

His breath was warm, sensual, against her ear, his erection pressing into her bottom as she took a deep breath. There was nothing she wanted more than to stay here with him.

Which was exactly why she needed to succeed at pushing from his arms to slide off the bed. "I need to go."

"Not yet." His teeth found her lobe and tugged at it. "I need you again."

She barely stifled a needy moan as she felt the immediate answering throb at her breasts, between her legs. She needed him, too.

Only hours after he'd given her a shocking amount of pleasure, she was desperate for more. For the slow caress of his large, calloused hands over her skin as he lazily filled his hands with her.

"You have the most beautiful body, Heather."

Wanting to stop her stupid heart from swelling at his heated praise, she made herself say, "How can you tell," as if she were cogent, rather than already sinking deeper and deeper beneath his spell, "when you haven't even seen it properly yet?"

She loved the sound of his soft laughter against her neck, far too much.

"I can see in the dark, remember? But I could be blind and know how beautiful you are. Just from this." He let his fingertips play across her breasts. "And this." He slid his hand down over her stomach muscles into the already damp curls between her legs.

She couldn't believe how desperate he made her feel with his hand between her thighs and his lips plotting a course of sensual destruction across her neck and shoulders. Thank God, the next thing she knew he was shifting on the bed to reach for another condom.

When she heard the familiar tearing of the small package, she spun to yank it out of his hands in the dark. Desire gave her perfect aim, even though she could still barely see a thing.

Zach helped guide the condom in her hand to his erect shaft and together they rolled it down over the thick, throbbing length.

Last night she'd let him take control and it had been amazing, but now that she knew the pleasure he could give her, she couldn't possibly sit back and wait for him to tease, to tantalize, again.

Laying her palms flat on his chest, she pushed him back onto the bed and moved over him to straddle his hips. A breath later, she was sinking down on him.

"You feel so good." She'd never been a talker in bed, but with Zach she couldn't seem to hold back what she was feeling.

Not when being with him really was *that* good.

Her inner muscles clenched around him and she loved the sound of his almost-helpless groan as she began to move.

"So do you." She felt him throb inside of her, growing bigger with every word he spoke. "So good I can't believe it."

She loved the way he moved with her, loved the feeling of hard muscles rippling beneath her fingertips as she braced herself on his chest and stomach as she rode him. She loved the feel of his big hands stroking over her flesh in the darkness, the way he seemed to know exactly where to touch her to elicit even more sighs of pleasure.

And even though a part of her desperately wished

the sun could rise quickly so that she could see him beneath her, coming into her, the truth was that nothing had ever been as good as the sweet carnality of making love with Zach, darkness all around them creating a world that was pure sensation. If she could have, she would have made it stretch on forever, where nothing existed but their elemental connection.

But everything was tightening too quickly, building too fast inside her again, heading toward the peak he'd sent her hurtling over so many times already. And when he settled his large hands on her hips to shift her pelvis slightly before thrusting up in a secret place inside that sent her reeling even further, she knew she had no choice but to give in to the mastery he already had over her body.

"What did you just do?"

He did it again and she almost came right then and there.

"You like it, don't you?"

*Like* it? Was he crazy?

She freaking *loved* it.

But she couldn't manage words anymore, not when he was thrusting up into her again, right in that beautiful spot that took her breath completely away. A quick learner, she quickly figured out how to move with him to make it even better, the push and pull of pure ecstasy as he withdrew, then came back to drive her even crazier with every powerful thrust.

If that had been all there was, it would have been enough. More than enough. Beyond amazing.

But Zach, she had quickly learned, never did anything by halves. And if he was intent on rocking her world, by God, he was going to all but blow it to smithereens.

The next thing she knew he was sitting up, his arms moving around her waist as he adjusted her so that she was sitting on his lap, her legs now crossed behind his hips. He was so deep like this, deeper than she could have imagined she could take him.

"Hold still."

She was glad for the momentary pause, for the chance to appreciate being so close to him.

*Oh!*

The slow slide of his tongue over the tip of one breast had her sucking in a breath before he moved to the next and it whooshed back out of her lungs. Back and forth, he aroused her with his lips and tongue and teeth, the bristles across his chin an utterly delicious scraping against her sensitive skin.

He hadn't told her she could move again, but there was no way to stop her hips from rocking against his. Everything inside her drew up so tight she thought she would shatter.

And then, on the next strong pull of his lips against her, she did.

# *Nineteen*

Zach had to pull Heather closer, had to try to erase any space left between them as he followed her over the edge. He continued to hold her close as they fought for breath in each other's arms. He didn't want to let go of her, would happily have held her on his lap forever, but when she shifted over him, he forced himself to loosen his hold as she began to lift herself from him.

The sun was just starting to rise, and even though his night vision was good, seeing Heather's incredible beauty in the light of day took away the breath he'd finally regained.

"Let me look at you."

"The dogs need to be let out."

He wasn't willing to let her use them as an excuse just yet. "They can wait a few more minutes."

Pulling her firmly back onto his lap, he began to get hard again as he let his gaze rove over her breasts, her waist, her hips. "Next time, we're going to have every light in the house on."

She went still for a moment before laughing out loud. He loved the way she felt—and looked—as her body bounced above him.

"I think I just might be able to stomach looking at you," she said as she scanned his body with her intelligent, appreciative eyes. "I really do have to go, though."

She pushed off his lap and he watched her walk naked toward the bathroom. The door closed behind her and he heard the lock click before the shower came on.

If she hadn't just locked him out, he would be in there with her, showing her how much fun they could have with the custom water jets that he'd had installed on the back wall of his shower.

Zach got out of bed and reached for his clothes. Sex with Heather had been phenomenal. But instead of feeling relaxed, he was wound tight.

He'd never, not once in his life, felt the urge to pin a woman down on their next date. But Heather didn't act like any other woman he knew, all of whom would have been pulling out the stops this morning to try to nail *him* down for another evening together.

Hell, even letting her fall asleep in his arms last night had been outside the bounds of his rule book. And he never took women to his place. It was easier to throw on his clothes and head out if he went to theirs.

But he hadn't thought twice before bringing

Heather to his house. Not when he'd been fantasizing about the way she'd look in his bed since the moment he'd set eyes on her.

The craziest thing of all, though, was the fact that he'd loved falling asleep with her. Almost as much as he'd loved everything that had come before…and after.

What was happening to him?

The only thing he knew for sure anymore was that he didn't have a prayer of keeping his hands off her. Not after the hours they'd just spent together had completely blown his mind. Only an idiot would willingly give up that kind of pleasure.

Zach wasn't an idiot. Not by a long shot. And he knew he needed to be extra careful about the complications that clearly went hand in hand with such extreme pleasure.

He liked Heather, and that wasn't going to change. But loving her was still out of the question. Now more than ever.

Because the thought of making a commitment of forever to Heather, and then leaving her behind to mourn him when he died suddenly just like his father had, made Zach's blood run cold in his veins.

He never wanted anything to hurt Heather ever again.

Especially not him.

He shoved on his jeans and headed into the kitchen, where Atlas and Cuddles were curled up with each other on his rug. Atlas looked up hopefully, then sighed when he saw it was only Zach.

"She's in the shower. You'll get her back soon."

And he shouldn't be jealous of the fact that her damn dog was going to get to spend the whole day with her. Slamming his coffeepot into the machine, he heard a *crack* and swore as he went to dump it out in the sink and toss the broken pot in the trash.

Cuddles freaked out at the loud sounds and started barking just as Heather walked into the room, her hair wet around her shoulders. She had on one of his clean button-down shirts, which hung to her knees. Her face was makeup free, her feet were bare…and she looked more beautiful to him than any of the perfect starlets that hung from his brother Smith's arm at his movie premieres.

"Poor baby," she said as she bent down for Cuddles to run into her arms. "Did that big, foulmouthed man scare you?"

Zach shoved away his envy at how naturally Heather opened her arms for his puppy. What if he'd run to her like that? Would she have been that receptive? Would her eyes have lit up and would she be kissing him now instead of the little fur ball?

"It's all an act," he told her, "the whole I'm-just-a-little-defenseless-puppy thing."

"I don't care." She pressed a kiss to the top of Cuddles's head. "I love her, anyway." She looked up and pinned him with a knowing glance. "And so do you."

"If counting down the days until I can give her back is your definition of love, then yeah, she's the dog I've been waiting for my whole life."

Her mouth moved up into a wide grin. "You're going to be lost without her."

Not bothering to dignify that ridiculous statement with a response, he plopped four pieces of bread into the toaster.

"So, were you impressed?"

She looked momentarily surprised by his question. She put down Cuddles before going to kiss Atlas on his long muzzle, then moved to the sink to wash her hands before eating.

"Yes. Very." She shot him an innately sensual look over her shoulder. "Both times."

"Good," he said, but when the seconds ticked by and she didn't move over to him, he had to add, "You missed one."

She looked confused. "What did I miss?"

He nodded toward where the dogs were standing by the door, pawing at it. "You kissed everyone but me."

Surprise softened her pretty features and Zach actually found himself holding his breath as he waited to see what she would do.

Technically, good-morning kisses weren't in their sex-only agreement, but that didn't mean he didn't want one.

Slowly, she moved toward him, his chest tightening down even further with every step.

"I didn't mean to make you feel left out," she said softly, and then she was putting her hands on either side of his face as she went up on her toes to press a kiss to his lips.

Their kisses until now had been all about sex and desperate need.

This one was different.

The desire was still there, riding between them the way it had from the first moment they'd met, but there was a softness in this kiss that he'd never shared with anyone.

When she stepped back, she looked as stunned as he felt. Turning quickly to the dogs, she went to open the sliding glass door to let them out into his yard.

Zach moved beside Heather at the door to watch the dogs play. "Your mutt likes it here."

Heather sighed before agreeing, "He does."

"What about you?" Zach didn't know where the question had come from, just that he needed to know.

The toast popped up and she started to move away from him to get it, but he reached out and grabbed her hand, turning her toward him. She looked down at their linked fingers.

"You know exactly how much I liked last night." She sounded resigned and a little bit upset about it. "The sex was great."

He dropped her hand, stupidly upset with her answer. What the hell was wrong with him? She was exactly the woman he'd been looking for. Up for ridiculously great sex with none of the other junk attached to it. Like feelings. Or wanting more. Or trying to angle things to be his girlfriend.

Heather was perfect.

The whole damn thing was perfect.

He yanked the bread out of the toaster, slapped on butter and jam, then dropped the plates out on the breakfast counter.

"So then, we're on for doing it all over again tonight?"

Jesus, first he was trying to get her to write him poetry about being together, and then when she didn't give him the answer he wanted, he was actually begging for a second night.

She slid onto the leather barstool and picked up a piece of toast. "Sounds fun, but the big auction for the animal shelter is tonight."

If she was trying to blow him off, she'd have to work a hell of a lot harder than that.

He got up to let the dogs back in, but instead of returning to his seat at the bar, he stood in front of her. "What time should I pick you up?"

She frowned. "I didn't ask you to go with me."

"I like animals." He looked down at Cuddles, who had found a shoe from his closet to chew on. He took the shoe out of the puppy's mouth and replaced it with a plastic chew toy.

"I've put a lot of work into this event, and I can't let anything distract me from bringing in as much money for the shelter as I can." She put down her unfinished toast. "It won't work for you to come with me, but I'm happy to get together for sex afterward if you want."

Heather was saying exactly what he'd always wanted a woman to say, was offering precisely what he'd always dreamed a woman would offer. Only, now that his wish had finally been granted, it turned out that getting exactly what he wanted grated like a son of a bitch.

"What are you going to wear?"

She blinked at his non sequitur. "A dress."

She was beautiful even when she was frowning at him. He didn't see any point in checking the urge to lean forward to kiss the lines between her eyebrows.

"What color?"

He didn't think she was aware of reaching up to press her fingertips to the place he'd just kissed as she said, "Blue."

Zach wound a lock of her hair around his index finger and slid his thumb over the silky softness. "I've never seen you in a dress."

"You've seen me naked. Isn't that good enough?"

He didn't think before answering, "No, it isn't."

She slid off her seat and backed away from him. "What are you doing, Zach?"

"Working on getting an invitation to your party."

She shook her head. "If you came with me, everyone would think we were dating."

"So what?"

*"So what?"* She sounded more than a little aggravated. "We're not dating and you're not my boyfriend. We agreed," she reminded him, "that this thing we're doing is just sex." Her gaze was too steady as she held his. "Tell me now if you've changed your mind and we can stop right here."

Zach's gut twisted at the thought of not seeing

Heather again. One night with her wasn't nearly enough, but hot sex wasn't all he'd miss if she decided not to be with him anymore.

He'd miss her laughter.

He'd miss the way she softened around the dogs.

He'd miss her smart mouth ripping into him just like the people he loved the most in the world always had.

But he knew why she was wary. Her father was an asshole who had lied to her his whole life. Zach couldn't love her, wouldn't make the mistake of promising her a forever he didn't have, but he would never lie to her.

"I'm not going to hurt you, Heather."

She went perfectly still. "I know you're not. Because I'm not going to let you."

She grabbed her bag, picked up her car keys and made a sound that had Atlas leaving his game with Cuddles and moving to her side.

Zach grabbed her hand before she could walk away from him. "I'll see you tonight." He knew what she wanted to hear, so he made himself say, "For sex." He let his mouth curve up into a grin. "Really, really great sex."

He knew it could go either way at this point. All he could hope was that she'd enjoyed the time she'd spent in his arms enough to want to do it all again.

Finally, she said, "It will probably be really late by the time everything is over."

"Late-night sex is one of my specialties."

He was beyond glad when she finally smiled again. "Only you would have *sexual specialties*."

"Here's another," he said before he gave her a goodbye kiss that he intended she remember for the rest of the day.

# *Twenty*

The first thing Zach noticed that evening when he stepped into the large ballroom at the Fairmont was Heather's laughter. She was speaking with an older couple and, even from across the room, the sound of her joy washed over him, just as it had that morning when she'd been on his lap in bed and he'd made her laugh.

*My God,* he thought as he took in her long, silky hair flowing down her back and the long-sleeved, dark blue dress that ended just below her knees to showcase her perfectly toned and tanned calves and ankles. *She's so beautiful.*

He loved her in shorts and had more than one fantasy about all the fun he could have with that long braid of hers in bed. She'd always taken his breath away, without doing a damn thing to try to accentuate her natural beauty. All around her, women were decked out in sequins and sky-high heels intended to draw eyes to them. But in her simple blue dress, Heather outshone them all.

She hadn't wanted him here as a distraction, but he'd come, anyway, because that was how he'd always run his life. Putting what he wanted—and his own happiness—first.

Only, now that he was here, as he watched her move through the crowd to speak with people who clearly admired the hell out of her, he realized he couldn't go through with his plan to surprise her, then kiss her into not being mad at him for ignoring her request to stay away.

It was one thing to rearrange her seat at the ball game so that she'd have to sit next to him. It was another to screw up an important event she'd worked long and hard on just because he was a selfish prick who couldn't make it another hour without seeing her.

Tonight he wanted Heather to be happy.

Moving to a shadowed part of the room, he drank in her grace, her confidence, as she took the stage. He'd always gravitated toward younger women who didn't demand anything from him apart from a good time. Heather was the polar opposite of them all. She didn't need him, didn't need any man to take care of her or to tell her she was worthy.

A few seconds later, the music playing over the speakers turned off and the spotlight went to where Heather was standing on the stage.

"Thank you, everyone, for coming here tonight to support the San Francisco Animal Shelter. I know each and every one of us in this room is shocked to know that animals are still being abused and neglected, household pets most often of all."

Behind her, a screen showed pictures of dogs walking with their owners, cats playing with children, puppies cuddling with babies. Some of the dogs and cats were missing a leg or an eye, but anyone could see how happy they were now that they'd finally found families who loved them.

"That's why we're all here tonight, to raise money to support those animals who are brought in to the shelter hurt and afraid. With the right love and care, it's our hope that they will all find loving homes and owners who will care for them the way they should have been cared for from the day they were born. Every penny of the proceeds from tonight's auction will go straight to the shelter and the animals who so desperately need our help. Thank you for reaching deep into your checkbooks for them."

As she stepped away from the podium to let the auctioneer run through the list of items up for bidding, Zach pulled his valet parking tag from his pocket and headed for the front of the hotel.

"I need you to bring my car around and leave it out front."

"Aren't you going to be driving it, sir?"

"No," he said without even needing to give it a second thought, "I won't."

Heather was pleased at how well the bidding was going on the auction items. Still, as the auctioneer called out the final items on the list, she calculated that it was going to be a close finish to reach their fundraising goal.

And then, suddenly, one of the partners from the auction house motioned to the auctioneer with a piece of paper.

Heather frowned. What was going on?

The auctioneer unfolded the paper and whatever he read on it made his eyes widen. Without taking the time to confer first with Heather, he quickly moved back behind the podium.

"I'm pleased to let everyone know that we have a last-minute addition to our auction items. A truly excellent addition." It was as if he needed to catch his breath first before saying, "The classic 1967 Lamborghini 400 GT is in mint condition." The approximate value he listed had Heather's jaw dropping to the floor. The room rumbled with sounds of amazement as the auctioneer grinned and said, "It is currently parked in front of the hotel for your viewing pleasure. The owner is available to answer questions. Bidding will begin in precisely ten minutes."

It was a stampede as every man and half the women made a dash for the ballroom doors.

The auctioneer turned to Heather and said, "This is truly extraordinary. If I had the funds, I'd bid on it myself."

Needing to know who would give the animal shelter something so precious, just moments before the auction ended, Heather quickly headed away from the stage and pushed her way through the crowded lobby. There were so many people crowded around the car that she couldn't really see it. But standing out among the crowd of people was one man who was almost a head taller than the rest.

*Zach.*

Shock had her stopping in her tracks dead in the center of the lobby. The Lamborghini had to be his.

Her heart thudded to a halt in her chest as she realized she couldn't let him give it away, even if it meant the shelter would have almost an entire extra year of operating expenses taken care of with the money that car would bring in. Not if he was giving it away for all the wrong reasons…and not if the donation meant he'd now expect things from her that she simply couldn't give him.

He already had her body, for as long as he wanted it.

But her ultimate trust—and the secret, walled-off parts of her heart—would always be off-limits.

She had to push through the people to reach him. "Zach!" she called, needing to get his attention to tell him it was too much, but before she could, the auctioneer's voice could be heard over the crowd.

"The ten minutes are nearly up, folks. Bidding will begin right away."

The excited group rushed back into the ballroom, leaving only Heather and Zach standing alone outside. His eyes roved over her face, her hair, her dress, her legs.

"You're just as beautiful as I knew you'd be."

She felt herself flush with pleasure at his compliment, even as she said, "You shouldn't have done this, Zach." Flustered, she blurted, "Why did you do it?"

"I had to."

"Did you—" She couldn't believe she was actually going to say this. "Did you do it for me?"

His eyes were dark as they held hers. "Yes."

Her breath caught in her throat. "Giving away an expensive car won't change anything between us. You know that, right?"

"If I thought I could buy you, I would have done it that first day I met you. Don't insult us both." The bite of his words softened as he added, "You were very convincing up on that stage, Heather."

She flushed, biting back the apology on her tongue. Instead, she said, "It's too much, Zach. Especially since you didn't exactly take much time to think over the donation."

"No," he told her in as serious a voice as she'd ever heard from him, "auctioning off one of my cars isn't nearly enough. Just thinking about what might have happened to Cuddles if she'd ended up in the wrong hands makes me sick."

"Still," she insisted, "you could have given away something else, like free car service for a year at your garage. I'm afraid you're going to regret giving away something so precious."

"It's just a car, Heather. A hunk of metal that's put together to drive fast. I would never give away anything truly precious." His eyes darkened even further with heat and a flash of emotion that hit her just behind her breastbone. "You must know by now that I'm far too selfish for that."

He always did that to her, made it hard for her to find her breath at the same time that she couldn't help but give in to a smile. "You are pretty selfish," she agreed.

"Greedy, too," he said as he finally moved close enough to pull her into his arms.

If she'd managed to forget how good his goodbye kiss had been that morning, the kiss he gave her in front of the Fairmont was the perfect reminder.

Of course, she hadn't forgotten a thing about that earlier kiss. And she wouldn't be forgetting anything about this one, either.

When he finally let her go, she was glad his arms were around her to hold her up on shaky legs.

"Besides," he murmured against her earlobe, "getting to see you in that dress—and knowing I'm going to strip it off you later—is worth every penny."

Heather liked him so much more than she should. He made it so hard not to. If he'd given away the car because he wanted people to be impressed with him, if he'd done it to try to buy a part of her heart, she would have written him off as just another rich blowhard with more money than sense.

But he'd clearly done it simply because he believed it was the right thing to do.

And this time she was the one kissing him before grinning and saying, "I would have let you take off my dress for free."

# Twenty-One

"Time for bed."

Heather looked up from where she was sitting. "But there's still so much to do," she said, gesturing to the disarray in the large ballroom.

"The catering staff can take care of the rest of it." He took her hands in his and pulled her to her feet.

The heat in his eyes immediately drew her in and she knew there was no more fighting the inevitable. She wanted to sleep with Zach again, of course, but she was worried that she was going to forget to keep it to just sex, their previous night together seared into her mind. After his selflessness tonight, she was very much afraid that her heart was going to do something stupid in response.

She was surprised when he led her to the bank of elevators with his large hand on the small of her back. She was tall enough that she rarely felt small around a man, but between his height and broad shoulders—and his air of confident masculinity—she'd always felt incredibly feminine around Zach.

"Where is Cuddles tonight?"

"Hanging with Atlas at your assistant's house. She'd already mentioned that she was going to be watching Atlas and said she was happy to have them both."

Heather turned to him in surprise just as the elevator door opened. "Have women always been unable to resist giving you whatever you want?"

He pretended to leer at her. "Whatever I want, huh?"

She rolled her eyes. "I was talking about other women, not myself. I can resist you just fine," she lied with a flourish.

His grin told her he knew otherwise as he slid the key card to the penthouse suite from his jacket pocket.

"You booked the penthouse for tonight?" On top of giving away a shockingly expensive car just hours ago? "Have you completely lost your mind?"

"Most women not only give me whatever I want, but they also know my net worth within five minutes of meeting me." He slid the fingers of one hand into her hair and tugged her closer before saying, "You're the first one who doesn't care about my money."

He was right—she didn't. And maybe if she weren't so tired, she would have moderated her thoughts a little better before blurting, "You're hardly ever serious. How can you run a business that big without working all the time like everyone else?"

True to form, he didn't look upset about what she'd just said or how she'd said it. "Like I said before, they're just cars. And trust me, Heather," he said in that low voice that always sent shivers running up and down her spine, "whenever I decide to focus on something I want, I always get it."

She believed him, especially when he pressed her back against the wall of the elevator. His mouth was sinfully delicious against hers as his stubble rasped against her cheeks and chin. She immediately wound her arms around his neck to pull him closer as their kiss deepened.

"Is there a stop button in this thing?" she found herself asking against his lips, even though she'd never done something crazy like having sex in an elevator. Then again, she would never have felt safe enough to do that with anyone but Zach.

But before either of them could find it, they reached the top of the building and the doors slid open. Together, they moved out of the elevator, not separating or stopping their kiss. Feeling bold, she grabbed the room key from him, pressed it against the card reader beside the double doors and used his tie to drag him inside.

Last night he'd run the show.

Tonight, she wanted her turn at being in charge.

The last thing she expected to see was a massage table set up in the middle of the expensive-looking carpet. "Do we have the wrong room?"

"Nope," he said with a soft kiss to her lips. "You've been working so hard all day. I don't want you to be sore tomorrow."

She couldn't believe he'd arranged a masseuse for her.

Or that he was planning to make her wait to have him.

"You don't play fair, do you?"

"You wouldn't want me to," he said against the curve of her neck, where he'd started nibbling on her skin.

And he was right, she thought, even though her entire body buzzed with arousal, with the desperate need to have him inside of her *right now*. Every other man that had come before Zach now seemed boring. Unimaginative. She couldn't remember a single reason she would want to be with anyone else.

He gave her one of those evil grins she was beginning to dread…and wish for at the exact same time. "Before I call in the masseuse, I'd better get you undressed."

He turned her around, found the zipper at the back of her dress and drew it down. The dark blue fabric fluttered away from her body and all it took was one soft tug for it to slide down her shoulders, over her arms, past her hips and to the floor. Turning her around with his large hands on her waist, he took a step back to look at her in her bra, panties, thigh-high stockings and heels.

"You're the most beautiful woman I've ever seen."

She hated to break the spell, but she didn't want there to be any lies between them. Especially when he didn't need to say things like that to get her into bed with him.

"I'm not." She fought the urge to try to cover her arms, and the old scars, by hiding them behind her back.

*"You are."*

He said the words with such intensity that even though she couldn't possibly see how it was true, she had no choice but to believe he meant it.

And then he was reaching for her hands. But instead of threading his fingers through hers, his thumbs caressed her old scars, one by one, as he moved his hands farther up from her wrists, over her forearms, to the soft underside of her elbows.

It was too much for her, the way he seemed to adore even her imperfections, and she made a sound of protest. "Zach, I—"

He kissed her before she could say anything else, but he didn't stop touching her, didn't stop exploring her battered skin with his fingertips. She'd been right about a mechanic's hands, about how talented they could be. He was turning her to putty again, but she didn't want to just sit back and feel.

She wanted to be right there with him, an equal in passion, a partner in desire. And she didn't think she could stand for him to be that gentle, that sweet, another second longer without her heart falling.

Sliding quickly from his grasp, she undid the clasp on her bra. As the straps fell from her shoulders, and her bra began the slow slide from her breasts, she loved the hunger in Zach's eyes.

And loved even more that it seemed the most obvious thing in the world to drop slowly to her knees in front of him.

* * *

Zach had planned to keep his hands off Heather until she'd had her massage. He'd witnessed first-hand tonight how hard she'd worked for the fund-raiser, and even though he'd wanted her every single second since she'd left his arms that morning, he'd been trying to wait to take her again until she was relaxed and ready for him.

He should have realized his plans were shot to hell when she yanked him inside the suite by his tie. But he was so used to doing things his way, it still hadn't occurred to him that Heather might not let him get away with that tonight…or that she'd actually drop to her knees and lick her lips in pure sensual need as she unzipped him.

He had to slide his hands into her hair as her tongue found him first and then she—

*Jesus, her mouth.*

A few minutes later, Zach somehow managed to pull back and lift her into his arms. But as he moved toward the bedroom and kicked open the door, he had to lean over her to take one beautiful breast into his mouth.

She wrapped her arms around his neck and cried out his name as he laved first one, then the other. They sank down to the mattress like that, with his greedy mouth on her soft skin as her hands held his head over her chest, groaning when his lips and tongue met her warm, sinfully sweet flesh.

Zach had always loved sex in every form—slow sex, rough sex, playful sex, quick-and-dirty sex—

but he'd never before felt this desperation, this primal need to claim a woman as his. And when he finally looked up to see Heather's long, dark hair fanned out on the pillow, her cheeks flushed with excitement, her eyes dark and hazy with arousal…he lost it.

All those plans to heighten her anticipation by making her wait, to take his time learning her curves and hollows all over again with the lights on this time, shattered in the face of his overpowering desire to take her.

To make her *his*.

His hands were shaking as he slid his fingers into the sides of her panties, his erection growing even bigger at the shockingly sexy view of Heather's nearly naked body on the bed. He wanted her full breasts pressed into his chest, her long legs wrapped around his hips as he took her up, up, up, then over with him.

"Hurry," she urged him, but how could he resist the scent, the taste, of her? Her panties were only halfway down her thighs when he bent his head down to run his tongue over her.

She bucked up into his mouth as he laved the center of her arousal and a split second later he had to use his hands on her hips to hold her still as she began to cry out and quiver beneath his mouth. Ripping her panties the rest of the way off, he pushed her legs open wider to wring every ounce of pleasure out of her beautifully unexpected climax.

Zach loved the way she trembled beneath his lips. She was one of the strongest women he'd ever met, but when they were making love, she was all soft-ness and pleasure.

He wanted to take her up over that edge again, could have listened to her gasps of pleasure all night long, and would have forgone his own orgasm to do just that had she not already ripped open the con-dom he'd thrown onto the bed and sat up to slide it over his erection.

"All night long, I needed you inside me, Zach. I can't wait another second."

This time it was her hands that were shaking as she pulled him down over her. Their mouths con-nected at the exact moment he slid into her, and he swallowed her gasp of pleasure with his kiss.

Again and again they rocked together, hard flesh against soft, Heather possessing him every bit as much as he was possessing her. They rolled so that she was on top, her strong muscles flexing as she rode him harder, faster, their mouths still fused in passion. His hands couldn't decide where to go, to her breasts or her hips, and he ended up stroking her again and again from curve to curve, her skin grow-ing hotter, slicker, beneath his palms, as he drove higher into her with every caress.

And just as he felt her inner muscles tighten down over him, he confessed, "I need you, too. More than I've ever needed anyone."

He could hardly believe the beauty before him as his heated words gave her the final push she needed to tumble into a powerful climax. One so strong that despite how badly he wanted to stay lucid enough to watch her, to drink in every second of her pleasure, Zach had no choice but to join her.

It took a long while for them to catch their breath, and when he moved to lift her up again, she was half-asleep against him as he carried her into the bathroom.

"Too tired for a massage," she murmured against his chest.

He kissed her forehead, then turned on the tub, making sure the water was warm before lowering them both into it. She sighed as she felt the water move over her naked skin, but she didn't open her eyes. Instead, with her back to his front, her hips between his thighs, she leaned her head back farther against his shoulder.

"So comfortable with you," she said in a sleepy voice.

He smiled against her hair, happy to be her pillow for as long as she liked. Another time, he'd show her all the fun they could have in the tub together, but knowing she'd appreciate waking up clean and fresh, he softly ran the bar of soap over her beautiful skin.

She practically purred beneath his touch, but even though he knew she was enjoying the sensuality of their bath, nothing could trump her need for sleep right now. Still, he wasn't even close to being a saint, so when her thighs instinctively opened for him to soap her up, he let himself play over that soft skin a little more than he had everywhere else.

Even half-asleep, she bucked up into his hand and made little pleading noises for pleasure that he couldn't help but want to fulfill. Dropping the soap, he swirled his fingers into the curls between her thighs.

He could tell she was somewhere between a dream and the bathtub as she breathed out his name. God, he loved hearing her say it. Whether she was horny or angry, laughing or irritated, he wanted her.

*Needed* her.

He already knew just how she loved to be touched. Moments later she was shuddering against him, her eyes still closed, a smile curving up her lips before every muscle, every bone, in her body finally went lax against him.

He lifted her from the tub, toweled her off and tucked her into bed. As she curled against him, one thigh over his, her face pressed into the crook of his shoulder, her arm across his chest, he was surprised to realize he actually didn't mind going to bed without having her take care of his pleasure again.

Not when the chance to be with Heather like this, when she was soft and supple and perfectly trusting, was already more than he thought he could ever have.

# *Twenty-Two*

Heather was just waking up when she realized Zach wasn't in bed with her. She couldn't believe how late it was. She never slept past 6:30 a.m., so how could the clock say 10:00 a.m.?

Sitting up in bed, she looked through the slightly open bedroom door into the penthouse living room, where she could hear Zach speaking on the phone.

"I don't know if I can do this one, Tommy. Are you sure no one else is available?" came before a slightly resigned "Sure, I can be there by this afternoon for some practice runs with the crew."

She grabbed a supersoft robe from the armoire and walked into the living room just in time to hear Zach curse as he dropped his phone onto the coffee table.

"Good morning to you, too," she teased him.

He reached out and grabbed for her so fast that she found herself sprawled on his lap with his mouth on hers. She should have gotten enough of him already.

Instead, every time he kissed her, touched her, she only found herself wanting more.

"I had so many plans for a Sunday alone with you," he murmured against her mouth when he finally let her up for air. "My buddy Tommy just screwed them all up."

Heather had to work hard—*really* hard—to keep from showing her own disappointment knowing that he had to leave already. She hadn't planned to spend any part of the weekend with him, but after the way Friday night had turned into Saturday morning and was then repeated all over again Saturday night, she'd started to get used to having him around. Enough, at least, that a Sunday together wouldn't have killed her.

She almost asked him where he needed to rush off to, but it was the kind of thing a girlfriend needed to know. Not a sex buddy like her.

Fortunately, he told her, anyway. "Tommy was a good friend of my father's. My dad taught me how to build an engine, and then Tommy showed me how to drive one real fast." He was pressing soft kisses along the underside of her jaw as he spoke. "Tommy's doctor wouldn't sign off on him racing the car this time around and he needs someone to sub for him in a stock-car race on Monday morning. I've got to get to Southern California by this afternoon to do some practice runs with the crew."

Of course he raced cars, she thought. A man like Zach wouldn't be content with just being a business mogul. It wouldn't be enough that he could slay at least half the human population just by glancing in their direction. He would need the rush of testing the limits of the fast cars he built, too. And she had a pretty good sense that he wasn't afraid of getting hurt, that those kinds of fears wouldn't hold him back the way they might with other people.

But just thinking about Zach getting into a race car and *driving real fast* had her heart pounding. What if he got hurt? What if these past few days with him were the only ones she ever got to have?

She was surprised to realize the scars on her arms were tingling, like a main line from her emotions to her body.

Working to sound as if it was no big deal, she asked, "How long have you been racing?"

Just because she was sleeping with him didn't mean his grin had any less impact. If anything, it hit her even harder now. Because she knew how fast that grin could bend into a sensual look that melted her should-stay-icy core.

"Pretty much since the day I got my driver's license."

"Sounds like fun," she said, but then couldn't stop herself from adding, "but isn't it dangerous?"

His eyes flashed with something she couldn't quite read before he shrugged. "We're going close to two hundred miles per hour. Of course it's dangerous."

Her fingers itched to smack him for his devil-may-care response. "I'm sure your family would be really upset if anything happened to you."

His eyes narrowed on her as if he knew she was really saying *she* would be upset if anything happened to him. But instead of calling her on acting more like a possessive girlfriend than she had any right to be given their arrangement, he said, "You should come. I'll strap you in real tight and take you for a ride."

Just that fast, the wicked glint in his eyes got her heart to racing for reasons that had nothing to do with his getting hurt in a speeding car.

Both a shiver of need and a thrill at the thought of letting loose in a speeding car were there as she teased, "You just like the idea of strapping me into something."

He abruptly stood up with her in his arms and carried her over to the massage table. "Unfortunately, there are no bindings on this, but I'm sure we can improvise." She tried to clutch the robe to her chest but he quickly had it off her shoulders. "Ready for your massage?"

Her breath was already coming too fast and her mouth felt dry as she said, "Don't you need to go race a fast car?"

"I promised you a massage first, and I always make good on my promises."

She tried not to read too much into his talk of promises. It was just sexy talk. He was being playful, the way he usually was. People threw around a lot of words they didn't mean when they were having really awesome sex with someone.

"In that case, I'm not going to turn down the

offer," she said in a deliberately light voice. "How do you want me?"

His eyes darkened with desire at her provocative question. "Let's start with you on your stomach."

Trying not to feel self-conscious about being naked on the padded massage table, she got into position. He left the room for a moment, and when he came back to stand in front of her, she looked down at his bare feet through the hole in the padded headrest. She wasn't surprised to note that his bare feet were as perfect as the rest of him.

"Usually the masseuse puts a sheet over me."

"I sure as hell hope so," he growled as she suddenly smelled lavender. "You'd better never let anyone else see you like this."

He was the most possessive man she'd ever met. But any protests she might have made about no one owning her but herself were lost in a moan of sheer bliss as his hands began to massage her shoulders.

"I thought sex with you was the best thing I'd ever felt, but this might actually be better."

She was so lost in the throes of the sweet pleasure of Zach's hands breaking down her stiff muscles that it wasn't until he said, "The best thing you've ever felt, huh?" that she realized what she'd just admitted.

"Massages are worse than drugs for me," she improvised, the way he was touching her making her words surprisingly true. "I get loopy and say things I don't mean."

His laughter washed over her just as he moved down over her shoulder blades to the middle of her back. His hands were so large that they easily spanned her rib cage. "I wonder what else I can get you to say?"

No matter how good he made her feel, she was keeping her mouth shut from here on out. God only knew what he was going to do with the information she'd just accidentally handed him on a silver platter. The last thing a guy like Zach needed to know was that he was *the* sexual champion on top of everything else.

"Do your worst," she challenged him, but her words were muffled by another low moan of pleasure.

"Don't you mean my best?" he asked in a silky voice that should have had her tensing to prepare her defenses.

But how could she when he chose that moment to press his thumbs into the small of her back, where she'd been aching from lifting and carrying everything in the ballroom to set up last night's fundraiser?

"Oh. God. Yes."

But her utter and complete capitulation obviously wasn't good enough for him, because a moment later he had slid his hands down to her hips and was massaging her glutes. She gasped at the shocking pleasure of her sore muscles beneath his fingertips, along with the sensuality of knowing whose hands were on her…and that he could choose at any moment to do so much more than just massage her muscles with them.

"Can't even form words now, can you?"

He sounded incredibly pleased with himself, and yet, she could hear the way his confident words broke at the ends. As if he was holding on to *his* control by a very thin thread.

From the first moment she'd met him, she'd wanted to snap that control, wanted to best him by knocking him off his pedestal. And even though she liked him a whole heck of a lot more now than she ever thought she would—and despite the way he was turning her muscles and mind to mush with hands down the best massage she'd *ever* had—she still couldn't resist that urge.

Frankly, she didn't want to.

The truth was that if she ever let down her defenses around Zach, Lord knew how he'd take advantage of that.

"This is when I usually turn over," she informed him in what she hoped was a fairly steady voice.

This time he was the one left speechless as she rolled over onto her back and deliberately lifted her arms above her head. Zach's eyes, she was pleased to see, blazed with fire.

Before he could pick a place to rub, she boldly said, "My arms are sore."

She'd hidden her scars from everyone else, but every time Zach touched them, caressed the marks of old pain, she felt soothed.

Healed.

The only sounds in the room came from both of them breathing, faster and louder with every second of the sensual massage, and she wasn't sure anymore which of them was making more noise as he worked out the tension in her biceps and triceps. When he moved his hands down toward her breasts, she was sure he'd decided to go for the gold, but instead he found a muscle just below her collarbone that had her practically sobbing with gratitude.

"You're amazing."

She opened her eyes and saw him staring down at her with such intensity as he replied, "So are you."

The reverence in his words, combined with the fact that he still didn't touch her breasts as he moved his hands lower down her rib cage, had her eyes closing again, her lower lip sliding between her teeth as she tried not to beg him for even more pleasure.

"That's my job," she heard him say, and then his teeth were replacing hers on her lower lip and he tugged it in between his lips. "God, you taste good," he said, and then he was kissing her some more, an upside-down kiss that stole the rest of her brain cells away in perfect choreography with his hands as they moved from the bottom of her rib cage to feather over her stomach, then lower still.

She opened up for him, moaned into his mouth as he slid one hand past her damp curls and into her, while the other moved in perfect circles over the point of arousal between her legs. Just that quickly, she went off beneath him. Somehow, he managed to be there not just with his hands, his fingers, but with his mouth, too.

Too impatient to let her climax run its course, she

pulled him up over her so that both of them were lying on the narrow massage table. She ripped at the zipper of his jeans and he was ready with a condom the second she had him free.

Wrapping herself around him was so natural, so perfect, that it was almost as if he'd always been there with her, in her arms, holding her.

*Loving her.*

# Twenty-Three

A short while later she dropped Zach off at the airport so that he could fly down to Southern California. Heather went to pick up the dogs at Tina's house, and after a reunion where they both acted as if she'd been gone for one year instead of one night, she took them to the park and the dog bakery and the coffee shop. By then, they were tired enough for her to accept that she couldn't avoid going home any longer.

She loved her house. After being around people all week long at her office, it had always been a wonderfully quiet, peaceful respite on Sundays when Top Dog was closed.

So then, why did it suddenly feel too quiet?

And how could she possibly feel lonely when she had two absolutely wonderful furry companions?

She couldn't already be missing Zach, could she? It wasn't at all okay that he could have taken a spot in her life that quickly, or that thoroughly.

Her phone rang and her hands were too full with

bags of dog food to look at the call display screen before answering.

"Hi, Heather, it's Lori. Zach's sister. We met at the baseball game."

Heather had given Lori her phone number to pass on to a friend who was thinking about getting a new puppy, but she hadn't expected Zach's sister to call herself.

"Of course I remember who you are," she told Lori. "How are you?"

"Are you free tonight? We're doing an impromptu girls' night here and I thought you'd be a great addition."

Any other time Heather would have made her excuses, but her empty house still loomed way too big. Besides, Lori and Sophie had been really nice. Why shouldn't she spend some time with them? Just because she and Zach would eventually run their course and go their separate ways didn't mean that she couldn't make a couple of friends along the way.

After a quick shower, she grabbed a bottle of wine and a container of brownies she hadn't been able to resist at the farmer's market. Female laughter rang out as Lori opened her door.

"Heather's here," she called out to everyone, and a moment later Heather found herself being openly studied by several sets of eyes. "Heather, this is Chloe, Nicola, and you already know Sophie. Chloe is married to my brother Chase. Nicola is dating my brother Marcus."

Oh, no. Why hadn't she realized she'd be walking into Sullivan Significant-Other Land? Had Zach scrambled her brain that much with his supersexy massage that she couldn't think straight anymore?

"Look, she brought brownies. What did I tell you? Is she a good one, or what?"

Chloe, who was *extremely* pregnant, nodded. "It's so nice to meet you."

Nicola echoed the sentiment as she handed her a glass of red wine. Heather knew enough about Zach's family to remember that his brother Marcus owned a winery in Napa Valley, but he was often on the road with his pop-star girlfriend, Nicola. She tried not to be too starstruck and prayed she wouldn't make an idiot of herself around the girl by admitting to the way she and Atlas liked to dance around the room to Nico's songs.

Lori pinned her with a knowing glance. "A friend of mine was at the fundraiser last night and said it went really well." She raised her eyebrows. "She also mentioned something about a kiss."

Clearly, word had spread—quickly—not only about Zach donating his car, but also about the scorching kiss outside the Fairmont. Heather was glad Lori wasn't the type to beat around the bush, because now that she had finally clued in to what was going on, she had to make sure they didn't have the wrong idea.

"Zach and I are still just friends." As the three other women blinked at her in surprise, she clarified, "With some benefits." Despite the fact that she knew she was blushing, she wanted them to understand.

"But we're still just friends." She looked at Lori. "Sorry, I know you were hoping for more than that, but—" she shrugged "—it's all either of us wants."

Nicola recovered first. "Lori and Sophie said I would really like you, but they were wrong. I *love* you." She grinned. "Seriously, I think I'm going to dedicate my next song to you."

"Unless I beat you to it by having a girl and naming her Heather," Chloe said.

Heather realized she must have been sitting there with a shell-shocked look on her face when Sophie explained, "They've never seen a woman resist falling head over heels in love with Zach before. Especially when he puts on the charm by giving away an expensive car to try to impress her." Sophie thought about it for a moment. "I haven't, either, actually. Women always get so stupid around him, just because of what he looks like. It's got to be kind of weird for him, even though I guess he's used to it by now."

Chloe nodded her agreement. "At my wedding, you should have seen my girlfriends. I thought they'd all be trying to get at Smith because he's a movie star. But they were practically forming a line in front of Zach. Chase told me that Smith loves having him around as a foil. I heard he once offered him a full-time job on the set of his movies just to hang around and deflect attention."

Heather laughed. She could picture it all too easily. But she couldn't let them think Zach had given away the car for selfish reasons.

"He really wanted to support the animal shelter with his donation," she insisted.

"Of course he did. Like I told you at the game, he's nice," Lori said, talking around the brownie she'd shoved into her mouth. "Even when we were kids, Sophie and I couldn't tell who wanted to hang out at our house because they wanted to be our friends, or who was just there to drool over Zach."

"You've got to tell us your secret of staying so resistant to him, so we can pass it on to our friends," Nicola said.

Heather worked to keep her smile intact even as a picture of her father coming back from one of his business trips all smiles, with false words of love, slammed into her.

Her "secret" wasn't one she would wish on anyone else. It was better that all of them believed love was real, that they held on to hope rather than cynicism.

But she knew they wouldn't let her off without giving them an answer, so she said, "Well, despite the fact that he isn't hard to look at and he makes me laugh, he's also way too possessive." At the perfect silence that followed, she turned to Lori and Sophie and said, "No offense. For all his faults, he can be a really nice guy."

"For all his faults?" Sophie echoed with wide eyes.

"Way too possessive?" Lori looked around at the other women before turning back to Heather. "Are you sure we're talking about the same Zach Sullivan?"

Heather couldn't believe they'd miss something that obvious about him. "Haven't you noticed that *mine* is practically his favorite word?"

Nicola started choking on her sip of wine, and as Chloe patted her back, she told Heather, "Chase and I tried the friends-with-benefits thing." She looked down at her belly. "Pretty obvious how well that worked for us, isn't it?"

Heather wasn't sure if that was supposed to make her feel better or worse about her agreement with Zach. But before she could decide, Nicola said, "Cover your ears, girls" to Lori and Sophie before telling Heather, "Marcus and I skipped the whole friends thing and went straight for the benefits. It was just supposed to be a one-night fling."

"I still can't believe you fell asleep on him during your one-night stand," Lori said.

Nicola shot her a mock frown. "Can't you at least pretend that you don't know all the details of my whirlwind romance with your oldest brother?"

Lori rolled her eyes. "We're Sullivans. It's our code to know absolutely everything about one another. Right, Soph?"

Sophie took a sip from her glass of sparkling grape juice. "Unfortunately, yes." Just as Lori's mouth opened, likely to say something incriminating, Sophie beat her to the punch by telling Heather, "I seduced Jake at Chloe's wedding and ended up pregnant. But it turned out he'd been in love with me for as long as I'd been in love with him, so it all ended up working out."

Heather was overwhelmed, not only by how open each of the women was being with her—and one another—but also by what they'd told her about the other Sullivans. Each of their one-night-stand and friends-with-benefits attempts had turned into long-term relationships and marriages.

*Oh, no...*what was she doing?

And, really, just how far out of her depth was she?

"Zach's racing for Tommy's team tomorrow in L.A., isn't he?" Lori asked.

"I hate it when he does those races," Sophie admitted. "At least when Gabe is running into burning buildings, I know he and the other firemen are facing danger to help people. But if Zach crashes, it's all supposed to be for fun. I swear, I'll never forgive him if he gets hurt in one of those stupid races."

Sophie's concerns echoed the ones Heather had been trying to push away ever since Zach had mentioned the race.

Lori dismissed it with a simple "Zach is indestructible."

Maybe it was the wine, maybe it was the way just thinking about him made her endorphins shoot off into the stratosphere, but Heather wouldn't be surprised if it turned out Zach actually *was* indestructible—physically and emotionally.

Unfortunately, she was pretty sure that she wasn't... and when the day came when friends with benefits turned to just friends, or to nothing at all, she was no longer sure she'd walk away from that crash in one piece.

# *Twenty-Four*

Monday morning came too bright and too early for Heather given the little sleep she'd had. She told herself it was one too many dark-chocolate brownies that had kept her awake, rather than the way the bed already seemed too big without Zach holding her as she slept.

They'd only spent two nights together. She couldn't believe how much she missed him already, and that she was on pins and needles worrying about him getting hurt in the race that morning.

An hour later, after checking in with her staff and accepting their congratulations on the successful fundraiser, she settled in behind her computer in her office. Atlas immediately took his place on the big dog bed in the corner and closed his eyes to take his morning nap. But instead of draping herself over Atlas the way she usually did, Cuddles stood in the middle of the room and gave Heather one of those pathetic little whines she'd started last night when she realized Zach wasn't back yet.

Heather scooped up the puppy and gave her a kiss on her muzzle. "Don't worry, he'll be home soon." When the puppy still looked sad, she found herself echoing Lori's words from the night before. "Zach is indestructible. He'll be just fine. How about we watch him win the race together?"

She kept the puppy on her lap as she clicked on the live streaming link he'd emailed her. A bunch of men in colorful racing suits were walking around the fancy cars, but it wasn't hard for her to spot Zach. He was taller, broader, a thousand times sexier, than any of the other drivers.

Her heart beat a little faster just watching him run one big hand over the body of the car, and thrill bumps lifted across the surface of her skin as if he were touching her instead of the vehicle.

Cuddles let out a soft yap that made Heather think she could see Zach on the screen, too, and it made Heather's stomach hurt to think of how the puppy was going to react when Zach gave her back to his brother.

There was no way for the young dog to understand that she shouldn't have let herself get so attached to him, that she shouldn't have made the mistake of falling in love with him.

Good words of warning for all females everywhere.

The drivers got into their cars and Heather gripped the puppy tighter, burying her chin in the supersoft fur on top of Cuddles's head as the cars zipped away from the starting blocks. Zach was in the Sullivan

Autos car, of course, the now-familiar blue-and-gold logo a blur as he pushed the pedal to the metal.

She couldn't believe how close he got to the other cars as he did one lap, then two, then three. He wasn't in the lead yet, but something told her he was simply biding his time, taking it easy the way he always did, before going all in for the win.

She remembered what he'd said to her in the elevator: *trust me, whenever I decide to focus on something I want, I always get it.*

No question about it, Zach Sullivan wouldn't race if he wasn't in it to win it.

Again and again the cars wove around the track, until seemingly, from out of nowhere, Zach's car shot out ahead of the pack, and they were all eating his dust.

For a moment, she forgot to be scared about his getting hurt as she chanted, "Go, go, go!" at the screen.

Cuddles was standing with her front paws on the desk, joining in with Heather in dog language. And when Zach finished the race a good car length ahead of the rest, she lifted the puppy up and cheered.

Only, it turned out the two of them weren't the only ones who were happy with Zach's performance. Because as he unfolded his large body from the car, several scantily clad girls rushed over to him and wrapped their perfect bodies around him in congratulations.

Just then, Tina knocked and popped her head in.

"I thought I heard you call for me. Is everything okay in here?"

God, no, it wasn't okay. How could it be when she was literally being eaten up, inside and out, by jealousy? She wanted to rip the other women's hands off Zach.

He was *hers!*

She clicked on the little X at the top of her screen to close the streaming video and nodded at Tina. "Everything's fine, thanks."

It would be, at least, once she'd set her brain back to rights and refocused her attention where it should be.

She put Cuddles on the floor. "I'd like to go over the final numbers for the shelter this morning, so that I can draft up a press release on it in time for the six-o'clock newscast."

Looking at the spreadsheet, Tina exclaimed over the Lamborghini that Zach had donated and marveled at the final tally. The proceeds far exceeded the expenses. The results were everything Heather had hoped for but, somehow, all this success seemed to pale.

Because somehow, in the span of one short week, Zach Sullivan had infiltrated every part of her life and she could think of nothing else.

On the flight back home to San Francisco Zach had some time to think. He had always believed that there were few things better than the rush of being in a race car.

But being with Heather was better. Much, much better.

When Tommy had called to ask him to race, for the first time ever, instead of jumping at the chance, Zach had tried to turn him down. He'd told himself it was because he wanted to stay with Heather in the hotel room to spend the entire day exploring every inch of her skin, to make her laugh between acrobatic bouts of lovemaking, to watch her eyes light up and her skin flush with joy with the heat of desire again and again.

But even as he tried to deny the truth, he knew his reasons for not wanting to race were bigger than that.

What he couldn't stop wondering was, what if his number came up on the racetrack…and he didn't get to see Heather again?

*No.* This was an idea he did not want to consider— ever.

He'd been careful. So had she. They'd agreed not to fall in love with each other.

Besides, he hadn't died in the race. Not this time, anyway.

Zach jumped out of the airport taxi in front of her building and nearly knocked over a group of poodles as he ran inside to get to her. Her assistant was in the middle of saying hello when he barged past her into Heather's office.

It nearly killed him to take the time to lock the door behind him and pull down the blinds on her window before he grabbed her from where she was standing at her file cabinet. The papers in her hands scattered all over the floor as he slid his hands into her hair.

A second later, her legs were around his waist, and he was lowering her down over her desk, his mouth locked to hers while she kissed him back just as passionately as he was kissing her. She made a small sound of pain and he shoved a stapler out from under her. Using his hands to caress the softness of her hip where it had dug in reminded him of the way she'd felt when he'd been massaging her in the hotel.

"Missed you," he said between nipping at her lips and yanking off her long-sleeved shirt. He pressed a kiss right between her breasts. "Needed you."

He thought he saw her eyes flash with something more than desire as she followed suit by roughly yanking his T-shirt over his head. She leaned into his chest and he thought she was kissing him until he realized they were little bites that she was giving him all over. Jesus, it was hot, but a whole hell of a lot more aggressive than she'd ever been before.

Despite how badly he wanted her, his internal radar was going off. "What's wrong?"

"Nothing," she said, but again there was that flash in her eyes that looked too much like anger, and when she followed it up with "Just shut up and do me already," he knew a hell of a lot more than *nothing* was wrong.

Somewhere between their extraordinary hours together at the Fairmont and now, he must have screwed up. He didn't have the first clue how, just that he had.

With any other woman he wouldn't have cared, would have just finished doing her and then gotten out of there. But he and Heather were more than just bang-buddies.

"What did I do?"

"You went and did your stupid race, even though you could have been hurt." The lingering worry in her eyes was quickly masked as she snarled, "Congratulations on your big win."

It was hard trying to think around the low level of blood in his brain, with her legs still around his and her beautiful breasts bounding around in a white cotton bra that shouldn't have been sexy but was blowing his mind. The whole package made it nearly impossible for him to form a coherent sentence.

Still, he knew he'd better figure out how to get his brain to work real quick, because he had a feeling a whole lot more than a hot quickie was at stake.

"You watched me race?"

"Cuddles wanted to."

She pressed her lips together hard as if she dared him to challenge that silly statement, and he barely checked the urge to lick across the firm line of her pretty lips.

"So you saw me blow the other guys out of the water?"

"Among other things," she muttered. "You certainly don't need me to keep congratulating you, when everyone else did such a good job of it on the racetrack."

He was a guy. And he was horny as hell around

Heather, especially with her stripped half-naked. But he wasn't stupid.

She'd obviously seen the trophy girls congratulating him on the track. And it had upset her.

"I'm not going to screw around on you, Heather."

He watched surprise and hope flicker in her eyes before she tamped them down. "You don't owe me any promises. It's just sex. That's all we're doing. *Having sex.*"

Anger rose in him, just as hot as hers. "Are you going to sleep with anyone else while we're together?"

"No." She looked as if she couldn't believe he'd asked her that question. "God, no."

"Then why are you assuming I'd do it?"

She looked at him as though he was a complete idiot. "It's what every guy does."

"No," he told her, "not every guy. Not *me.*" Frustration had him saying, "I'm not your father, damn it."

But she was shaking her head and trying to push him away. "I saw you with those girls at the racetrack. I saw you put your hands on them."

"To push them away, not pull them in closer!"

He wouldn't let her go, wouldn't let her leave his arms in anger when the only thing that had gotten him through the past thirty hours was the thought of having her back in them. "Can't you see you're the only one I can even think about? The only one I want? Don't you understand that I'm losing my mind over you?"

She looked stunned by what he'd just said, as stunned as he felt himself.

"Please kiss me, Zach. Just kiss me."

Just as willing as she was to let his words go, he kissed the breath from her lungs while stripping off her jeans and making short work of his own.

Jesus, he loved her mouth against his, loved her softness, loved those little sounds she made when he touched her just right. He slid into her slick heat, and she was so responsive she was coming almost the second he touched her between her legs.

At the last second, he realized he'd somehow forgotten to put on a condom. Somehow he managed to tough it out through her orgasm. She made a sound of protest when he pulled out, and he pressed a kiss to the inside of her thighs as he knelt down to grab a condom from his pants.

He sat down on her desk chair and quickly shoved it on, then reached for her and pulled her onto his lap, loving the feeling of sinking deep into her all over again. He could tell how much she liked it from the way she gasped as he filled her all the way up.

"It's your turn now," she said as she wiggled her perfect rear end over his thighs.

"My turn," he growled against her neck, licking, kissing, nipping his way down to her breasts, which were still trying to come free from her bra, "and yours, too."

He found he liked her breasts trapped behind cotton like that, liked having to work to taste her, to run his tongue inside the top edge of the fabric to tease the taut flesh. Then her inner muscles tightened down over him and he finally gave up his own control and came with her.

"I love it when you smell like sex." He buried his nose in the crook of her neck and licked at the sweat drying on her skin. Their quickie should at least have taken the edge off his need for her…but it hadn't done a damn thing to make him want her less. "I love it when you taste like sex, too."

Unfortunately, it wasn't long before he realized Cuddles was at their feet, rubbing against his shins.

On a gasp, Heather shifted and looked over her shoulder to find Atlas lying on the pillow in the corner, blinking up at the two of them.

"Oh, my God, I forgot about the dogs." She hopped off his lap to search for her clothes. "Atlas has never seen… I've always been really careful to go into the bedroom when I…"

She looked horrified as she stuttered out partial sentences. And so damn adorable with that flush on her cheeks that he had to go give her a kiss even as he laughed at her.

"He's a big boy. He'll get over it."

"I'm surprised he didn't freak out, actually, seeing you over me like that." She was flushing even more now as she pulled her jeans back up and grabbed her shirt from the floor.

"He didn't freak out because he knows who the boss is."

She yanked down her shirt. "Me. I'm the boss."

He pulled on his clothes, then scooped up Cuddles, who licked him with undisguised glee all over his face and neck. "Right. You're the boss."

She pushed her damp hair off her face. "I should have known you'd be even more insufferable after winning your completely pointless race." She moved over to her desk and began to put it back to rights. "Some of us have work to do."

He was about to reach for her again when a knock sounded on her door.

"Heather?" Her assistant sounded worried about something more than just interrupting her boss having sex in her office. "Your parents are here."

# Twenty-Five

*Oh, God.* She'd forgotten about her father's phone call earlier last week. Working to try to keep her panic from taking over, Heather looked down at herself, then over at Zach.

"They're going to know what we were doing."

What had she been thinking, having sex in her office? She silently berated herself as she made sure everything was zipped and buttoned.

That was just the thing. She hadn't been thinking. The second Zach had walked in, she'd lost all control of her synapses—and her hormones. Her reaction to him was that instinctive, that primal.

He put the puppy down and moved closer to undo the tangles he'd just put into her hair.

"You look great, just like you always do." His mouth left hers tingling again before he said, "Don't worry, Heather. It'll be all right." She just shook her head at him, but he gently cupped her cheek and said, "I've got your back."

She didn't know how he always managed to do that, to completely turn her inside out no matter the circumstance, but for once she was glad for the way just one soft kiss—and a handful of sweetly confident words—had her unable to focus all of her energies on being completely freaked out about her parents' visit.

He put his hand on the doorknob. "We've got this, Heather."

Strangely, even though they'd been caught barely seconds postsex, she did feel a whole lot more able to deal with her parents with Zach than she normally did on her own.

She'd seen him in action enough by then not to be surprised by the way he had her mother eating out of his hand within seconds of saying hello. Her father, however, was slightly less than his usual charming self.

Then again, had any man ever come even close to outcharming Zach Sullivan?

"Heather?" Her mother's eyes moved from Zach to Heather, then to the desk they'd made a mess of. "Is this a bad time?"

Belatedly, Heather realized she'd forgotten to put her shoes back on. She moved to quickly slip them on, but not quickly enough for her parents not to notice what she was doing.

Her father pulled her into a hug before she could act fast enough to step out of reach. "My precious girl. How your mother and I have missed you."

When she was actually a girl, she'd loved the way

he'd come home from a business trip and hug her and tell her how much he loved her, that she was the center of his world. But she hadn't been that naïve for a very long time. She now knew better than to think anyone was the center of her father's world but himself.

Her father didn't take his arm from around her waist, as though he was trying to make some kind of statement to Zach about whom she really belonged to. Atlas stood up, his ruff bristling, and she was glad to be able to use him as a reason to move away from her father.

He frowned at her dog. "Does he sit in your office all day?"

Heather ran a comforting hand down her dog's back. Atlas had never liked her father. "Yes."

Clearly not impressed with her answer, he asked, "Didn't you get my message last week?"

"I apologize for not calling you back. This week has been really busy." She tried not to flush at the memory of what she and Zach had just been busy doing, especially when her father looked between the two of them again, his frown deepening.

If only she'd remembered to call him back, then she could have invented a bulletproof excuse. Maybe even taken an impromptu trip out of town for a few days to somewhere she couldn't be reached.

"I hope you're not too busy to spend a few hours with us," he said, effectively trapping her into an evening together.

Thankfully, Cuddles chose that moment to start

barking, pulling attention away from her for just long enough to regain her equilibrium and to figure out how to respond. Zach had watched the exchange in silence and she guessed that he had quickly taken her parents' measure.

She shot him a look that she hoped he could read as well as he read her thoughts in bed: *please don't leave me alone with them.*

Zach picked up the barking puppy and smiled at her before turning that beautiful face of his on her parents. "Heather and I would be very pleased if you joined us tonight at 212 Stockton."

Heather tried not to act surprised that he'd just named one of the hottest new restaurants in San Francisco. Even now that she knew how wealthy he was—and how well connected via his famous siblings—the fact that he did absolutely nothing to broadcast his wealth had her completely forgetting about it.

She could tell from the look on her father's face that he knew just how hard it was to get a table at that restaurant. Clearly, he could not believe a guy in wrinkled jeans and a T-shirt had the pull to get a reservation like that, and it was obvious he wished he'd thought to do it first.

Her mother's eyes were wide as she responded, "I just saw a piece about 212 Stockton on TV. It's owned by a group of movie stars and billionaires."

Her father's expression darkened. "All I want is to spend quality time with my little girl, not rub shoulders with a bunch of stars with more money than morals."

Fairly certain that Zach's brother Smith was likely one of the "moral-free movie stars," Heather said, "Why don't I show you some of the improvements I've made to the training areas?" No doubt her parents would quiz her endlessly about Zach, and nit-pick all the parts of her business that weren't shiny and perfect, but even though she would have loved to lean on him, her parents weren't his battle to fight. They were hers.

But Zach didn't look the least bit upset about her father's comment. If anything, he looked more re-laxed than usual…reminding her of a deadly preda-tor about to strike.

Turning the full focus of his attention to her, Zach said, "I know you have some important business to finish up," as he gently brushed a lock of hair back from her forehead and tucked it behind her ear. It was a move made even more spectacularly protective—and possessive—by how casual it was.

"I'll show your parents around so that you can get back to work."

Heather knew firsthand that Zach was a master at getting exactly what he wanted. But to witness him outmaneuvering her father made her glad.

And scared the bejesus out of her.

A few moments later, when her mother and father had no choice but to follow Zach and Cuddles out of her office, Heather sat down on the office chair that would never look the same after what she and Zach had done on it.

Yet again, she reflected on the way Zach Sullivan had infiltrated every part of her life in one short week.

*Thank God.*

Zach wasn't used to worrying about other people. He always made sure to treat his employees right and his family was never far from his mind, but ultimately he knew his siblings could take care of themselves. Besides, if they needed his help with anything, they would call.

But the expression on Heather's face when her assistant announced that her parents were outside haunted him for the past several hours since he'd left her office.

Heather was so strong, so confident. Sassy and beautiful and so damned smart she'd kept him on his toes every single second that he'd known her. No one and nothing should ever make her look that sad. She was completely on guard with them, as if she was trying to prepare for an emotional blow that would come at any moment.

Before he even raised his hand to knock on Heather's front door, Atlas announced his arrival with a few loud barks. Heather opened the door and she was so breathtakingly beautiful in her dress and heels with her hair flowing around her shoulders that a split second after Cuddles leaped out of his arms to go play with Atlas,

Zach was ruining her perfect hair with his hands as he kissed her.

She kissed him back with the same heat before saying, "Thank you for coming with me tonight."

"I wouldn't have missed it," he said, and it was true. He couldn't stand the thought of leaving her alone with her parents. Not when he knew how upset they made her. "I get how family can be."

"I wish we were like your family, but we're not. We don't actually love one another." Her voice was thick with unshed tears as she said, "We just lie about it."

"You've never lied about anything," he said, hating the way she said *we*. "They're your parents. They're not you." He pulled her closer. "Tell me what you need from me tonight."

"Just this," she said, but her voice was shaking as she repeated, "Just be here for me, like this. Just please don't let me think about the way he treats her and how she always lets him—"

His mouth covered hers to cut off the rest of the sentence, her wish immediately his command. If she didn't want to think about her parents' screwed-up relationship, then he would do whatever was necessary to keep her mind on other things. Now and throughout dinner, whatever way he could.

Because he was her friend. And that was what friends did. They looked out for one another.

And yet...even as he slid his hands under her dress and Heather let out a soft gasp of pleasure as his fingers found her, he could almost hear the rumbles in the distance. Rumbles of something big, heavy and impossible to avoid as it sped toward him.

He moved his hands to her bottom to lift her up from the floor, and she wrapped her legs around him. But even the intense pleasure of having her heat all around him wasn't enough for him to get some distance from the emotions that were trying to nail him straight in the middle of his chest. Right from the first moment they'd met, he hadn't been able to keep his mind, hands or mouth off Heather.

And his heart was rumbling in the same direction, whether he wanted it to or not.

It was pure, practiced instinct for Zach to fight these feelings. To pretend they weren't true. To tell himself as he undid his pants and was inside of her seconds later that Heather was the perfect friend to have sex with, and nothing more.

She kissed him with a wildness that told him how much she needed this distraction, this outlet, this chance to let herself be fierce, bold, without risking retribution. He knew she wanted to be taken with that same fierceness, so he didn't hold back as he slammed against her, pushing her into the wall even as she pushed right back at him with her hips.

He'd never wanted anyone like he wanted her— more every time they came together—and yet even though he could have lost it at any second, he made himself focus on her reactions so that he'd know when she was close.

Tonight wasn't about his feelings. It wasn't about his fear for the future that had always been wrapped up in his father's untimely death. No, tonight wasn't about him at all.

On the contrary, it was about making sure Heather survived her parents' visit with minimal damage. And he knew exactly what would keep her on the edge of her seat all night, regardless of whom they were having dinner with.

Heather gasped into his mouth as her inner muscles began to tighten down around him. Lord, it killed him to pull out of her right then…but the knowledge of just how physically painful the next several hours were going to be didn't stop him from doing it, anyway.

He wouldn't have made the sexual sacrifice for anyone but her.

Her eyes flew open as he gently set her back on her feet and pulled her dress down before doing up his pants.

"Zach? What are you doing?"

He had a hell of a time keeping his voice steady. "We need to go."

She was looking at him as if he'd lost his mind as he grabbed her purse from the counter, told the dogs not to cause any trouble and dragged her out to his car. And maybe he had lost it, purposefully stopping just before the big finale like that.

Only, tonight, something bigger was at stake than getting off with a beautiful woman.

Heather's heart was on the line, and he was going to make damned sure it remained in one piece, no matter what her father tried to pull.

* * *

Heather was going to kill Zach. Her parents had already seen her once today looking as if she'd just stepped out of his bed. But the way she felt right now was almost worse, the persistent wanting that buzzed through her, making it virtually impossible to not only appreciate the glass of fine red wine from the Sullivan winery, but to nurse her frustration at her parents for acting the way they always did.

She narrowed her eyes across the table as her father stroked her mother's hand and gazed at her as if he were the luckiest guy in the world. Anyone looking at them would think he was the most devoted husband on the planet.

God, it all was so false. So fake. It made her want to—

"Too bad we didn't have enough time to finish what we started at your house," Zach murmured, his breath hitting her on the spot just below her earlobe that instantly melted her every time he came near it.

She couldn't decide if she wanted to kick him under the table to get him to stop…or if there was some reason she could invent to pull him into a dark hallway and *make* him finish what they'd started.

Still, even though she was practically jumping out of her skin from wanting him, once she'd calmed down a bit during the short drive to the restaurant, she'd finally figured out what he was doing.

And she couldn't help but adore him for his brilliant distraction technique.

"So," her mother said as she beamed at the two

of them, "your father and I are dying to know how you met."

Thank God, that was an easy one. "Zach lost his puppy—"

"—and Heather found it."

"Aren't they adorable, the way they finish each other's sentences. Just like we do, sweetheart," she said to her husband.

Heather suddenly wanted to puke.

Zach slid his hand up her thigh beneath the tablecloth, to a spot that was not appropriate for public viewing.

"No," he said in an easy tone. "We're nothing like the two of you." He grinned at Heather. "You hated me on sight. Didn't you?"

She couldn't explain why Zach's honesty made her so happy. Especially when it was guaranteed to upset her parents. But, oh, how she loved what he'd said.

*No, we're nothing like the two of you.*

She wanted to grab him and kiss him in front of the whole world for that alone.

"It's true. He was yelling at the puppy, so I tried to take Cuddles away from him."

"Cuddles?" Her father laughed with faint derision. "That's some name for a dog."

Rather than rise to the implied challenge to his masculinity, Zach simply refilled the wineglasses and said, "I still owe your daughter for saving Cuddles."

Her mother looked confused. "If it all started

off so badly, I don't understand how the two of you started dating, then?"

Heather *hated* lying. She'd grown up in a liar's house, after all.

"We're just friends." It was the truth, although, unlike the night at his sister's apartment, she decided to leave off the *with benefits* part.

"Just friends?" Her mother looked between the two of them. "But today when we dropped by your building—"

Her mother didn't have to finish her sentence for it to be abundantly clear that she'd assumed since they had been having sex in Heather's office that they were an item.

Just as she'd known it would, Heather felt the evening begin to crash in around her. But then Zach slid his hand higher up her thigh and said, "Our dogs can't stand to be apart. It was love at first sight for the two of them." His eyes held hers a moment too long. "Which means Heather is stuck with me. Aren't you?"

Her father's frown would have normally made her feel like garbage. Any other time she would have felt sick at the fact that after all he'd done, it still mattered to her what he thought.

But yet again, Zach somehow managed to turn everything inside out and upside down. Enough that she found herself smiling in the face of barely averted disaster.

"It really was love at first sight for Cuddles and Atlas." She raised an eyebrow at Zach. "Fortunately, you've grown on me since that first day at your garage."

Her mother tried to nod as if it all made sense, and her father was still glowering at Zach, but when the waiter came to tell them the specials, she found it surprisingly easy to tune them all out.

Brilliant man that Zach was, he made sure the feel of his fingers on her skin, the way he was playing with the hair lying between her shoulder blades, kept her focus more on him than on anything her parents were doing during dinner. And as he purposefully steered the conversation to his famous siblings, and her mother practically lost her mind at learning he was Smith Sullivan's brother, she was amazed to realize that Zach had come through for her in a way no other man ever had.

Right when she needed him the most.

# *Twenty-Six*

It was still dark outside when Zach's cell phone started buzzing on her dresser. When he ignored it, the call came through again.

Heather turned in his arms. "Sounds important." Her words were muffled by his biceps.

Even as he shifted away from her to reach for his phone, he enjoyed running a hand over the curve of her hip. She made a small sound of pleasure at his touch and he couldn't believe how much he liked having her in his bed. In his arms.

In his life.

When he saw the name on his phone's screen, he came instantly awake, thoughts of early-morning sex with Heather moving to the back burner for a few seconds. "Chase? Are congratulations in order?"

He could hear the satisfied grin in his brother's voice. "Chloe and I want you to come meet Emma. We're at home."

Pure joy at hearing about the newest Sullivan

warred with his sudden realization of what day it was: the twenty-third anniversary of his father's death.

Zach's chest clenched tight as he heard Chase's wife speaking in the background. "She wants you to bring Heather."

It took Zach a few moments to force thoughts of his father out of his head before he turned back to Heather.

She was sitting up in the bed. "Your brother and Chloe had the baby?"

Her long hair was flowing around her shoulders, tangled from the previous night's lovemaking. Things had been crazy when they'd gotten back to her house after all the hours of teasing. He'd taken her against her door, finishing what he'd started before dinner in the same place, driving into her so hard that the doorframe shook with every thrust as he took both of them to heaven and back.

For the second time in one day the dogs had gotten a show, but she hadn't seemed to care quite as much. Not, he thought with a satisfied grin of remembrance, when she'd been too overwhelmed with pleasure to do much thinking—or worrying—at all before falling into an exhausted sleep in his arms.

Yet again, he couldn't keep his hands out of the dark silk as he moved back to her bed and pressed his mouth to hers in a good-morning kiss.

"Her name is Emma and he wants us to come meet her."

Pleasure lit her face at the idea of seeing a new baby. Still, she asked, "Us?"

He knew better than to tell her that she was a special request. "Come with me to meet my niece, Heather. Please." He would have wanted her there, anyway, but now that Emma's birth and his father's death were forever entwined, he needed Heather there to keep him grounded.

She slid from his hands and the bed, beautifully naked. "Race you to the shower."

He got under the water just behind her. He loved to wash her hair, couldn't get enough of her little gasps and moans of pleasure as he soaped her up and rinsed her off, but despite the inevitable arousal that built from a few hot kisses neither of them could re-sist giving and getting, they quickly rinsed, toweled off and put on their clothes. Heather let the dogs out into the backyard to take care of business while he poured food and water into their bowls. She grabbed two bananas from the kitchen counter and handed him one as they left the house.

Zach didn't bother to knock before walking into Chase's house. It seemed to Heather that everyone inside was talking and laughing at once and she clutched to her chest the teddy bear that she'd pur-chased for the baby.

Showing up with Zach at his brother's house first thing in the morning was akin to wearing a T-shirt that said Yes, We're Sleeping Together. Of course, she reminded herself, after drinks at Lori's house, they all knew that, anyway.

*It was just sex. Great sex with a friend. A really good friend. But nothing more than that.*

Heather had reminded herself of this so many times in the past few days that it had become a mantra in her head. Only, it was so hard to keep her guard up when Zach was so playful, so easy to laugh with, so tempting to kiss. And on nights like last night when he'd been nothing short of her knight in shining armor…well, she simply couldn't get her head—or heart—around the confusing swirl of emotions he inspired.

Hour by hour, she felt him creeping in further and further, past the thick, strong walls she'd built so many years before, and she was powerless to stop it.

Fortunately, before she could feel weird about walking into the middle of a Sullivan family celebration, Lori spotted her and ran over with open arms.

"Yay, I'm so glad you're here!"

Heather hugged Zach's younger sister and smiled at her. "Congratulations on your new niece."

Lori was glowing with pride. "She's gorgeous and obviously a Sullivan since she couldn't wait to get to the hospital to make her big appearance. Good thing they had a fantastic midwife on call."

The brother she hadn't yet met shook her hand. "I'm Marcus." His eyes were warm and she noticed he didn't let go of Nicola's hand. "It's really nice to meet you."

Nicola hugged her with her free arm. "How are the benefits going?" she whispered into her ear.

Heather couldn't help but laugh and say, "Good."

Ryan, Sophie and Jake came by to say hello again, and she was both glad, and uncomfortable, when Zach moved beside her again, his hand warm on her lower back.

"Chase had to go take care of a diaper change," Zach said, scrunching up his face in disgust, "and then we can see Chloe and the baby."

"Even with these two in me," Sophie said, looking down at her stomach, "I can't believe Chase actually has a baby now." She paused before adding, "And that she was born today."

It didn't take long for Heather to learn that their father had died on this very day.

Zach's hand tightened on hers as Marcus said, "I can't help but think he had a part in this, somehow."

Each of the siblings seemed to pull together more tightly. All but Zach, who slipped his hand from hers and moved from the circle of Sullivans, his expression completely shuttered in a way she hadn't seen it before.

Heather wanted to pull him into a quiet corner to ask him if everything was okay and to let him know she was there for him the way he'd been there for her with her parents. Before she could, Ryan popped the cork on a bottle of champagne and a beautiful woman with gray hair walked into the room from the back of the house.

Heather quickly realized the photo she'd seen of

Zach's mother, while stunning, hadn't come close to doing her justice.

She loved the way Zach so easily moved to hug his mother, with soft words said only for her ears, before turning to introduce them. "Mom, this is Heather. Heather, this is my mom, Mary."

"Congratulations on your new grandchild, Mary," Heather said as Zach's mother regarded her through warm and intelligent blue eyes. Heather was mesmerized and more than a little stunned by the close relationship this woman had with all of her children.

"Thank you," Mary said, looking both radiant and sad as she smiled. Was she also thinking about Zach's father and the grandchild he would never meet? "I'm so glad you're here to share this moment with us."

A dozen words was all it took for Heather to feel perfectly welcome in what should have been a family-only event. One day, when Heather had kids of her own, she vowed to love them the same way this woman had obviously loved hers, enough to welcome their friends and lovers into the fold with open arms.

"I'm thrilled to be here."

She took the glass of champagne Zach handed her and raised her arm in a toast as Sophie's husband said, *"Sláinte!"*—the Irish version of "Cheers."

They were all drinking when Chase walked out, looking exhausted and rumpled...and beside himself with happiness. Zach grabbed her hand and pulled her through the crowd. Okay, so not only did she love the way he clearly cared about his mother and siblings, but the fact that he was in a rush to go meet his new niece?

Unbelievable.

Especially considering her opinion of him that first day they'd met. She couldn't believe how wrong she'd been.

"Hi, Heather," Chase said. "It's great to see you again."

Even though she'd barely met him for thirty seconds at Zach's garage, she had to hug him. "I'm so happy for you and Chloe."

"Thanks, we're thrilled. Want to meet Emma?"

Zach was already halfway down the hall to their bedroom, and she could hear Chloe laughing at something he said as he pushed open the bedroom door. A few seconds later Chase held the door for her, but Heather didn't walk through it.

How could she, when she was utterly mesmerized by the sight of Zach holding baby Emma, staring down at her pretty little face in absolute wonder.

Heather's heart—and her soul—was captured as she watched Zach slip one finger into the little fist and raise it to his lips.

He looked up at Heather, his eyes utterly intense and full of love. "You've got to come see her. She's a freaking miracle."

The pull of his low voice was the only thing that could possibly have gotten her feet moving again. But she couldn't breathe quite right as she moved closer, and she felt her legs shaking as he shifted the baby in his arms.

Emma was perfect and so beautiful that Heather knew she didn't have a prayer of stopping the tears that were coming. She hadn't cried since she was a teenager, but the sight of the baby in Zach's arms pulled at a part of her that was supposed to be shut down, closed off, impenetrable.

Suddenly realizing just how deep she was in the quicksand, she yanked her gaze from Zach and the baby to hand Chloe the teddy bear.

"I'm sorry. I should have said hello and congratulations first."

"Thanks, Heather. It's great to see you again," Chloe said in a tired but happy voice.

As Chase sat down on the edge of the bed beside his wife and brushed her hair back from her face, Heather was amazed by the incredible intimacy—and unconditional joy—between the two of them.

She should have left, knew she didn't have any right to be a part of this family for even a few more seconds, but when the baby gave a sweet little yawn in Zach's arms, the yearning was too strong for Heather to leave just yet. "Could I hold her?"

Chloe smiled. "Of course."

Handling the baby with surprising ease, Zach slid the warm, blanket-wrapped bundle into Heather's arms.

The little girl opened her eyes and blinked up at Heather with perfect innocence.

"Oh, my," she said, "aren't you pretty?"

"You're in big trouble with this one," Zach told his brother.

"I know," Chase replied. "And I wouldn't have it any other way."

The baby immediately turned her head at the sound of her father's voice, and even though Heather wanted to nuzzle Emma's cheek and keep breathing in her fresh baby smell, she forced herself to move across the room to give her back to Chase and Chloe.

"Congratulations," she said again, tears close enough again that she knew she had to get out of there. Not just from their bedroom, but out of the house, away from the rest of the Sullivans and everything she'd told herself she never wanted, but so desperately did.

"I need to get back to the dogs. Zach, you should stay. I'll watch Cuddles as long as you need me to."

She practically broke into a run as she fled the bedroom. She thought she heard his siblings, maybe even his mother, say her name as she made a beeline for the front door, but apart from blurting out something unintelligible about needing to get back to the dogs, she didn't stop to acknowledge them.

She couldn't let Lori tell her how great Zach was again.

She couldn't let Sophie look at her so sweetly and say they were all really hoping for a normal sister-in-law.

She couldn't let herself fall deeper into the fantasy that she should have been smart enough to keep away from in the first place.

Zach had driven them here in one of the dozen cars he seemed to have in his underground garage, but a walk would do her good, would help her clear her head and help her figure out what the heck was wrong with her.

Only, she already knew she could walk all day and all night for the next year and never be able to erase the picture of Zach with the baby in his arms.

Heather loved kids enough that, despite not wanting to do it the traditional way, she had always planned to have children of her own. Not only because she wouldn't dare risk trusting a man enough to pledge a lifetime to her, but also because she couldn't possibly risk her children's hearts, either, the way her mother had risked hers.

But as soon as she'd seen Zach and the baby, when she'd witnessed the complete adoration, the pure, unconditional love in his eyes…she'd stupidly *wanted* that dream family. With him.

Because she'd fallen in l—

*No.*

*God, no.*

Horrified by what she'd almost admitted to herself, she was startled by Zach's strong hands on her waist, pulling her against him out on the sidewalk. Of course, her body had to betray her by instinctively curling into his heat.

She felt his mouth in her hair, and then his kiss on the top of her head, before he asked, "What's wrong?"

"I can't do this." Knowing she needed to be strong, that she should have faced him head-on rather than running, she forced herself to turn around and look him in the eye. "This thing we're doing—" she sucked in a shaky breath to get it out "—it's a mistake."

How she wished she'd never laid eyes on the man who had turned her world completely upside down. But that was a lie, too, because she couldn't imagine not having had the chance to be with him.

Still, that didn't change the fact that she needed to get out while there was still a chance of preventing one small sliver of an unbroken heart.

"I thought I could do this, but seeing you with the baby and the dogs and your family—it's too much. I let myself get in too deep. I shouldn't have been in there today with all of you."

"They all wanted you there, Heather. And I needed you with me." He slid the pads of his thumbs across her cheeks to wipe her tears away. "Seeing you with the baby—" He paused, his gaze intense and filled with emotion. "You're going to be such a beautiful mother, Heather. So damn beautiful."

The reverence in his words made her tears fall faster, made it even more imperative that she say, "I'm sorry. I can't see you anymore."

"Why?" he demanded fiercely.

*Because I can't keep pretending I'm not falling more in love with you with every breath you take, with every caress from your strong hands, with every sweet word from your lips.*

Instead of saying any of those things, she forced herself to shrug. "It was fun, but—"

"Fun?" he growled. Any trace of the teasing man

completely disappeared as they faced each other down on an early-morning San Francisco sidewalk. "We both know it's been a hell of a lot more than fun."

She couldn't let him say anything more. Not when Zach Sullivan was hands down the most charming, charismatic man on the planet, to the point where he actually made her father look like a rank beginner by comparison.

And not after she'd just watched a fantasy flash before her eyes of him holding *their* baby one day.

Desperate to try to save what was left of her heart, frantic to try to keep her soul from being utterly destroyed along with it, she said, "That's why we should stop seeing each other—before either of us gets any deeper."

"Too late." His eyes flashed with surprise and he stared at her in the same stunned disbelief that she'd just experienced moments before. "Holy hell, I think I'm already in love with you."

Her entire body tingled at his words, especially the several square inches just beneath her breastbone.

She'd never seen Zach look less than steady on his feet. Or maybe he just looked that way because she was spinning so fast from having heard the one four-letter word she'd been certain Zach Sullivan would never, ever say.

His emotional confession knocked the breath right out of her. Joy at his words of love warred with disgust at herself for wanting to hear him say them again, to insist that they would remain true no matter what she said or did to try to push him away.

"We agreed," she said just above a whisper, her throat raw, the words hoarse. "Just sex. No emotions. *No falling in love.*"

## *Twenty-Seven*

It was crazy, but the more horrified Heather was by his being in love with her, the more Zach realized his feelings weren't going anywhere. She hadn't tricked him into this. His falling for her had happened all on its own, despite the fact that love wasn't supposed to be in his plans.

His chest clenched tight at the thought of leaving both Heather and the kids he couldn't imagine not having with her now behind too soon. But even though he knew he should be letting her go find some guy who could really give her forever, it turned out he was just as much of a selfish bastard as he'd always been.

Which was why even thoughts of how crushed his mother had been by his father's sudden death couldn't stop him from saying, "I changed my mind."

He slid his hand into her hair the same way he always did when they were making love. Because that was what it had always been, right from the start.

Not just sex, but *love*.

"You changed my mind."

"No," she protested in her beautiful, stubborn way. He wouldn't want her any other way, even as she said, "You can't change your mind about love when you don't even believe in it, remember?"

"I never said I didn't believe in love," he clarified. "I just said I wasn't looking for it. But I didn't know you were coming into my life. I couldn't have known." He looked into eyes that were so beautiful, whether lit with laughter or hazy with passion. "I meant it when I said you were mine. From the first moment I set eyes on you, I knew it. You knew it, too, Heather. That the first time we met, the first time we touched, the first time we kissed, I was yours."

She didn't try to deny it this time, simply said, "I wasn't looking for this. I don't want this."

Didn't she see how strong she was? Strong enough to make better decisions than her mother ever could have? For the millionth time he wanted to tear her father apart for the way he'd hurt his beautiful daughter. She'd been innocent, pure, like Emma once... until her father had destroyed her faith.

"I love you, Heather."

Love for her had been there, inside of him, all along. Seeing Heather surrounded by his family, and then with Emma, and knowing how perfectly she fit in with everyone else he loved, had just made his feelings for her all the more undeniable.

Her beautiful face was full of so much emotion

as she looked up at him that his throat clogged just looking at her.

"How do you always do this to me?" she whispered.

Hope lit in him, warring with the dark knowledge that making her profess her love to him wasn't fair. Not when he'd go and die on her too soon, just like what had happened between his father and his mother.

Shoving the darkness away as he had a thousand times before, he whispered back, "What do I do, Heather?"

Finally, she reached for him, putting her hand over his heart the same way she had their first night together. "You make me feel so much."

She wasn't running anymore, and that should have been good enough. But it wasn't. He wanted to hear her say she loved him, too.

"How much?"

*"Everything."*

Nothing could have stopped him from kissing her then, and as his mouth covered hers he realized he didn't need her to say the words, after all.

Because the love she felt for him was right there in her kiss.

The trip back to Zach's house was a blur. Heather's phone kept buzzing with reminders of meetings she needed to attend and voice mails from her assistant. Zach's siblings texted and called to get the dirt on why the two of them had left his brother's house so abruptly.

Without even discussing it, it was clear that work, family—all of the usual things that made up their days—would have to wait.

Only the dogs couldn't possibly be ignored, not when they needed to be fed again and taken on a walk to the park to run off some energy. Throughout, while Heather told Tina to cancel everything for the rest of the day, and she threw Atlas's rope and watched Cuddles tackle it with her entire body, the only thing Heather could focus on was the way Zach never let go of her hand for one second.

And the fact that he loved her.

*Love* was a word that hadn't meant anything to her since she was seventeen. She'd been certain it could never impact her again, not after so many years of hearing her father throw it around like sparkly confetti.

But when Zach said it, she'd felt the resonance of those four letters so deep in her soul that her entire world shifted on its axis.

She'd tried for so long to pretend love didn't matter.

But it did.

She'd tried for so long to keep that part of her cold. Untouchable.

Zach had touched her, warmed her.

She'd embraced being alone.

Only to find a man whose smiles, off-color jokes and sensual whispers as she was coming apart in his arms meant the world to her. Without him, she'd be lost.

By the time they got back to the house and Atlas plopped down on his doggy bed with Cuddles lying across him the way she loved best, Heather felt as if her insides were a volcano on the verge of exploding.

Her hand was still in his as they headed for the bedroom. Zach closed the door with a soft click that sounded like a bullet going off inside her head.

Feeling shaky, she had to reach for him, had to wind her arms around his waist and back, knowing he'd be strong. Solid.

She'd never let herself lean on anyone before.

Zach caressed her cheeks, his thumbs brushing over her mouth before his fingers moved into her hair, to the spot that felt just right whenever he held her there.

"I've never made love to anyone before," she whispered, overwhelmed by what she was feeling, how strong, how unstoppable, her emotions were.

He leaned closer and his mouth hovered over hers. But instead of kissing her, he whispered across her lips, "Yes, you have. Every time we've touched, you've let me love you." His voice was even deeper than normal and raw with emotion. "And you've loved me right back."

His reply was utterly unexpected.

And, amazingly, just as true.

Just because she hadn't wanted to let herself love him didn't mean she'd even come close to succeeding. From that first brush of their fingertips in the park, to the kiss she'd given him on his cheek, to passion exploding in the alley at the ballpark…no matter what she'd told herself, no matter how she'd tried to pretend none of it really mattered, every second with Zach had shifted the walls around her heart.

Until they'd come crashing down.

"Love me again, Zach."

His mouth covered hers a heartbeat later with a kiss that was so sure and warm and utterly sinful it made her toes curl in her tennis shoes. He loved her mouth the way he loved every inch of her skin— with complete possession, unbridled pleasure and pure male satisfaction.

His tongue slipped and slid against hers before moving back out to run a sensual path across her lips, from one corner to the other. "So sweet." He nibbled on the flesh of her lower lip. "So soft." His tongue laved over the small bites, soothing her at the same time he built her arousal even higher.

And then she was in his arms and he was carrying her over to the bed, pressing her back into the duvet as he covered her body with his. Both of them were still fully clothed, but that didn't stop her from wrapping her legs around him and pulling him even closer.

He deepened their kiss with a possessive growl that sent the dials on every last nerve in her body into the red zone. There was no space in their kiss for thinking, for worrying, only the sweet release of feeling herself open all the way up, inside and out.

For Zach.

He lifted his head to stare into her eyes. *"Mine."* The word was rough, ragged, from his lips. Fire burned in his gaze, hotter, more intense, than her beautiful charmer had ever been before. *"You're mine."*

Before she could tell him yes, she was his and always had been, his mouth was stealing her breath away again and his hands were pulling at fabric, unzipping where he could, ripping when fabric didn't come off easily enough.

Heather loved every one of his rough demands, the same ones she was making of him as she kicked off her shoes, then yanked his shirt off and shoved his pants down with her feet.

She'd never felt this wild, or this free, before.

Only with Zach.

She had to run her hands over his hard muscles, his chest and arms, his back and shoulders, to make sure it wasn't a dream. His hands were just as greedy as they stroked every inch of her skin, his mouth following his fingers from her ankles, then up her legs to that spot behind her kneecap that had her trembling and gasping at how sensitive it was, before he moved even higher to the needy flesh between her thighs.

Emotions crashed into her as his tongue slid over, then into her, until the combination of heart and body, mind and soul, had her release going on and on until she was begging Zach to stop with one breath and asking for more the next.

She was lost—and then miraculously found— as he slid his mouth and hands from her to replace them with such hard heat it took what was left of her breath away.

She was amazed by the beauty of their connection, the way her body had always recognized his as its mate every single time they'd come together, even when her head, and her heart, had wanted so desperately to remain unsure.

His mouth covered hers again as they rocked together, their bodies slipping and sliding in a perfect rhythm of strength. And surrender.

*To love.*

Heather's hair spilled around them as she came over him. Even caught in his need to possess her, Zach could feel her need to possess him right back, to claim the heart he'd given her. As they shifted together so that he was lying beneath her and she was sitting up on her shins to take—and give—so sweetly, so beautifully, he could barely do anything but stare in wonder at the woman who had rocked his world so completely.

Her hands were pressed flat on his chest, her head thrown back as she rode him, and he shifted his legs so that she could lean back against his thighs to go deeper, to fly higher. Her gasp of pleasure at the small change, and then at the feel of his hands on her breasts, her belly, between her thighs, was almost more than he could take as her body tightened around his.

*"Heather."*

At the sound of her name, she opened her eyes to look down at him.

"I need to hear you say it."

Her eyes darkened with passion. And with all the emotion she'd finally stopped holding back from him.

"I love you."

They were the three most beautiful words he'd ever heard.

"Again," he demanded, even as he tightened his hold on her hips and slid in deeper.

"I love you."

"Give me more." He would never grow tired of hearing her say the words, of having her become one with him like this.

"I love you." She leaned down to kiss his mouth. "I love you" preceded another kiss on his shoulder. "I love you" landed on his chest along with her lips.

Everywhere she could reach, she whispered her love for him, then sealed it with a kiss. Throughout, their bodies were joined, moving together.

"Don't stop loving me," he begged her, even though it wasn't fair to ask her for this. "No matter what happens, promise me you won't ever stop."

Her smile wobbled at his request as she leaned down so that her breasts were pressing against his chest and her mouth was almost on his.

"How could I stop loving you," she said so softly he could barely hear her words over the blood rushing in his ears, "when I've never been able to do anything about the way you make me feel? I'll love you forever, Zach."

He could hear the surrender, but also the joy, in her admission as their passion hit its sensual crescendo. Knowing just how much the words cost her, he wanted to give her more than just another climax, more than just the pleasure he knew she'd found in his arms as she lay soft and supple over him while they both worked to catch their breath.

He wanted to give her the same gift she'd just given him. He wanted to give her a promise of *forever*.

But he couldn't.

All he could give her was what he felt today. Here. Now.

"I love you," he whispered into her ear.

And this time, she whispered it right back.

# *Twenty-Eight*

Heather had never been able to sleep during the day, not even back in college after pulling all-nighters to finish a paper. But as she lay sprawled across Zach's bare chest with early-afternoon sunlight streaming over the bed, she was so physically spent that she could have closed her eyes and kept them that way until the next morning.

Of course, there was no way that was going to happen with the dogs pawing at the bedroom door.

On a groan, Zach pressed a kiss to her forehead. "Go take a shower. I'll take care of the fur balls."

Now that she was awake and temporarily sexually sated, her worries about Zach's reaction to the anniversary of his father's death came right back.

"Can I ask you something?"

He took her hands in his, brought them up to his mouth for a kiss. "Yes," he answered, "I'll be ready for another round soon."

It would have been easy to use their incredible

attraction to skip over the hard stuff, but she didn't want that. And she was pretty sure he didn't want that, either.

So even though she couldn't help but smile at his teasing, she still said, "This is a hard day for you, isn't it? Despite the baby," she clarified, "and us. Because of your father."

His hands tightened on hers for a split second before he shrugged. "It's a good thing that we have something to celebrate now, instead of being bummed out every year on this day."

The dogs were all but throwing themselves against the door, and when he pressed one more kiss to her knuckles, then let her go to let them out, she really couldn't stop him.

Wishing that love came with instructions, she went to the shower and got under the warm spray. If only she knew how to help him heal with his father the way he'd helped her with hers.

She sighed as she faced the truth. Yes, she'd been brave and had opened up her heart to Zach. But just because she'd said "I love you" to a man for the first time in her life didn't mean there wasn't more to say.

And how could she expect him to be completely open with her when she hadn't been completely open with him?

When she'd told him a flat-out lie.

Zach found her forehead-to-wall as he joined her in the shower. He wrapped an arm around her waist.

"Already regretting it all?" he teased against her

neck, but she could hear the real worry beneath his joking words.

She turned in his arms so she could press her face to his chest and hear his heart beating strong and steady in her ear. "Have I ever told you that I love the way you make me laugh?"

Maybe that was why she knew she could tell him anything; because he wouldn't let her take anything too seriously, would always find a way to show her the joyful side of life.

"You mean like this?"

He tickled her rib cage until she was giggling as the water splashed down on both of them and made everything too slick for her to get away from his teasing fingertips.

And when laughter inevitably turned to passion and he pressed her back against the wall, she welcomed the chance to clear her mind of anything but the sweet ache of taking him inside her yet one more time, letting him fill up all her empty spaces with his heat, his kisses.

And his love.

Good thing Sullivan Autos was a well-oiled machine, because if it were a choice between hanging out under the engine of a car or spending time with Heather—naked or not—Zach would happily blow off every future day at the office. He was in the bedroom pulling on a T-shirt when he heard Heather speaking to Cuddles.

"Uh-oh, did you find another yummy shoe?"

He walked into the living room just as she picked up a slobbery hunk of brown leather.

She gave him a crooked, very cute smile. "I suppose we've been a little lax with training her the past few days."

"I've got this," he said as he grabbed a tiny chew toy from the floor and held it out for the puppy, who immediately latched on to it with her sharp little teeth. Cuddles shook it with her tiny mouth, her fur flying around her face, and he told her what a good girl she was.

Heather leaned back against the counter. "It used to really annoy me how good you were with her. The fact that she so easily accepted that you were the boss."

He grinned at her. "I liked annoying you."

She laughed. "Liked? Don't you mean you still like it?" Her laughter fell away as she asked, "You're not going to give her back on Saturday when your brother comes back from his trip, are you?"

He gave the other side of the chew toy to Atlas so he could take over. "She's not my dog."

Heather made a face. "I know your niece-to-be will probably be disappointed, but she only had her a couple of days. It's incredible the way the two of you have bonded." She pinned him with a serious look. "Cuddles is your dog, Zach."

As he washed his hands at the kitchen sink, he reflected on the fact that two weeks ago he'd been a bachelor with nothing bigger to worry about than where he was going to drink his next beer.

"I was going to watch her, keep her fed, take her on a few walks and then hand her back." He figured he should have felt grumpier about it and made himself say, "This wasn't how it was supposed to work out."

"Things don't always work out the way they're supposed to."

He knew that firsthand. His father dying so young shouldn't have been in the cards for his family. But it had happened, anyway.

Heather looked really serious. The same way she'd looked in the shower when he'd thought she was regretting loving him.

"There's something I need to tell you," she said softly.

His gut twisted. She wasn't going to leave, was she? She hadn't decided it was a big mistake, after all?

But when she held out a hand for him to take, he gave silent thanks. If she'd been planning to tell him she'd changed her mind about the two of them, she would have kept her distance.

He pulled her closer before threading his hands into her hair and leaning his forehead against hers. "You can tell me anything."

"I lied to you," she whispered before lifting her eyes to meet his. "I didn't get the scars on my arms in an accident. I made them myself. With razor blades."

Just the thought of anything hurting Heather tore up Zach's insides. But knowing she'd done it herself? "Why would you hurt yourself like that?"

"After I found out about my father, I was still keeping it together in school, pretending with my mother, but every time he came home from a trip I found myself locked in my room. Almost like I was trying to bleed out the pain. Trying to control something. And to find a way to distract myself from all the anger."

Zach had to reach for her hands, had to press kisses to the soft skin of her pulse, along the tendons and muscles on her forearms. He'd heard about kids cutting themselves, but he'd never known anyone who did it.

At least, he'd thought he didn't.

"You don't have any new scars, do you?"

"No." She shook her head, almost smiling at him as she said, "I'm sure you would have found them by now if I did. There was a guidance counselor at school who could tell something was wrong. We all had to take one of those vocation tests and she suggested I should try working with animals. So instead of going home to cut myself that day when my father was coming home from a trip, I went to the local animal shelter."

"That's why you do so much for them," he said in a low voice as he now realized what she'd been through. And how brave she'd been to come out on the other side so strong. Braver than he'd ever been. "Those dogs and cats in that shelter helped you the way you've always helped them, didn't they?"

Finally, a tear fell. The first he'd ever seen her cry.

"I never trusted a man with the truth about my

scars before. I never thought I could." Her mouth wobbled at the corners as she tried to smile. And failed. "Until you." She shook her head, half laughing as she said, "I still can't believe it ended up being you."

"Thank you for telling me. For trusting me."

"I don't know why I'm still crying," she said as her tears fell one after the other. "Especially when telling you has made me feel so much better, so much lighter, than I've been in a long, long time."

He wished he could come clean about his own demons, wished he had half the guts Heather did. But after twenty-three years of holding the darkness deep inside, he just didn't see how sharing his fears would do anything but upset her. He also knew there was nothing he could say to take away her scars or to change the man her father was.

Fortunately, he had a couple of backup reinforcements that were naturally equipped to comfort the woman he loved.

"Cuddles, Atlas, come!"

Three pounds of fur and bone and teeth flew into his arms. He handed the puppy to Heather while Atlas leaned his big head on her thighs. Zach put his arms around her and the two dogs to let her tears fall on all of them.

And like the family they'd become so quickly, the three of them loved her tears away with the kind of slobbery kisses that only a couple of dogs—and a man who'd been likened to one many, many times—could.

# Twenty-Nine

Heather had never been so busy with dogs and work...and Zach. She wasn't even coming close to getting enough sleep, not with a sinfully gorgeous man in her bed, or her in his. But the rest she did get, when his body was wrapped around hers, or when she was using his rock-hard muscles as a pillow, was better than a full night of sleep without him had ever been.

And every day he surprised her. Not just with laughter. But with more love than she could have ever imagined would be hers.

On Wednesday night, he took her and the dogs to an outdoor concert on the green. The band members were friends of his and he'd scored amazing tickets. Together they'd laughed at the way the dogs' tails wagged in time to the music. And when the sun set, he pulled her between his legs and kept her warmer than any blanket could have.

Thursday found them out on Smith's sailboat, the

dogs in their own fitted life vests, Cuddles under one of Zach's arms, his free hand holding hers tightly as Atlas lay at their feet. She'd never realized before just how beautiful the Golden Gate Bridge looked in the setting sun...or how nice it was to be able to share that beauty with someone she loved.

By Friday, when she thought she was ready for whatever he had planned, he completely blew her mind by suggesting they hunker down at home on the couch and watch movies together. He made her watch *Hoosiers,* and even though she could have sworn nothing would ever get her interested in basketball, she had to admit she was hooked by the end of the movie. As payback, she cued up *The Sound of Music,* and even though Zach wouldn't admit how much he liked it, she caught him humming "My Favorite Things" as he was brushing his teeth.

Heather had to give credit where credit was due. Zach was amazingly good at everything he did, from loving her senseless, to getting her to talk a little more every day about her feelings about her parents. Safe in his arms, she'd started to realize that even though blood tied her to her father and mother, she'd succeeded at building up a real family for herself via her close bonds with friends, coworkers and the animals she'd taken in over the years.

A part of her still couldn't get over the fact that Zach Sullivan was the one who had helped her see things more clearly. He was so far from the self-absorbed, vain man she'd once assumed he was.

Was he charming?

God, yes, he was charming. With charisma to spare, enough that her eyeballs sometimes hurt from all the eye-rolling he—and the reactions of women who constantly drooled over him—inspired.

But was he a liar and a cheat?

No, he wasn't.

On the contrary, he was one of the most honest people she'd ever met. Everything was right there on the surface with Zach. He didn't make you guess; he just told it to you like it was.

Still, she was nervous come Saturday morning. Not only because he was going to be racing again—this time at the raceway in the wine country near Marcus's winery—but also because this was the first time she would spend an entire day with his family after last seeing them the day that Emma was born.

She remembered insisting to Lori and Sophie that she wasn't going to date Zach, but she had blown that by doing the friends-with-benefits thing. Then she had capped it all off by flipping out at Chase and Chloe's house. She had actually yelled at Zach on the sidewalk, telling him he couldn't possibly love her because they had an *agreement*.

Ugh.

"Looks like you need a little help relaxing." They were walking onto the racetrack, hand in hand, and he was giving her the grin that told her he had wicked plans.

*Very* wicked plans.

"I'm fine," she told him in the same firm, no-nonsense voice that she used with particularly rambunctious dogs when they needed to know she was not in the mood to play.

Of course, the truth was that she was *always* in the mood to play with Zach.

And, unfortunately, he knew it.

For all his teasing, she thought he seemed a little tense. As if he didn't really want to do this race.

Maybe, she found herself thinking, it wouldn't be so bad to find a private spot behind the stands where they could relax each other. Thankfully, before she could give in to the insanity that Zach's hands and mouth always inspired, Lori called out to them from the stands.

"Saved by a brat," he muttered as he made a beeline toward his firefighter brother who had given him Cuddles. "Gabe, Megan, Summer, this is Heather."

She smiled at the couple and the pretty little girl between them, but before she could even say hello or ask them how their trip to Europe had been, Zach said, "You can't have Cuddles back."

Heather's gaze shot to the little girl, worried about how she'd take the news. But instead of getting upset, Summer gave Zach a smile so smug it might have actually outsmugged him at his worst.

"I knew you'd love her!" Summer said as she threw her arms around Zach's waist. "When we saw her with all the other puppies, I knew right away that she was just what you needed so you'd smile more and be happier."

Zach frowned as he looked from the top of Summer's blond head to his brother's smirk. "I was set up."

"It was like taking candy from a baby."

This was the kind of family Heather had often wished she belonged to. One where even the tricks they played on each other came from the heart.

Then again, Heather's version of the perfect family hadn't included a movie star. Her friend Brenda would die right now. Because Smith looked just like he had last week on the big screen. Only better.

Zach slid his arm around Heather's waist and pulled her tightly against him. So tightly that it almost felt as if she were wearing a corset.

"Smith, this is Heather."

Smith Sullivan gave her the smile that she was sure had melted a million panties. Interestingly, hers were fine. Well, they would be fine, if only Zach would stop rubbing his fingertips against the underside of her breast.

She tried to shift out of Zach's arms but he only held her tighter. He was always possessive, but for some reason, today he was taking it to a whole new level.

As Smith's hand curled around hers and he said a low "Hello," she felt Zach tense against her.

Wait a minute. Did he actually think his movie-star brother would be interested in her?

Ryan appeared next to Smith and grinned at her. "Great to see you again, Heather."

Just like Zach, Ryan was the picture of good-looking charm. But that was where the similarities ended. Where Zach thrived on his sarcastic edge, Ryan was all laid-back ease. She could see why women fell for him, beyond being impressed with his skill on the pitcher's mound.

Smith nodded toward the track. "Looks like they're ready for you down there, Z."

Ryan grinned. "Don't worry, we'll take care of Heather."

Zach's jaw clenched. "Don't flirt with her."

Had they forgotten she was still there? She was just about to remind them when Zach's hands were in her hair and his mouth was on hers and he was kissing all the breath from her lungs.

And then he was gone, leaving her to gasp for air in the middle of a half dozen Sullivans, all of whom were grinning at her.

"Come, sit with me," Smith said, leading her to one of the padded folding seats out on the bleachers. Ryan snagged the seat next to her, and her butt had barely hit the seat when Zach's two famous, single brothers started flirting.

Big-time.


Photographers were out in droves to catch the pro race-car drivers who'd come out in support of the San Francisco food bank. Zach figured he only had to put up with their flashbulbs until they realized Smith was in the stands.

Barry Jones made a crack about getting a run on him in turn two, but Zach didn't have a comeback for him. Not when he was too busy staring up at the bleachers to make sure his brothers didn't try anything with Heather.

He trusted her, of course. It was Smith and Ryan he was going to kill if he saw even one picture come out with their hands anywhere on her.

Zach slammed his helmet on and pushed through the other drivers to get into his car. He'd worked with this crew enough to skip the prerace speech. He hadn't wanted to do this damn race, but he was a man of his word and had to make good on it.

The race started and he drove like a man possessed. Not just to win, but because he wanted to get the race done, then take Heather back to bed, where it was just the two of them. Where nothing mattered but her laughter, her sweet little sounds of pleasure.

The sound of metal against metal came first, a split second before it slammed through his body.

Damn it, he thought as the car started spinning, he'd known his luck was going to run out one day, but he hadn't thought it'd be this soon. Or that it would end like this. He'd always figured on having an aneurysm like his father, had believed every headache was one step closer to the inevitable.

Zach's brain and body went into autopilot, something any racer worth his shit immediately reacted to in a crash situation. His hands worked the wheel. His feet worked the brakes and clutch. But as the colors all around him spun together, and his brain and body followed the do-or-die instructions his crew were yelling at him through his earpiece, his heart remained with Heather.

A dozen quick flashes of beauty, of pleasure,

swelled behind his breastbone, pushing even deeper, all the way into his soul.

Heather with scratches on her knees, her shirt ripped, dirt smudged across her cheek as she clutched Cuddles to her chest and glared at him.

The feel of her soft curves beneath him as he rolled them out of the way of the skateboarder, and then her fingers slipping into his as they stared up at the blue sky together.

Her mouth warm beneath his at the ballpark as he stole that first kiss, the desperation that had flared to life between them and only grown hotter every time they touched.

Running after her on the sidewalk to tell her he loved her, and loving her even more for the way she'd yelled at him, for how hard she'd tried to insist their love wasn't real.

And then, later, the taste of her tears on his lips as she'd cried in his arms, the dogs there with them, all of them comforting her.

People had always joked that nothing could touch Zach and his charmed life, but as the battle he was waging to control the car and the heat of the engine's flames burned through metal and leather, he knew better.

He'd always known better.

After all, his father had died young, and everyone always said that Zach was exactly like Jack Sullivan.

Jack Sullivan's life had been perfect. He'd had a beautiful wife he loved and eight great kids. He'd been the definition of *charmed*.

But he'd still died.
And left them all behind.


Heather blindly pushed through the people on the bleachers to get to Zach. She was at the entry gate to the racetrack when Ryan's arms came around her.

"You can't go out there."

She fought Ryan's hold with every ounce of strength she had, but Smith was there, too, and the brothers' muscles were like steel clamped around her.

*"Let go of me!"* she screamed at the two superstars while a dozen photographers spun back and forth to film the crash and then her and Smith and Ryan.

But his brothers just held her tighter as she watched flames engulf Zach's car.

He was supposed to be indestructible...and hers forever.

She'd known he wasn't, that nobody was bulletproof. But it had been easier to lull herself into a false sense of security than to have to face the utter loss of control that came from sitting helpless in the stands while he raced a car at dizzying speeds.

She could still feel the imprint of his lips on hers, from the kiss he'd left her with. She'd stopped praying a long time ago, had substituted hard work and focus and reality for those prayers.

Now her lips wouldn't stop moving, wouldn't stop repeating, "Please, God. Please."

The smoke from the fire extinguishers grew thick and dark around the car as the emergency crew attacked the flames. Her tears mixed in with the smoke and the dust from the track as cars skidded to a stop one by one. The other drivers got out to watch the scene unfold, horror on their faces as they yanked off their helmets.

Suddenly, she saw boots. Legs. And then a man throwing himself to the ground, rolling out of the way of the flames.

Shock made Smith's and Ryan's hands loosen just enough for her to slip free, to hurdle the gate. The roar of the crowd mixed with the pounding of her heart in her ears as she sprinted toward Zach. His crew had dragged him away from the car; they had all backed away as the flames only grew taller, brighter.

The explosion rocked the ground, but even though she stumbled, she got right back up on her feet.

Zach pushed up from his knees to pull off his helmet. She crashed into him at the exact second his eyes met hers, and she pressed her mouth to his face again and again. "Lori said you were indestructible. I didn't believe her. Now I do. Thank God nothing ever touches you."

His eyes flashed with darkness before he pulled her so tightly to him that it almost hurt.

"I love you so much," she told him in their last private moment before the track doctors, the other drivers and the rest of the Sullivans descended. Heather didn't want to let go of Zach's hand, didn't want to lose that connection, but she knew he'd be all hers later.

Believing he'd been spared from the car crash and fire so that they could have their forever, when his fingers started to slip free of hers she let him go.

# *Thirty*

After the emergency crew checked Zach out and he'd convinced his brothers and sisters that he was okay, Heather had known without being told that all he wanted was to get away from the racetrack. She'd thought she would be the one to drive home, but when he'd headed for the wheel she'd realized it was probably best that he dealt with driving a car sooner rather than later.

There were so many things she wanted to say to him, so many things she wanted to tell him—how much she loved him and how she wasn't sure about these races, but would try to be open to them in the future if they were really important to him— but just as she buckled into the passenger seat and they headed off toward the city, his mother called.

Mary Sullivan's distress over the accident was palpable. And yet, Heather admired the calm that lay at the foundation of her love for her son. If Zach had seemed a bit short, even a little irritated with the mother Heather knew he loved, she figured it was one of a dozen natural responses to the crash. There had been so many people hovering around him wanting reassurance that he was okay. He had to be exhausted.

But even though she hadn't been the one fighting like hell to right the car, and then to escape it, Heather still couldn't find her own calm. It would take time to stop seeing the man she loved go up in flames every time she closed her eyes. And until that day came, she wanted to live every single minute with him to the fullest. She was done holding back a part of her heart from him, done waiting for that other shoe to drop.

Today she'd learned just how precious life—and love—truly was.

As Heather stood in Zach's kitchen cooking dinner, the knife almost sliced through the tip of her finger instead of the bell pepper as another image of him spinning out on the track zinged through her head. Just as she put the knife down, Zach walked out of the bedroom. His hair was wet from the shower, his perfect face scratched on the right side.

Thank God he was alive.

Despite her lingering distress over his crash, she couldn't help smiling at him. The truth was that she'd always grinned like a fool whenever he was around. Only, Zach didn't smile back.

It was the first time he'd ever not smiled back.

"Gabe's coming over."

She was surprised to hear he was up for a visit from one of his siblings when she could see how beat he was. "Is he going to bring over the rest of Cuddles's things?"

"No." The word shot like a bullet from his lips. "He's coming to take her back."

Even as he said it, Cuddles was rubbing against his calves trying to get his attention. But he wasn't scooping her up into his arms.

Instead, he was ignoring the puppy completely. He wasn't even looking at her.

"I don't understand," she said, and she didn't, couldn't possibly believe that he was serious. "You just told them you were keeping her."

He shrugged, the shrug of a man who didn't seem to care what he'd said to a seven-year-old girl...or what other promises he might have made along the way to anyone else.

"She's better off with them. The dog needs a kid around to play with."

*The dog?*

The way he said it was different than when he called Cuddles and Atlas *fur ball* or *mutt.* He was affectionate, teasing, when he said those things. But this was just plain dismissive.

The paramedics had said he didn't have a concussion. Had they been wrong?

"Zach." She started to move toward him, but the remote expression on his face stopped her in her tracks. "Are you feeling okay?"

"I'm fine."

He sat down on the couch and grabbed the remote, flipping on the TV. The sound of another car race immediately started up. Bile rose in her throat at the sight of the cars racing in circles around the track.

She wanted to scream at him, wanted to throw something at his big, thick head. She yanked the controls off the coffee table to jam her thumb over the red off button.

"I can't watch that right now." The TV screen went back to black. "How can you? Don't you remember you almost died out there today?"

Before he could answer, Cuddles walked over with one of Zach's leather shoes. The puppy plopped down in front of him and started chewing it, her big brown eyes trained on him as if she were waiting for a command to do otherwise.

"Aren't you going to stop her?"

Zach barely glanced down at the puppy. "No. Summer will figure out how to get her to stop making mistakes."

"She's a puppy. She's going to make mistakes." But wasn't the truth that some mistakes were so big that they couldn't be undone? Like trusting someone to actually love you right. "She trusts you, Zach. Gabe and Megan and Summer are just strangers to her. You're her family."

And hers, too, or so she'd thought. Finally, she'd had the family she'd never thought could be hers. A future filled with laughter. And love. So much love it had made her head spin.

Now, though, it was spinning out of control for reasons that had nothing to do with love.

*Please,* she thought, the word running around and around in her head just the way it had hours earlier. Only this time she wasn't begging God—she was silently pleading with a flesh-and-blood man. *Please don't do this.*

His face was like granite. "She'll be fine."

Every one of Heather's instincts told her to run. To flee. To get out and protect whatever was left of her heart while she still could. But something was obviously wrong.

Very wrong.

Zach hadn't cracked a smile, hadn't given her one of those smug looks she always wanted to kiss right off his face.

And, she realized with a dark hit of pain in the pit of her stomach, he hadn't so much as touched her since they'd left the track.

He was *always* touching her.

She forced herself to move toward him, rather than away. "There's something you're not telling me. Something that happened out there on the track."

"I'm alive" was his offhand reply. "Everything's great."

His eyes were so cold, so shuttered. All she'd wanted was to have him back, but not like this.

Not when he suddenly seemed to be a shell of the man she'd thought he was.

The pain in her stomach grew bigger, but the need

to have the real Zach Sullivan back—*her Zach*—
was bigger. Big enough that she kept moving closer.

"I can't imagine how it must have felt to be in
that car, trying to get out while it burned. But you
walked away from it."

Whenever she'd gotten stuck in darkness, he'd always fought for her. He'd made her laugh, held her
when she'd cried, taught her how to trust again and to
believe in love when she'd thought it wasn't possible.

Now *she* needed to fight for *him*.

"Talk to me, Zach. Tell me what's going on." The
word *please* was on her tongue when the doorbell
rang.

She could barely stand to watch as Zach shoved
all of the puppy's things into a grocery bag, picked
up Cuddles and pushed both the bag and the puppy
into his brother's arms.

The little Yorkie whimpered as she looked from
Gabe to Zach.

"You sure about this?" Gabe asked his brother.

"I agreed to keep her while you were gone. You're
back now."

Gabe's eyes moved from his brother to Heather.
She could see worry in them, and disappointment.

The same disappointment that was choking her
until she could hardly breathe around it.

"Summer told me you needed a dog because she
thought you were lonely," Gabe said. "She was so
happy that you were going to keep her. She thought
you wanted the puppy."

Heather waited for Zach to soften at the men-

tion of the little girl…or for him to at least acknowledge the way Cuddles was struggling to get from his
brother's arms into Zach's.

"I don't need a dog."

He didn't say anything else, but he didn't need to
for Heather to hear what he was really saying.

*I don't need anyone else.*

She wanted to be anywhere but there, with Gabe's
eyes taking in her devastation. But she was glad she'd
stayed, glad she'd actually witnessed Zach doing
what he was doing, because it was the only way she
could ever have made her heart face the truth.

She didn't realize Atlas had gotten up from his
nap on his dog bed and moved to her side until she
felt his big head nudge her hand. She put her hands
on his neck and shoulders, letting his steady warmth
give her the strength she needed right then.

Hadn't she known the other shoe would drop at
some point? That it had to because it always did?

Oh, how she'd wanted to believe that it wouldn't,
it couldn't.

Just as badly as she'd wanted to believe in Zach.

He closed the door on his brother, walked back
into the room, picked up the shoe Cuddles had been
chewing on and dropped it into the garbage can with
a *thud*.

All the while the puppy's cries could be heard as
his brother put her in the car.

"I told you everything." Her voice shook with
emotion she couldn't contain. "I loved you enough
to tell you my secrets. To trust you with them." And

with her heart. Which was why she had to try one more time to see if he would be honest with her about what was hurting him. "I know something's wrong, something to do with today's crash." She clenched her hands at her sides to keep from reaching for him, because if he pushed her away she would shatter into a thousand pieces on his kitchen floor. "Won't you trust me, too?"

He went completely still, and for a moment as she stared into his bleak eyes she thought he might be about to tell her why he was acting so weird.

Only, when he finally spoke, it was just to say, "Trust me, it's better this way. It was only a matter of time before something happened to her at the shop." He paused. "Or before something happened to me. Like today, out at the racetrack. If I hadn't been able to get out of the car, they would have taken her back, anyway. Better if it happens now, before she gets any more attached to me."

She blinked at him, trying to make sense of what he was saying. "Wait a minute. Are you actually trying to convince me you got rid of the puppy for her own good?"

When he nodded, she shook her head in disbelief. "That's crazy. Can't you see how much she loves you? And that she doesn't want to be with anyone else on the off chance that you'll crash a race car one day?"

But with every word she spoke, she could see Zach shutting down more and more. To the point where it was like talking to the cement wall he'd driven into today.

Only this time, it was her heart going up in flames as he shut her out completely.

Heather had thought she'd found him—the one guy who could prove to her that they weren't all the same. But she'd never know if she had or not, would she? Because he wouldn't talk to her.

Just like her father, Zach made all the rules and she was expected to follow them.

This was why she'd been trying so hard to resist him, to argue away his love…and her own.

Atlas silently moved beside her as she found her bag and put her things into it. She walked into the bedroom to retrieve the extra clothes she'd started to leave at Zach's house. The bed mocked her, told her what she hadn't wanted to believe was true.

It had just been sex.

Friends with benefits…only, maybe they hadn't even been friends when it came right down to it.

Zach's eyes were dark as he watched her gather up her things, a muscle jumping in his jaw, right beneath one of the scratches she was so tempted to reach out and run a finger over. Just to be close to him one more time.

"You're leaving?"

Before tonight, Zach would never have asked her if she was going. He simply wouldn't have let her go, would have pulled whatever tricks out of his sleeve to convince her she was better off staying with him.

"I've got a big backlog of work at the office."

Work had piled up due to all the time she'd been spending with Zach. It had seemed worth it at the time, the trade-off between love and growing her business.

Worth it, that was, until the mirage of *love* disappeared like a puff of smoke.

"You're that pissed off at me for giving the damn puppy back?" At last, she could see the veneer he'd tried to put around himself cracking. But it was too late. Especially when he said, "It wasn't even my dog. I never asked for it. They just dumped it on me."

*It.*

"No, I'm not pissed off." And she was being perfectly honest. She was far more heartbroken than she was angry. "Just like you said, she'll be fine." Heather would make sure of it, would personally assign her best trainer to work with Megan, Summer and Gabe so that Cuddles could forget that Zach Sullivan ever existed.

"Then why are you leaving?"

Because she needed to save herself while there was still a ghost of a chance that she could recover.

Because if he could give away a puppy she'd thought he absolutely adored without so much as flinching as it cried for him, then she wasn't sure she knew who he was at all.

Because she didn't think she rated a whole heck of a lot more than the puppy had to the man standing in front of her.

Because, in the end, it turned out love wasn't enough. Just like she'd always known.

But since she could no longer trust him enough to say any of that, all that came was an honest "I'm glad you're okay, Zach."

So glad, in fact, that she'd felt as if her own life had been saved out there on the racetrack when he'd scrambled free of the burning car.

She was about to start crying, knew any second she'd be falling apart.

Heather couldn't do that here. Not in front of Zach. She couldn't let her guard down around him ever again.

All those years ago, when she'd found out what her father had done, she'd vowed to never feel that way again, to never let anyone make her feel so terribly unloved, so unimportant. She'd renew that vow, make sure she stuck by it in the future.

She needed to get out of there looking as if she were still in one piece and then, when she was far, far away from him, she'd deal with the shattered insides beneath her skin.

When Zach had nearly died she'd finally admitted to herself just how much she loved him. She'd finally confessed down deep in her soul that she loved him more deeply, more truly, than she'd ever thought she could love a man.

Only to have him prove her cynicism about love was right.

She hated him for that, but hated herself more for falling for him.

"Good luck with the rest of your charmed life."

# *Thirty-One*

Zach's life had turned into a goddamned train wreck.

After he put the wrong fluid in a customer's transmission and it burned to a crisp, his staff wouldn't let him near any of the cars in the garage. He did something on his computer that gave it a virus and his executive assistant asked him, politely but firmly, to please stay away from the rest of the computers in the office while she got the hard drive repaired. His vocabulary shrank to a handful of curse words when reporters covering his accident at the racetrack called to ask what he thought about the pictures of Ryan and Smith holding Heather back from the track as his car burned, and now the press was pissed at him, too.

On top of everything else, Gabe had ratted him out to the entire family. As soon as Lori and Sophie learned that he'd given the puppy back—along with a clear visual of the horror on Heather's face that Gabe had likely recounted to all of them in vivid Technicolor—they began to tag-team him with messages wanting to know what his problem was.

Lori went so far as to threaten him with bodily harm if he continued to blow it with Heather. In her last message she'd made it perfectly clear that she had plenty of brothers already, so it was an easy decision for her to stick with Heather if he was going to keep being too much of a fool to figure out how to love her right.

*"We all know how you feel about her"* was what she'd said in her most recent message. Loud enough that her voice was still ringing in his ears. *"Heather and I were getting to be friends, but now she won't call me back. Jerk."*

He was tempted to delete all future messages from his siblings without listening to them, but he couldn't. Not if they were calling to say they'd heard from Heather.

But no one said a word about seeing her, not even Gabe, who he figured was doing training sessions with Cuddles at Top Dog.

*It wasn't even my goddamned dog* was what he kept telling himself over and over. *They shouldn't be getting their panties in such a twist over my giving it back to Summer.*

Only, all the old lies he'd always told himself weren't working anymore. Not when he knew exactly why they were all so angry with him.

Because he'd lost Heather.

*Hell.* It was worse than that.

He'd convinced Heather to walk to the edge of a

hundred-story building, went out of his way to convince her she was safe…and then he'd shoved her off.

God, that last night at his house he'd hated seeing her spark fade, hated even more that he was the cause of it, but he couldn't stop, couldn't just shut up and pull her into his arms the way he was dying to.

Not when he'd been gripped with the need to save them both before they went too far, too deep, into a forever that could—or couldn't, depending on the same bad luck and shitty fate that had befallen his father—be out there for them.

Exactly one week after Heather had left him, Zach pulled over in front of his mother's house. His tire jammed into the curb with a sharp pop.

A flat.

Figured, the way his luck was going.

Just as he'd thought at the racetrack, he'd finally used up his share of good fortune.

His *charmed life* had officially ended the moment Heather walked out of his house.

He grabbed the brightly wrapped baby gift from the passenger seat and shoved the pink and yellow balloons tied to his mother's mailbox out of his way as he headed for the front door. The last thing he was in the mood for today was a baby shower, regardless of how cute Chase and Chloe's kid was.

If only he could see Emma without the rest of his family around, poking at him.

If only he could forget the way Heather had looked with Emma in her arms. So beautiful, so natural, so amazed by the perfect little life.

When he closed his eyes at night just to lie there until the sun came up, that was what he saw. Heather and the baby. The wonder on her face. The joy.

The longing.

How could he have done anything but fall in love with her?

And how could he do anything now but let her go?

The front door was half-open and he plopped his gift on the pile in the living room. Planning to see Emma, give her a kiss and then get the hell out of there, he had just stepped out into his mother's back-yard when Gabe intercepted him.

"Here." His brother shoved an overjoyed ball of fur at him.

Zach grabbed Cuddles before she fell out of his arms. "What the hell?"

"She's yours. We're not taking her back." Gabe scowled. "You couldn't pay us to take her back."

The puppy was losing its mind licking Zach all over his neck and chin. It didn't matter how he shifted her, she just kept showering him with her slobbery love.

"What kind of trouble could she have caused? She was trained when I gave her back to you."

Megan appeared at Gabe's side. "She wouldn't stop crying, Zach. No matter what we did, she wouldn't stop." She watched Cuddles turn herself inside out to show Zach just how pleased she was to see him. "Now I see why. You two are obviously a match made in heaven."

Zach wanted to argue, wanted to tell them either

they kept the dog or he was taking it to the pound. But, damn it, he'd missed the little fur ball all week. He'd look down at his lap, expecting to see her there, and had hated how empty, how sterile, his living room was without her chew toys, the dog bed empty in the corner.

And yet, even as excited as the puppy was to see him, she kept looking around and whimpering between licks.

He knew why. She was looking for her friend Atlas.

And for Heather.

The four of them had been such a tight unit that the puppy couldn't possibly understand where everyone had gone.

Or why only he had returned.

"Fine," he growled, "I'll keep her. Where's the baby?"

Gabe and Megan shot each other a look before gesturing over their shoulders. Chloe was sitting with the baby on her lap. She looked exhausted and radiant all at the same time.

Zach put Cuddles down and the puppy immediately, frantically, started jumping up on his leg. "Down!" The puppy put her front feet down and waited for his next command. "I'm just going to wash your slobber off my face and hands. Don't worry, I'm not going anywhere. You'll be coming back home with me later."

He could have sworn the little Yorkie nodded at him as if she understood precisely what he'd said.

Just the way, he found himself thinking, Atlas had always been so perfectly in tune with Heather.

In the kitchen, he shoved the faucet up so hard that water sprayed all over him. He pumped half a bottle of soap into his hands, then stuck his hands and face under the water before yanking a clean kitchen towel out of a drawer and drying off with it.

Cuddles trailed after him as he headed toward the baby. Chloe smiled up at him. Chase's wife was the only one who didn't seem disgusted with him.

He sat beside her and took the baby into his arms. Big blue eyes blinked up at him and chubby little legs kicked. Zach dropped his mouth to the super-soft skin on her forehead. "Pretty girl. Your uncle Zach is going to spoil you rotten."

He heard Chloe laugh. "Look at her. She already knows it, doesn't she? I think she's even giving you her first smile."

And it was true—baby Emma's lips were curved up as she gazed at him and gave a little gurgle of happiness.

"Either that," he heard Chase say, "or she's going to give Uncle Zach his first lesson in changing a diaper."

To reinforce her father's prophetic words, Emma's face scrunched up and she grunted a couple of times while squirming in his hands.

Chase laughed and said, "Here's the diaper bag."

But Chloe was already standing up and taking the baby out of his arms. Zach watched the two of them walk away as Chase said, "Sounds like you've been screwing up big-time lately. Crashing cars. Losing women."

"You guys have been waiting long enough for me to blow something. Figured I'd finally come through for you."

He and Chase were close enough in age to get into it plenty of times over the years, but this was the first time he'd ever seen true concern in his brother's eyes.

"You know what makes you such a good mechanic? There's nothing you can't fix."

*Wrong.*

"Congratulations, again," Zach gritted out to his brother. "I'll be by to see you guys in a few days." When there were a half dozen fewer pairs of eyes on him. And when he had drunk enough booze to forget how badly everything he'd touched had gone wrong.

He grabbed Cuddles and they were almost to the front door when his mother intercepted him. She was fine-boned and delicate looking, but he knew first-hand that she had a spine made of steel.

"Zach, honey." Her arms came around him and the puppy and he breathed in her familiar floral scent. "I'm glad you're finally here. I've got something I've been meaning to give to you."

She turned and headed down the hall to her bedroom and he had no choice but to follow her. Family pictures lined the walls. Ryan in his first Little League uniform, taking it easy on the pitcher's mound a beat before he struck out another seven-year-old. Chase and Marcus heading out on Windsurfers on the bay at sixteen. Lori in her first ballet recital, just like Emma would be in a handful of years, so pretty it almost broke your heart to look at her. Sophie with her head in a book, lost in another fantasy world, another adventure. Gabe climbing the tree in their backyard in cut-off shorts with a hammer in his hand to finish building the fort. Smith as the star of the high school musical, his future already crystal clear. Zach's own cocky grin as he sat in his first race car, gazing out the window, certain the whole world was waiting at his feet.

Their mother had been behind the lens each and every time, had taken the picture of his father out on a hiking trail, a baby on his back, a toddler's hand in each of his. Jack Sullivan was looking over his shoulder at the camera with that same grin that Zach had seen a million times in his own mirror.

All those good times still to come, so much family to watch grow up…and life had still ended for his father in the blink of an eye.

Zach got to the bedroom door just as his mother opened the top drawer of her dresser. She didn't pull anything out of it right away. Instead, she closed her eyes and took a breath, her pretty face crumpling for a split second before she finally reached for something.

She turned and held out a small black box wrapped in velvet. "I think you should have this." She corrected herself. "I *know* you should have it."

Zach had never run from anything. Not a fight. Not danger. But the thought of opening up the box his mother was holding out to him had him wanting to run as fast as his legs would take him.

"It's okay, honey." She held it out so he had to take it. "He would have wanted you to have it."

Zach pulled the puppy closer with one hand as he reached for the box with the other. His hand shook as he flipped open the top and his throat tightened.

"It's your engagement ring." The ring she'd worn for so many years after his father died. The ring he still could see on her finger as if it were yesterday, as if she hadn't finally taken it off ten or so years ago. "You need to keep it."

"No, honey, I've had it just as long as I needed. The ring is yours now."

He shook his head. "I don't—" He was going to cry. Already was, actually. "I can't—"

She sat down on the bed and patted the coverlet beside her. "After your father died, I would look at you and it was like he was still there. Eating dinner with all of us. Playing ball in the background. Twirling the girls around in circles until they were dizzy."

Everyone who'd ever known their father had said that to him at one point or another. *"You're the spitting image of Jack."* He remembered how broken they all were over his father's death. How wistful about a life that had ended much too soon.

That was when he'd taken to trying to outrun the demons that chased him, but he hadn't succeeded. Not when he'd known all along that there was no separation between him and his father, because they were one and the same.

Something broke apart inside of him. "You always looked so sad. So damned sad."

"I know." Her voice broke. "I know and I'm sorry. Even rattled with grief, I knew it wasn't fair. I knew that you weren't him." She reached for his hands and gripped them tightly. *"You are not your father."*

"He was a saint." Whereas Zach had never been anything close to one. "He was a great father to eight kids. A wife he loved. The only thing he ever did wrong was die too early."

"Your father wasn't a saint."

Zach couldn't believe what he was hearing was true, but he'd never known his mother to lie.

"I loved him from the start, of course. He was impossible not to love, but the first time he gave me this ring, I threw it at him." Her eyes went hazy at the memory as she lifted her hand to her left eyebrow. "I clipped him right here, hard enough that he needed stitches. So, no, he definitely wasn't a saint. Not even close. And neither was I." His mother's gaze locked on Zach's. "But I loved him. He loved me. And in the end that meant we were both willing to give each other room to grow despite everything we both did wrong along the way. I know how close you were with your dad," she said softly. "He loved all of your brothers and sisters, but you were always so special to him. I know how special he was to you, too, honey. But what happened to him—" She searched for the right words. "It didn't have anything to do with you. It still doesn't, Zach. He helped make you who you

are, but only you can decide who you want to be…
and what you want from *your* life."

No one had ever said those words to Zach before.

Because he hadn't let them.

Heather had shared every last secret with him,
but he'd withheld his. And now she thought he didn't
love her, when the truth was that he loved her with
everything he had.

"He left you with no warning." Zach fought for the
words to explain something that had been so clear to
him since he was seven years old but was suddenly
growing fuzzy. "I can't do that to her."

"Do you think knowing your dad was going to
die would have changed the way I felt about him? Do
you think I would have stopped myself from loving
him?" She didn't wait for his answer before saying,
"If anything, I would have been absolutely furious
with him for thinking he needed to protect me from
my own feelings. To have missed out on the years
we had together would have been far worse than losing him too early."

Everything Zach had ever thought to be true
shifted around inside of him as he looked down at
the ring in his hand.

He'd had everything he could have ever wanted in
Heather. A lover. A best friend. A partner who wasn't
afraid to give him the kick in the ass he often needed.

Hadn't he known from the start that she was different?

And that a love as sweet as hers was something
you held on to, no matter what?

Unless, of course, you happened to be the world's biggest fool.

He closed the box with a snap before shoving it into the pocket of his jeans. "Thanks for the ring, Mom."

"You're welcome, honey." His mother gave him another hug. "Something tells me it's going to fit her perfectly."

# Thirty-Two

Heather waved the colorful rope at Atlas, but his ears barely perked up even though they were in the middle of the park and it was a beautiful day.

"You need to snap out of it." She put the rope down and sat on the grass beside her Great Dane. "Your whole world doesn't begin and end with Cuddles." At the sound of the puppy's name, he raised his dark eyebrows with hope. "No, she isn't coming here today."

No doubt, Cuddles was at Mary Sullivan's house for Chase and Chloe's baby shower. Lori had called and left a message with an invitation to attend, but Heather could only imagine how awkward it would be for everyone if she attended the family party.

When Atlas sadly lowered his big head back onto his paws, she said, "Don't you remember, you were a perfectly fine dog before her? You're going to be okay. It will just take a little time, that's all. Time heals everything. That's what everyone always says."

She stroked his soft fur as she looked out at the other people in the park. All happy couples, of course.

Refusing to acknowledge the pain zinging through her, the same way she'd been working to ignore the hollow ache in the center of her chest all week, she told Atlas, "You still have me. I still have you. We don't need anybody else. And just because those were the greatest two weeks of our lives, doesn't mean anything. We're going to be awesome again, just you and me."

She really did suck at lying. Just like Zach had pointed out that first night in her office when he'd brought her pizza and she'd already wanted him—and liked him—more than she should.

The truth was that, right now, she felt anything but awesome. Especially when what stretched out before her was an endless rinse-and-repeat of work and faking smiles for her friends and a bed that had never felt so empty.

Atlas missed his best friend terribly and he'd been sluggish all week. So had she.

Because she missed the man who had become her best friend.

In the span of two weeks, Zach Sullivan hadn't just managed to get into her pants…he'd charmed his way into her heart. Even worse, his laughter and warmth had taken up residence in her soul.

Just as Atlas couldn't seem to move on from Cuddles, she hadn't even come close to shaking herself free of the puppy's temporary owner.

The worst part about their breakup, though, was

that as the days crept by and the dust settled around her bruised heart, she couldn't help feeling that she'd let him down.

Those first few nights she'd hated herself for thinking she was *different,* that she could be the one woman a man like Zach could actually fall in love with. But that had been anger, and pride, spinning her wheels. Because regardless of the way the awful scene had played out between them, she couldn't deny that he'd been hurting.

And that was why he'd let her go.

Okay, so maybe love hadn't been enough for them…at least, not in that crucial moment of making the choice between staying and going, between keeping and giving away. But could it be? If she gave it another chance and stayed this time, to push past his walls and find out what had hurt him so badly?

Atlas's sighs turned to snores as he let the warm sun and her hand on his back lull him to sleep. Heather lay down, her head on his back, and closed her eyes. What she wouldn't do for an hour of restful sleep.

She took in the smells of leaves and fresh-cut grass, the sounds of birds chirping overhead, the laughter from strangers all around her. But instead of feeling a sense of peace at the soothing sounds and sensations, she saw her father's face in her mind's eye.

Heather found herself watching a seventeen-year-old girl confronting her father with his lies. The girl was so brave, so strong, as the man she had to thank for her dark hair, her long fingers, had told her that what she'd found out about his secret life on the road wasn't true, as he swore she and her mother meant everything to him.

From a distance, she watched that girl turn into a woman, one who believed her duplicitous father was the blueprint for all charming men. That laughing eyes and easy professions of love couldn't possibly be real.

And then, with perfect clarity, she cut to that moment in the kitchen when the man she loved wrapped his arms around her and the dogs to try to shield her from both past and future pain by simply *being* there for her.

She sat up suddenly, her eyes opening wide.

All along, Zach had fought for her. From that first moment when he'd insisted she work with him and Cuddles, until he'd gotten in that race car last Saturday, he'd been unrelenting in his insistence that they belonged together. At first, just as friends with benefits, until neither of them could keep denying that they were so much more than that.

Her stomach twisted as she realized what she'd done. Or, rather, what she hadn't.

*Don't stop loving me. No matter what happens, promise me you won't ever stop.*

He'd begged her for that promise as if he'd known it would all come down to one moment when he'd try to push her away.

But instead of fighting for him the way he always fought for her, instead of forcing him to own up to the reasons he was working so hard to push love out of his life, she'd decided it was safer to walk away from him instead. Safer for *her*.

Atlas opened one eye as she clipped on his leash and leaned in close to his muzzle. "Time to go get the girl and the boy. It's not going to be easy to win them back," she said with her first real smile in a week, "but they're worth it. And we're not going to give up, this time. No matter what."

"Goddamned flat tire!"

Zach should have been able to change a tire in his sleep. But the spare wasn't cooperating, kept slipping off the studs, while Cuddles sat on the sidewalk beside him and panted her encouragement.

He needed to get out of here to start figuring out a way to win Heather back. He couldn't stand to waste one more second without her.

A new spare dropped down next to his head and Zach looked up to see Ryan standing there, shaking his head. After all the cracks he'd made about his brothers falling in love during the past year, Zach had expected at least one of them to come out to heckle him.

"You're a mess. Can't even change a tire without her around, can you?"

Zach knew he should be thanking his brother for the new tire. Instead, he growled, "You're not safe, asshole. If this can happen to me— *this* being falling in love, of course "—it can happen to anyone."

But the brother that was close enough in age for

them to practically be twins didn't look worried as he walked away. He should be, thought Zach. And when the day came that Ryan lost it over a girl, Zach was going to make sure to rub his brother's guts in it.

Finally, with the new spare in hand, he started making headway. Five minutes and he'd be out of here and working out a way to make up for his colossal screw-up with Heather. There had to be some way to get her to accept his apology; he just wished he knew what it was....

Just then, something wet and sticky and overly warm moved over his cheek. He was so surprised, he banged his head on the side mirror. But even though his ears were ringing and it took his vision a couple of seconds to right itself, he could make out the huge paws.

Atlas's huge paws.

*Heather.*

He jammed his shoulder against hard metal as he shot to his feet. The woman he hadn't been able to stop thinking about for one single second stood on the sidewalk.

My God, she was beautiful. The most beautiful thing he'd ever seen.

His fingers itched with the need to grab her, to pull her into his arms, to thread his fingers into her hair and kiss her.

"Hi."

The one short word, more breath than sound from her lips, rocketed through skin and bone, straight into

Zach's heart. A heart that had finally started beating again. Just because she was near.

"I'm sorry." He'd never apologized for a damn thing in his life, but he would say the words over and over to her until she believed him. "I'm so damned sorry. I was just trying to get this tire on so I could come and tell you. I miss you. I love you. Please come back to me. And bring your mutt for Cuddles. I'm not going to hide anything from you anymore. I'm going to tell you everything, so many things that you're going to wish I'd never opened the floodgates."

She looked as if she could hardly believe what he was saying, but then shock turned to movement and the next thing he knew she was flying into his arms.

He put his hands in her hair and had his mouth a breath from hers when she said, "Don't kiss me yet."

Knowing he was covered in grease and sweat, he asked, "Because I stink?"

"No," she whispered against his mouth. "I love it when you have one of your rare imperfect moments. It's because once you kiss me I'll be too busy wanting you to hear what you have to say and I'll definitely forget everything I need to say."

*Jesus.* That almost pushed him over the edge, but he could see, could feel, how serious she was. "Who first?"

"Me."

"Talk fast."

Her mouth curved up into a quick little smile before she took a breath and said, "I'm the one who's sorry. For leaving you that night."

What was she apologizing for? "I made you go."

"You didn't make me. I could have stayed. I should have stayed and made you tell me what was wrong. I should have done whatever I needed to do to find out what happened to you out there in that burning race car." She pulled back enough to lift her eyes to his. "What happened, Zach?"

"You were the only thing I thought about during the crash."

"What about your family?"

"We've had my whole life together. But you and me—" he smiled at her "—we'd only had two weeks. It wasn't enough. I wanted a lifetime of memories with you, not just the ones we'd crammed into fourteen days. It's no excuse for the way I screwed up, but the thought of leaving you one day the way my father left my mother and all of us...I couldn't stand it. I'm so much like him that I always thought I was going to die the way he did—too young, without any warning. I was so afraid of leaving you behind that I made you leave me first." His chest felt tight as the old beliefs tried to take him over again. "I've never told anyone that before. Only you. Do you still want to be with me, even if I die the way my father did?"

"Oh, Zach." Her hand moved to his jaw, her thumb stroking over the fading scratches on his cheek. "You can be such a fool. One I love so much. Of course I still want to be with you."

That was when he knew for sure that she might

actually take him back. Not just because she was in his arms, not just because she'd listened to his apology…but because she'd just called him out on his stupidity, the way she had so many times before.

"Can I kiss you now?"

Her gaze dropped from his eyes to his mouth and he could already taste her sweetness when she said, "Almost."

He dropped his forehead against hers and groaned. "Would it speed things up if I mentioned how much I love you again?"

She grinned, her lips almost touching his—but not quite—as she said, "I fell in love with you so fast, so deep, I could hardly keep up with it. But even though I knew I loved you, I still didn't think it was enough."

"Because love never meant anything in your family."

She nodded, sighing. "I've measured every man against my father since I was seventeen. You seemed so much like him at first. So charming, so confident, that I had to keep my guard up all the time. Only, it turned out that you aren't like him at all. You're sweet and kind and warm and honest…and the only man alive who could have torn through my control and made it possible for me to love." She smiled at him, a smile so beautiful he lost his heart to her all over again. "But love is just one part of what I feel for you."

He was the one pulling back in surprise this time. "It is?"

"You taught me to trust. To have faith and hope.

How to laugh again." She ran the pad of her thumb over his bottom lip. "And when I'm safe and warm in your arms, just like this, I know the true meaning of peace."

Just as he'd been unable to wait so many times before, he had to take the kiss he wanted, devouring her lips with the hunger of a man who'd gone without for far too long. Heather kissed him back with the kind of passion that belonged between tangled sheets in dark bedrooms, not on suburban sidewalks.

He never wanted to stop kissing her, not when he had an entire week of lost kisses to make up for. Unfortunately, his family's clapping and cheering couldn't be ignored forever.

Heather looked over her shoulder and her eyes went wide. "Have they been watching the whole time?"

His brothers and sisters and mother and baby niece were all out on the front lawn now. "Through the windows for most of it, but I'm guessing they couldn't stand not hearing every word, or at least trying to read our lips. Which is a good thing, because I know how much they'd hate to miss this."

He dropped to one knee and her mouth fell open. "Zach? What are you doing?"

The dogs both nosed his hand as he pulled the black velvet box out of his pocket and opened it up. "Asking you for forever."

Her eyes lit up even as her mouth wobbled at the corners. He knew he wasn't playing fair by offering her the ring so soon after they'd made up. But from that first moment he'd set eyes on Heather, he'd pulled out all the stops to make her his. He wouldn't stop now, wouldn't ever stop loving her with every piece of his heart and his soul.

"My father gave my mother this ring."

She looked down at the ring, then back up at him. "It's beautiful, Zach."

"Will you be mine, Heather?"

"I've always been yours."

He loved the sound of it.

*Always.*

And then she said something he liked even more.

*"Yes."*

# *Epilogue*

Ryan Sullivan sprawled out on the lounger under the big oak tree in his mother's backyard, enjoying his beer.

Everyone was ecstatic that Zach had convinced Heather to take him back, but none more than Lori, who had been crowing about her victory on the bet they'd made to anyone who would listen, while the two dogs—one huge, one tiny—chased each other in circles on the lawn. Emma gurgled with happiness whenever the dogs came near.

It had been a heck of a year for his siblings. Weddings. Babies. Engagements. Even dogs.

Ryan didn't have anything against people falling in love, and he was glad it had worked out so well for everyone…but the whole thing looked like a heck of a lot of trouble. The sex part, he was game for, of course. But all the breaking up and getting back together, the anguish he'd seen on his siblings' faces when things went wrong?

No, thanks.

He was perfectly happy with the status quo. He liked his job on the pitcher's mound, enjoyed spending time with his family, friends and the pretty women who understood not to expect too much from a guy like him.

When his phone buzzed in his pocket, he was almost too relaxed to bother to pull it out. When it buzzed again a few seconds later, he reached into his back jeans pocket to shut it off. Before he could, he saw the text.

I need your help.

Vicki?

She'd been one of his closest friends in high school, but he hadn't seen her, or heard from her, in a long time. Too long.

Was she in trouble?

He quickly texted her back.

Where are you?

He was gripping his phone hard enough to crack it as he waited for her answer.

San Francisco. Pacific Union Club.

What was she doing back in the city? And at the exclusive, old-money cocktail lounge?

Ryan was out of the chair and heading for the front door when her next text buzzed through to his cell.

Come quick.

Gone was the relaxed Sullivan the world thought they knew. Because if anyone so much as touched a hair on Vicki's head, Ryan would kill them.

\* \* \* \* \*

*Turn the page for a sneak peek*
*of the next book in* THE SULLIVANS *series,*
*LET ME BE THE ONE,*
*available soon in print from Harlequin MIRA.*

# *One*

Victoria Bennett couldn't take her eyes off Ryan Sullivan, who was standing in the high school parking lot laughing with some of the guys on his baseball team. As she continued on her way toward the art store on University Avenue the image of Ryan kept playing on a continuous loop in her mind.

None of the other girls in her tenth-grade class could take their eyes off him, either. At least that was one thing that didn't make her stick out from the rest of her class. Her clay-stained fingers and clothes along with the "new girl" sign she felt as if she were wearing during her first few weeks at every new school did that with no help whatsoever from Ryan...or his ridiculously good looks.

Normally, she would have gotten over his pretty face without much trouble. As an artist, she always worked to look beneath the surface of things, to try to find out what was really at the heart of a painting or sculpture or song. That went for people, too. Especially boys who, as far as she could tell, only ever told a girl what they wanted to hear for one reason.

No, what had her stuck on Ryan Sullivan was the fact that he was always laughing. Somehow, without being the class clown, he had a gift for putting people at ease and making them feel good.

Before she could catch herself, she put her fingers to her lips…and wondered what it would feel like if he kissed her.

She yanked her hand away from her mouth. Not just because dreaming of his kisses was borderline pathetic given the utter unlikelihood of that scenario, but because she needed to stay focused on her art.

She wasn't just another tenth grader mooning over the hottest boy in school.

She was studying her muse.

Vicki had never been much interested in sculpting formal busts before. Old, dead, overly serious guys in gray didn't really do it for her. But it had taken only a few minutes near Ryan at lunch her first day on campus to be inspired to capture his laughter in clay. She wished she could get closer to all that easy joy—if only to figure out how to translate it from her mind's eye to the clay beneath her fingers.

Yes, she thought with a small smile, she was perfectly willing to suffer for her art. Especially if it meant staring at Ryan Sullivan.

She was almost across the school parking lot when she noticed the traffic light turned from red to green. She could pick up her pace and make it across the street, but she slowed down instead. She'd been having such trouble getting the corners of the eyes and mouth just right on her *Laughing Boy* sculpture. Knowing there wasn't a chance that Ryan or his friends would notice her, rather than leaving the school grounds she closed the distance between them in as nonchalant a manner as she could. Surreptitiously, she observed Ryan from beneath the veil of the bangs that had grown too long over her eyes during the summer.

A few seconds later, his friends high-fived him and walked away. Ryan bent down to finish packing up a long, narrow black bag at his feet, which she guessed held his baseball stuff.

What, she wondered on an appreciative sigh at the way the muscles on his forearms and shoulders flexed as he picked up the bag, would happen if she talked to him? And what would he say if she asked him outright to pose for her?

She was on the verge of laughing out loud at her crazy thoughts when she heard a squeal of tires seemingly coming from out of nowhere in the parking lot. In a split second she realized an out-of-control car was fishtailing straight toward Ryan.

There wasn't time to plan or to think. Without a moment's hesitation, Vicki sprinted across the several feet between them and threw herself at him.

*"Car!"*

Fortunately, Ryan's natural athleticism kicked in right away. Even though she was the one trying to pull him out of the way, less than a heartbeat later he was lifting her and practically throwing her across the grass before leaping to cover her body with his.

She scrunched her eyes tightly shut as the car careened past, so close that she could feel the hairs on her arms lifting in its wake. Breathing hard, Vicki clung to Ryan. Wetness moved across her cheeks and she realized tears must have sprung up from landing so hard on the grass.

The seconds ticked by as if in slow motion, one hard, thudding heartbeat after another from Ryan's chest to hers and then back again from hers to his. He was so strong, so warm, so beautifully real. She wanted to lie like this with him forever, more intimately, closer than she'd ever been with another boy.

Only, as voices rose in pitch all around them, suddenly, the reality of what had just happened hit her. *Oh, my God, we both almost died!*

She was starting to feel faint when he lifted his head and smiled down at her.

"Hi, I'm Ryan."

The way he said it, as if she didn't already know who he was, pierced through her shock. He acted as if it was normal to be sprawled all over a girl. Which, she suddenly realized, it probably was. For him.

Definitely *not* for her, though.

Her lips were dry and she had to lick them once, twice, before saying, "I'm Victoria." The words "But my friends call me Vicki" slipped out before she could pull them back in.

His smile widened and her heart started beating

even faster. Not from shock this time, but from pure, unfettered teenage hormones kicked into overdrive by his beautiful smile.

"Thank you for saving my life, Vicki." A moment later, his smile disappeared as he took in her tear-streaked cheeks. The eyes that she'd seen filled with laughter so many times during the first two weeks of school grew serious. "I hurt you."

She would have told him no, and that she was fine, but all breath and words were stolen from her the instant he brushed his fingertips over her cheeks to wipe away her tears.

Somehow, she managed to shake her head, and to get her lips to form the word *no,* even though no sound followed.

His laughing eyes were dark now, and more intense than she'd ever seen them. "Are you sure? I didn't mean to land so hard on you."

"I'm—"

How was she supposed to keep her brain working when he'd begun the slow, shockingly sweet process of running his hands over the back of her skull, and then down to her shoulders and upper arms?

One more word. That was all she needed to be able to answer his question.

"—fine."

"Good." His voice was deeper, richer, than any of the other fifteen-year-old boys she knew. "I'm glad."

But as he stared down at her, his expression continued to grow even more intense and she found herself holding her breath.

Was he going to kiss her now? Had her life just turned into the quintessential after-school-special fantasy, the one where the artsy girl caught the eye of the jock and the whole school was turned upside down by their unlikely but ultimately perfect and inevitable pairing?

"One day, when you need me most, I promise I'll be there for you, Vicki."

*Oh.* She swallowed hard. *Oh, my.*

He hadn't given her a kiss…but his promise felt more important than a mere kiss would have been.

Before she realized it, he was standing up again and holding out a hand to help her up, too. Instantly she missed feeling his heat and his hard muscles pressing into her softer ones. All the lies she'd been trying to tell herself about Ryan simply being a muse scattered out of reach.

"Can I walk you home?"

Surprised that he wanted to spend more time with her, she quickly shook her head.

He looked equally surprised by her response, likely because no girl on earth had ever turned him down.

"No, I can't walk you home?" he asked again.

She fumbled to explain. "I'm not going home. I was actually heading over to the art store to pick up some supplies for a new sculpt—"

She barely stopped herself from rambling on about her latest project. Why would Ryan Sullivan care? Besides, she reminded her racing heart with brutal honesty, he probably had some pretty cheerleaders waiting on him. And they wouldn't need an out-of-control car to get him to lie down on top of them.

No matter how tempting it was to believe that she had suddenly been cast in a happy-ever-after fairy-tale romance, the truth was that getting that close to Ryan had been nothing more than a fluke of fate.

And Vicki remained the star of her artsy, and often lonely, move-to-a-new-town-every-year-with-her-military-family teenage life.

Only, for some strange reason she couldn't understand, Ryan wasn't running in the opposite direction yet. Probably because he felt as if he owed her after she'd saved his life. After all, hadn't he just told her that he would be there for her one day when she really needed him?

"What are you getting supplies for?" He asked the question as though he were truly interested, not just acting like it because he felt he should.

"I'm making a—" Wait, she couldn't tell him what she was making. Because she was sculpting *him*. "I work with clay. Lately, I've been trying to capture specific facial expressions."

"Which ones?"

Never in a million years did she think she'd ever speak to him, let alone have this long a conversation. But what shocked her most of all was just how comfortable she felt with him. Even with all of her teenage hormones on high alert, Ryan was, simply, the easiest person she'd ever been around.

And she wanted more time with him than just five stolen minutes on the high school lawn.

Her nerves were starting to back off a bit by the time she told him, "I started with all the usual expressions every artist knows best." She played it up for him. "Tears. Pain. Suffering. Existential nothingness."

His laughter made her feel as if she could float all the way to the art store and back.

"Sounds fun."

"Oh, yeah," she joked back, "it's a riot. Which is why I'm trying something different now." She took a breath before admitting, "I'm working on laughter."

"Laughter, huh?" He grinned at her. "I like it. How's it going?"

Being so close to the full wattage of his smile made her breath catch in her throat. In an effort to cover her all-too-obvious reaction to him, she scrunched up her face. "Let me put it this way—I think I've started to resemble all those other expressions."

"Even the existential nothingness one?"

As if she were watching the two of them from a distance, Vicki knew she'd always look back to that moment as the one that mattered most. The one where she fell head over heels in love with Ryan Sullivan. And not because of his beautiful outside.

But because he'd listened.

And, even better, because he'd appreciated.

"Especially that one," she replied.

He picked up her bag from the grass. "Sounds awesome. Mind if I tag along?"

Okay, so maybe the two of them didn't add up on paper, but Vicki couldn't deny that they had clicked.

"Sure," she said, "if you don't have anywhere else you have to be."

He slung his equipment bag over his other shoulder and walked beside her. "Nothing more important than hanging out with a new friend."

This time, she was the one grinning at him. In the two weeks since she'd moved to Palo Alto with her family, she hadn't done a very good job of making friends at the high school. As an army brat who moved every year more often than not, she'd stopped making the effort. A long time ago, when she had realized how hard it was to break into fully formed cliques or maintain long-distance friendships, she had just stopped trying, knowing she would inevitably have to move again.

But Ryan made everything seem so easy, as if the only thing that wouldn't make sense would be if they didn't hang out.

By the end of their trip to the art store she knew all about his seven siblings, he knew she had two annoying little brothers, he'd told her what he liked about baseball, she'd told him what she loved about sculpting, and before she knew it she'd been invited to dinner at the Sullivan house.

It was the beginning of a beautiful friendship.

The best one she'd ever had.

*Present day, San Francisco*

Ryan Sullivan threw his car keys to the valet as he shot past him. The young man's eyes widened as he realized that he was not only about to drive a Ferrari into the underground parking lot, but that it belonged to one of his sports idols.

"Mr. Sullivan, sir, don't you need your valet tag?"

Ryan took his responsibilities to the fans seriously and made it a point never to let them down. But tonight the only thing that mattered was Vicki, so he waved off the valet's question as he hurried toward the entrance.

Even though a half dozen missed connections over the years after high school had kept them from meeting up again in person, he and Vicki had kept in touch through email and phone calls.

Vicki was his friend.

And he wouldn't let anyone hurt one of his friends.

Ryan pushed through the dark glass doors to the exclusive hotel foyer and made himself stop long enough to do a quick scan of the glittering room. The Pacific Union Club wasn't his kind of place—it was pretentious as all hell—and he hadn't thought it would be Vicki's usual stomping grounds, either.

So why was she here? And why hadn't she told him she was finally coming back to Northern California after so many years in Europe?

He'd been hanging at his brother Chase's new baby celebration when her texts had come in.

I need your help. Come quick.

Ryan had cursed every one of the thirty-five miles as he drove into the city from his mother's house on the peninsula. He'd called Vicki again and again to get more information, and to make sure that she was okay, but she hadn't replied.

He couldn't remember the last time he'd been so worried about anyone…or so ready to do battle. Vicki wasn't the kind of woman who cried wolf. She wouldn't have sent him those texts just to try to get his attention. She was the only woman he'd ever known, apart from his sisters and mother, who had ever been completely real with him, and who didn't want anything from him besides his friendship.

His large hands were tight fists as he surveyed the cocktail lounge, his jaw clenched tight.

*Damn it, where is she?*

If anyone had touched Vicki the wrong way, or hurt her even the slightest bit, Ryan would make them pay.

He was famous for being not only the winningest pitcher in the National Baseball League, but also one of the most laid-back. Very few people had a clue about Ryan's hidden edges, but it wouldn't take much more to set him off tonight.

He grabbed the first person in uniform, his grip hard enough on the young man's upper arm that he winced. "Is there a private meeting room?"

The young man stuttered, "Y-yes, sir."

"Where is it?"

His hand shook as he pointed. "On the back side of the bar, but it's already reserved toni—"

Ryan hightailed it through the lounge, and it shouldn't have been that hard to get through the crowd, but it seemed that every single person in the room either got up to buy another drink or was trying to get his attention.

When he found a subtly hidden door just to the side of the bar, he nearly knocked it off its hinges in his hurry to open it.

Ryan saw the flash of Vicki's long blond hair first, her killer curves second.

*Thank God. She is here and in one piece.*

But his relief was short-lived when he realized he'd interrupted her and her cocktail companion just as the man's hand was sliding onto her thigh.

Vicki jumped off her seat as Ryan strode into the room. The terror that had been on her face when the other man touched her leg slowly morphed into relief at Ryan's arrival.

Her companion, on the other hand, was clearly surprised to see Ryan…and he wasn't happy about it, either. The man was probably in his fifties and was obviously loaded. Or at least he wanted people to think he was, holding meetings in a place like this, wearing a handmade suit.

Quickly conjuring up an expression of surprise, Vicki said, "What are you doing here so early, *honey?*"

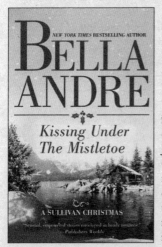

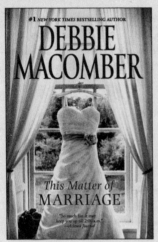

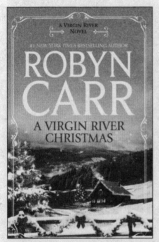

# sheila roberts

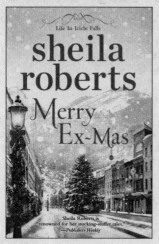

Life In Icicle Falls

sheila roberts
Merry Ex-Mas

Sheila Roberts is "renowned for her stocking-stuffer tales."
—*Publishers Weekly*

Cass Wilkes, owner of the Gingerbread Haus bakery, was looking forward to her daughter's wedding—until Danielle announced that she wants her father, Cass's ex, to walk her down the aisle. Even worse, it appears that he, his trophy wife and their yappy little dog will be staying with Cass....

Her friend Charlene Albach has just seen the ghost of Christmas past: her ex-husband, Richard, who ran off a year ago with the hostess from *her* restaurant. Now the hostess is history and he wants to kiss and make up. Hide the mistletoe!

Then there's Ella O'Brien, who's newly divorced but still sharing the house with her ex while they wait for the place to sell. The love is gone. Isn't it?

But Christmas has a way of working its magic. Merry Ex-mas, ladies!

## Available wherever books are sold.

# REQUEST YOUR
# FREE BOOKS!

## 2 FREE NOVELS
## FROM THE ROMANCE COLLECTION
## PLUS 2 FREE GIFTS!

**YES!** Please send me 2 FREE novels from the Romance Collection and my 2 FREE gifts (gifts are worth about $10). After receiving them, if I don't wish to receive any more books, I can return the shipping statement marked "cancel." If I don't cancel, I will receive 4 brand-new novels every month and be billed just $6.24 per book in the U.S. or $6.74 per book in Canada. That's a savings of at least 22% off the cover price. It's quite a bargain! Shipping and handling is just 50¢ per book in the U.S. and 75¢ per book in Canada.* I understand that accepting the 2 free books and gifts places me under no obligation to buy anything. I can always return a shipment and cancel at any time. Even if I never buy another book, the two free books and gifts are mine to keep forever.

194/394 MDN F4XY

Name                          (PLEASE PRINT)

Address                                                              Apt. #

City                          State/Prov.                    Zip/Postal Code

Signature (if under 18, a parent or guardian must sign)

### Mail to the Harlequin® Reader Service:
**IN U.S.A.:** P.O. Box 1867, Buffalo, NY 14240-1867
**IN CANADA:** P.O. Box 609, Fort Erie, Ontario L2A 5X3

**Want to try two free books from another line?**
**Call 1-800-873-8635 or visit www.ReaderService.com.**

* Terms and prices subject to change without notice. Prices do not include applicable taxes. Sales tax applicable in N.Y. Canadian residents will be charged applicable taxes. Offer not valid in Quebec. This offer is limited to one order per household. Not valid for current subscribers to the Romance Collection or the Romance/Suspense Collection. All orders subject to credit approval. Credit or debit balances in a customer's account(s) may be offset by any other outstanding balance owed by or to the customer. Please allow 4 to 6 weeks for delivery. Offer available while quantities last.

**Your Privacy**—The Harlequin® Reader Service is committed to protecting your privacy. Our Privacy Policy is available online at www.ReaderService.com or upon request from the Harlequin Reader Service.

We make a portion of our mailing list available to reputable third parties that offer products we believe may interest you. If you prefer that we not exchange your name with third parties, or if you wish to clarify or modify your communication preferences, please visit us at www.ReaderService.com/consumerschoice or write to us at Harlequin Reader Service Preference Service, P.O. Box 9062, Buffalo, NY 14269. Include your complete name and address.

# BELLA ANDRE

| | | | |
|---|---|---|---|
| 31558 | CAN'T HELP FALLING IN LOVE | ___ $7.99 U.S. | ___ $8.99 CAN. |
| 31557 | FROM THIS MOMENT ON | ___ $7.99 U.S. | ___ $9.99 CAN. |
| 31556 | THE LOOK OF LOVE | ___ $5.99 U.S. | ___ $5.99 CAN. |

*(limited quantities available)*

| | |
|---|---|
| TOTAL AMOUNT | $ _____ |
| POSTAGE & HANDLING | $ _____ |
| ($1.00 for 1 book, 50¢ for each additional) | |
| APPLICABLE TAXES* | $ _____ |
| TOTAL PAYABLE | $ _____ |

*(check or money order—please do not send cash)*

To order, complete this form and send it, along with a check or money order for the total amount, payable to Harlequin MIRA, to: **In the U.S.:** 3010 Walden Avenue, P.O. Box 9077, Buffalo, NY 1426-9077; **In Canada:** P.O. Box 636, Fort Erie, Ontario, L2A 5X3.

Name: _____

Address: _____ City: _____

State/Prov.: _____ Zip/Postal Code: _____

Account Number (if applicable): _____

075 CSAS

*New York residents remit applicable sales taxes.
*Canadian residents remit applicable GST and provincial taxes.

**HARLEQUIN® MIRA®**
™ www.Harlequin.com

MBA1013BL